Praise for the Laura Winslow novels by
DAVID COLE

"Dazzling."
Alfred Hitchcock Mystery Magazine

"Not for the squeamish. Keep the lights on!"
Glynco Observer (GA)

"Kept me reading far into the wee hours.
The author has a gift."
Sue Henry, author of *Murder on the Iditarod Trail*

"Full of memorable characters, convincing
dialogue, and enough dead bodies to keep
even the most jaded reader happy."
Lansing State Journal (MI)

"Compelling and readable . . . Laura Winslow
[is] a unique and gutsy sleuth."
Mary Jane Maffini, author of the Camilla MacPhee
and the Fiona Silk series

"One of the most complex and fully
realized protagonists around."
Donna Andrews, author of *Click Here for Murder*

"Haunting . . . Will leave the reader a
bit uneasy at the end."
The Mystery Reader

Books by
David Cole

DAVID COLE

FALLING DOWN

AVON BOOKS
An Imprint of HarperCollinsPublishers

AVON BOOKS
An Imprint of HarperCollins*Publishers*
10 East 53rd Street
New York, New York 10022-5299

Copyright © 2005 by David Cole
Excerpt copyright © 1999, 2001, 2002, 2002, 2003 by David Cole
ISBN 0-06-051197-4
www.avonmystery.com

First Avon Books paperback printing: July 2005

Avon Trademark Reg. U.S. Pat. Off. and in Other Countries, Marca Registrada, Hecho en U.S.A.
HarperCollins® is a registered trademark of HarperCollins Publishers Inc.

Printed in the U.S.A.

10 9 8 7 6 5 4 3 2 1

for
Mary Emich, my muse
and
Dympna Callaghan, my mentor

*"I do love thee!
and when I love thee not,
chaos is come again."*

—Othello to Desdemona,
in Shakespeare, *Othello*

FALLING DOWN

arívaca road

When you read this, please know that you became what you are today, you became my daughter, just eleven months ago.

On a typical monsoon afternoon in August, your pickup truck barreled past me at exactly two minutes before five o'clock, I know this time exactly because the Border Patrol nearly ran me off the road, they didn't swerve over, like your driver, a small courtesy at eighty miles an hour, the monsoon blowing heavily and rain clouding all my mirrors until the pickup roared past me, a Ford 250 diesel, *rapraprrrrrrap* of a blown muffler? an automatic weapon? an old diesel engine backfiring? when the driver tried to downshift, that's what I thought, but your driver gave up giving me room because of his speed.

Anyway, the backfires or weapon or muffler noise saving my life, snapping me from the meditative state I brought with me from my Reiki attunement in Arivaca along this two-lane road, one of the busiest smuggling back roads in all of Arizona, the road so busy the Border Patrol finally set up a permanent checkpoint.

My foot drifting off the accelerator and moving to the brake pedal. Stunned by the crowd beside you in the pickup long bed. So many people sitting up high, others crouching, two even standing as you all disappeared inside the heavy monsoon rain squall just as the first Border Patrol Jeep tailgated my Subaru Baja, cherry and turquoise lights flickering, heavy electronic siren bleating as the Jeep's grill flooded my mirrors and *wham* the Jeep's front crash bumpers nudged my smaller car ahead. I couldn't brake, just steered over the small dirt berm at the shoulder and headed off into a tangle of creosote bushes as three Border Patrol Jeeps sped past.

Angry, furious, frightened but *fur*ious, I punched the accelerator and used the car's momentum to get back on Arivaca Road. I came up on a hill, I could see half a mile in front of me, the monsoon swept across and behind me, wind pushing aside the rain so I could clearly see the first Border Patrol Jeep overtake and pass your truck, the Jeep passenger throwing something on the road and your pickup running across the object *pa-POW,* both right tires blowing and your pickup launched off the top of a small rise, glanced off a thick mesquite tree, still airborne, crashing against other trees until coming to earth exactly at the three-wire cattle fence, crunching and tilting onto the driver's side, that horrible metallic crinkle*thud* of metal buckling, you and all the people screaming as the pickup started rolling over and over, bodies flying out of the truck, it just wouldn't stop rolling.

After the first rollover, several wooden crates flew twenty feet into the air, slatted crates that disintegrated on hitting the ground, *and all these birds flew out,* bodies and birds commingling, flying through the air.

Later, a DPS accident-investigation team estimated that after hitting the spiked strip thrown down by the Border Patrol, after both tires blew out, your pickup rolled and bounced for more than three hundred yards.

I drove as close as I could to the scene. Pulled up, slammed my shift into park, and got out of the car. Deep within the monsoon, the rains so fierce they shrouded everything beyond ten or fifteen feet, so that as I ran through the rain my circle of visibility constantly shifted. I stumbled upon a mother spread-eagled against a boulder, her back broken and a baby girl hugged to her stomach and crushed against the rock. I was feeling for the baby's pulse when a Border Patrolman grabbed my arm, yanked me roughly backward, and quickly pinned my arms behind me to slap on a plastic quick-flex.

They're dead, I said. *Can't you see, they're dead. Let me go.* I tried to power myself up. He thrust me to the ground, put a boot on my neck, my face slammed into the dirt beside a dead bird. A chicken, no, I thought, face in the dirt, a rooster.

Are you insane? I said. *What are you doing?*

Stay put, asshole, he said.

He ran toward the pickup while I staggered to my feet, lurching after him, cursing him, sobbing, passing more bodies, dead roosters but many more just stunned, flying and running, several dozen, I couldn't count them all, I couldn't decide what to do, should I gather the roosters, stop beside every person? See if they were injured but alive? I knelt beside a dead man, half scalped, the hair and blood partially covering a large tattoo on his forehead. *Mara 27.*

The wind shifted, rolling the rain across the desert floor, a larger window of visibility suddenly appearing. I saw a man, his back to me, right arm extended with a pistol against the forehead of somebody lying on the ground. I saw the pistol recoil, but heard nothing as the rain swept in again to hide everything but the body at my feet. I looked closer at his forehead, saw an entry wound.

An execution.

I recoiled with astonishment, turned completely in a circle, turned again, saw nobody, and now terribly afraid.

An officer came toward me, looked me over quickly, saw I was in shock.

Were you in the truck? he said.

No. No, what have you done?

Red car? Slapped my face.

You ran me off the road, I said. *You sonuvabitch, then you ran them off the road. You murdered those people.*

Accident, he said.

Accident, hell! I said. *That was murder.*

They fired at us, we tried to stop them. What's your name?

Fired? What do you mean, fired?

Gunshots.

You're saying you heard gunshots?

When they fired at us. Yes.

Those weren't gunshots, I screamed. *The engine backfired.*

Gunshots, he said, nodding to himself. Certain he was right.

Why did you stop me?

You were speeding, he said.

On automatic, already in damage-control mode.

You rammed my car!

Go to Nogales, he said. *File an accident complaint. But right now, get back in your car and stay there.*

Smoldering with rage. Eyes clouded with tears. I lowered my head, tried to head-butt him. He caught me gently, held my arms tight, and I could see him closely, as frightened as me, both of us in shock as we stood there, frozen, his hands gripping my arms until I wiggled and he blinked, looked down, licked his lips, took out a knife, and cut the plastic quick-flex.

Just go away, he said. *Please? Just leave?*

I tried to dodge past him, his arms extending straight out, forming a barricade I couldn't cross. Kept thrusting against his arms, jumping sideways.

These people are smugglers, he said.

These people are dead! I screamed.

Smugglers. Weed, Afghani heroin, people, birds . . . these people smuggle anything. These are maras. *They smuggle anything and everything.*

Tried to run under his right arm, he caught me.

People die for roosters? I said.

Fighting cocks. Top-quality. Please. Go back to your car, he said. *We have three emergency ambulances and a chopper on the way. Please. Help us by not getting in the way.*

Finally gave up, walked backward to my car.

And then I saw you.

And your brother, both arms around a dead rooster.

Both of you, huddled behind a clump of teddy-bear cholla. Blood all over your brother's head, covering your hands and your thin white dress with little red ribbons around the neck and sleeves. Without any hesitation, instinctually, put a finger across my lips. *Shhhhh.* Got to my car, opened my door, saw all the Border Patrolmen far away, each near a body except for one officer with a microphone to his mouth, shouting, I couldn't hear the words, and just then another swirl of rain blew over them, covering them from my sight.

And me from theirs.

Come on, I said, jerking my head five times toward my open car doors until you ran to me and piled into the back seat, the blood on my seat cushions turning black as it soaked into the fabric but your brother's face covered with blood almost the same shade as my candy-apple-red Subaru Baja.

I turned around. Back to Arivaca. Stopped at the medical clinic. All the blood from your brother's head wound, we washed both of you, the first sting of grain alcohol on his gashes jolting him alert as another gurney rolled beside him, pressure packs on the man's legs and right arm, a huge tattoo on his face partially obscured by blood as the med tech tried to swab his face clean.

You blanched at that tattoo.

Your brother recoiled in fear, turning his body away from the wounded man, cuddling into a ball. He held a small card.

La Bruja, he whispered. I thought it was a Tarot card. *La Bruja,* he said and said again and again while we bandaged his head.

Saint Magdalena de la maras.

I don't understand. Is this your mother?

Shook his head. Offered me the card. Heavy plastic, not a tarot card, but like a miniature of an old movie poster. Hands shaking on the card, eyes dulled by shock and terror, not looking at the woman's image. He suddenly retched, spewing blood and bits of rubber balloons onto the floor.

La Bruja. Saint Magdalena de la maras.

The Witch. Saint Magdalena of the . . . what were *maras?*

We're going to lose him, the nurse said. She folded her arms around the boy, her bent wire-frame glasses falling off her face as she held him tightly until his body stopped spasming and he died. After easing him back on the gurney, the nurse bent to the floor, swore to herself, crossed herself, ran to get a bottle of purgative, and started feeding it to you from a measuring spoon.

Hours later, you exhausted from purging, the nurse folded my hands around your head. *You must take her,* the nurse said. *To St. Mary's Hospital, in Tucson. Tell them, just say you believe the girl has swallowed heroin.*

Heroin?

They're drug mules. They've been made to swallow balloons of heroin. Some burst inside the boy's stomach. The girl must be examined carefully. I've given her a laxative, but it will be some time before the balloons pass through her system. You must take her to Tucson.

No way, I remember saying. *It's not my responsibility.*

You initiated the responsibility, she said, *when you rescued them. The girl will live. She will, if you get to her to the emergency ward.*

I cannot take responsibility, I said.

The nurse held up the boy's card. *You know what this is?* I shook my head. *La Bruja. The witch, Saint Magdalena of the Maras. And these words down here? In the small black letters?*

no me jodas

This is a death card, she said. *Death to witnesses, death to anybody who talks about being a drug smuggler, being a mule.*

no me jodas

What does it mean? I asked.

Literally, it means 'Don't fuck with me.' Down here near the border, it's a warning. Like I said. It's a death card. I cannot jeopardize this clinic by keeping the boy and girl here. Get them to Tucson, get them to an emergency ward.

And I took you both.

Your brother dead.

And you lived.

I wrapped your hands around my Mother Teresa medal, I draped my rosary over your neck, and waited outside the St. Mary's emergency ward.

I prayed and prayed for three hours, that God would allow you to live. And you did. One bag of heroin ruptured inside your body and somehow damaged your central nervous system, screwed up the part of your brain that lets you talk. Neurologists say you may some day recover the ability for speech. I do not know, I only pray. Since you have never spoken of the accident to me, I never truly understood your brother's horror until this week.

I have seen the tattoo again.

So. I'm writing all this down, now that you've begun learning how to understand English and my Spanish is, well, improving. One day, I pray that in reading this, maybe you'll remember what happened on that day and so remember your life before we met.

I will protect you.

I *will* protect you.

—mary emich, 11 august 04 thru 29 june 05

1

Bob Gates followed me up the narrow bricked stairway to my roof.

"Let me get this straight," I said. "You've got a bad cop. A traitor, somewhere inside TPD. You want my help?"

"That's pretty much it."

Downslope from the house, trimming a blue Palo Verde tree, Nathan Brittles watched us carefully. Long-bladed clippers held in front of him as he watched, clippers snicking open and shut, open and shut, his body turning to see me on the roof, the clipper action mechanical without focus, and no longer anywhere near the Palo Verde, snicking open and shut on nothing but air.

His sadness and disappointment battered my heart.

I looked away.

I no longer knew where our love had gone.

On the roof, I sat at my battered redwood picnic table while Gates locked hands above his eyes and rotated slowly, taking in the view.

"Helluva view," Gates said. "Clear day like this, I can see Elephant Hill, all the way down past Green Valley. That's gotta be forty miles south. You *own* this place?"

"Yes," I said shortly.

Waiting him out, Gates a patient man, acting lieu-

tenant of the Tucson Police Department. Had a slow way
of talking, like he really didn't much care to say more
than he had to. Or just didn't like to talk.

"You must see a lot of wild life from up here."

"Javelinas, bobcats, foxes, coyotes," I said. "Lots of
pack rats, lots of snakes."

"I live in a condo, off a golf course," Gates said. "Saw
a rattler in my backyard, that snake was so big you
coulda put a saddle on it. I whacked at it with a shovel,
lost my TV cable service for a week."

"Why the stand-up comic routine, Bob? And don't tell
me you came here just for the view."

"Mmmm," he said, swiveling north to look up at the
Santa Catalinas, towering behind the house. Took in the
million-dollar homes stretching far into the dry foothills.
I let him ramble across the rooftop, noticed that he
stayed a good two feet from the low-bricked railings.

Yes, it was my own home.

Built by a surgeon in the '70s before the gold rush in
real estate. Southeast of Sunset and Swann, you drop
down into a small ravine and then climb a hill overlooking all of Tucson. Picnic table on the roof, a memory of
my early years in Tuba City. Random wooden chairs
from garage sales.

I'd sit up there and watch the sun rise, or set, or streak
through monsoon clouds and create double and triple
rainbows.

I helped the surgeon disprove a multimillion-dollar
malpractice suit brought by a family of nine, I didn't
care much about the details, I just uncovered a history of
past crash-car insurance scams. Buy four junkers. Cruise
along U.S.-10 at seventy miles an hour, lock on to a Benz
or Beemer, then box it between all four junkers and the
guy driving the front car, they've disconnected the brake
lights, he hits the brakes hard, and *wham,* it's a huge
lawsuit.

The surgeon had properties all over the world. Could have paid my fee with cash, but the guy was so grateful, he gave me the home on the hill with the view. He never told me the place was lousy with pack rats. After five weeks they chewed through several cables on my Jeep Cherokee.

Gates circled back to the table, pulled out a ladder-back wooden chair.

"Sorry I had to come here," he said. "Tried your office for a week."

"I'm retired."

"Still. I hate bringing this to your home, instead of your office."

"I don't want to contract out to TPD. I really am retired. I quit."

"Not what I hear."

"I've got a good life here."

"Laura, I know you've got a good man, a loving daughter, and you're gaga over a granddaughter. And where are your girls?"

"Spider's got a full-time job with flex hours, her baby always with her."

"And this baby, this granddaughter, what's her name?"

"Sarah Katherine."

As Gates settled into the chair, two of the lower rungs popped out and he nearly fell over when the chair collapsed. Not bothered, he pulled another chair over and sat down. Quick mover for a big guy. Gates somewhere in his fifties. He'd been with TPD for a thousand years. Instead of wearing his lieutenant's uniform, he dressed for himself and not the job:

pressed khakis
Tommy Bahama silk Hawaiian shirt
Paul Bond lizardskin boots

The shirt had a blue flower-and-bird pattern, buttoned at the neck and color-coordinated with his light gray jacket. He removed his jacket, folded it across the back of another chair.

"Want some sun tea?" I said.

"I'd love some."

"No ice."

He shrugged. I pulled two large jelly glasses from a wooden cabinet, poured the tea. Set the glasses out on some paper napkins from Risky Business, poured the tea, and sipped it while Gates rotated his glass around and around, adjusting the napkin, finally tasting the tea. People mask and delay their real intentions by eating or drinking, by fiddling with glasses and plates and utensils and napkins, getting them in some order while they carefully work out in their head just how and what they're going to say.

Usually, the more they fiddle, the worse the message.

"You read the local papers?" he asked.

"Not much."

"But you've heard that we've got problems with drug smuggling?"

"Drugs?" I said. "Yeah. The *Star* runs a drug story every day now."

"Reporters don't know jack. A bust in South Tucson, front-page news. How much do you know about the *mara* cartels laundering money through Arizona banks?"

"I quit hacking into bank records two years ago. I do nothing illegal anymore."

"And what if it *was* legal?"

He'd been fiddling with a naugahyde briefcase under the table. Reached down, laid it flat but unopened on the table.

"Heard you also quit taking autopsy photos," Gates said.

"You brought pictures of dead people to my house?"

One hand hesitated on the briefcase, waiting for encouragement.

"Drugs and dead people," I said. "Not my line of work."

"Nope. But bank records, you can track money transfers. Legal or illegal."

"Illegal? Drug money?"

"Drugs, extortion, gambling . . . we don't yet understand the size of this operation. Bodies piling up, somebody new taking control of organized crime, from Nogales north to Tucson. It's backward logic. With so many bodies, there has to be a lot of money moving somewhere."

"Where?"

"No idea," Gates said. "Our people can't find anything."

"But it's connected to a bad cop?"

"I *think* it's connected." Hands out, palms up, shoulders rising and falling a few inches, the universal shrug of *I don't know*. "We've been friends a long time, Laura. You know a gut feeling when it hits. My gut tells me, this is all connected."

"Please tell me you've checked this out on your own."

"As far as I can, without telling anybody . . . yeah, I've looked."

"And?"

"Nothing."

"You've come at the wrong time, Bob. I'm trying to phase out of my business, not take in more work."

"You're the only licensed PI in your company."

"That's a poor argument, you know it. Computer searches, data mining, it's a whole new world. Half my employees are MBAs. And a lawyer on board, to keep us strictly legit, and to get court orders and financial search orders. PIs aren't like Sam Spade anymore."

"So there's no use appealing to you as a good citizen?"

I snorted, poured myself some more sun tea. A blend

of Red Zinger and slices of jalapeño peppers. Gates wandered around the rooftop, shaded his eyes to look over the Santa Catalina Mountains piled high behind the house. Seated again, he pulled off his lizardskin boots and socks, stretched his feet into the sun.

"Would you do it as a favor to me?" he said.

Briefcase on his lap, opened, one hand inside, waiting.

"I think I saw this movie," I said finally. "*Manhunter*, from that Harris book *Red Dragon*. Where the FBI man brings photos of two happy families, wanting to sink the hook of interest for a retired investigator."

"TPD needs your help."

"I don't work drug cases."

"It's not about drugs. Or bank records. We've got a bad cop."

"Whoever it is, you know how to deal with them. You've got Internal Affairs, or whatever you call it."

"Office of Internal Affairs."

"So? Deal with the *it*."

"Don't know who *it* is."

The whole thing shaped up, right then, I realized what he wanted, my eyes opening with the insight, and Bob saw my eyes and nodded.

"Oh, no," I said. "Bob, that's, you want *me* to run an investigation?"

"Computer records need checking. Got to be done by somebody from outside TPD."

"No way, Bob."

Stroking his briefcase, still making no move to open it.

"You ever hear of these new gangs called *maras*?" he said. "All kinds of facial tattoos?"

"El Salvador, Guatemala, Honduras . . . probably in LA?"

"For the last five months, the *maras* have been systematically taking over all Tucson drug networks. Weed, coke, white and black tar heroin."

"That's *not* been in the papers," I said. "Bob. You've

got a lot of TPD people working this. I can't see where I'd help in any way. I'm retired here. I want to shuck off most of my life."

"The presidential vote," Gates said. "Just last fall. You volunteered to help detect electronic voting fraud."

"That was politics. I didn't want my guy to lose."

"He lost anyway. Besides, knowing you, Laura, it's mainly *you* that doesn't want to lose. Look. If you don't want to hear any more about why I'm here, I'd understand that. I'd leave. Will you hear me out first?"

He unsnapped the brass clasps of his briefcase, raised the top, swiveled the briefcase around for me to look inside. Two tabbed manila folders. A Glock nine.

"Two propositions on the table," Gates said, removing the folders. "Help us. You get back your PI license. And you get back your Glock."

All sound stopped. No breeze, no birds, no traffic, Nathan wasn't *snipsnipping*. One of those moments where people say:

An angel just fell.

I nodded.

He'd set the hook well. My computer forensics business depended, in part, in being legal, on my having a valid Arizona private investigator's license.

"After that casino deal last year, where you and your boyfriend hustled the casino manager out of his own place with guns in his back, well, the ISB assistant chief wants you totally out of business. Cancel your PI license, cancel your gun-carry permit."

He opened a folder. The top page was the TPD organizational chart.

"Professional Standards Division," Gates said. "See this blank box down here? Narcotics Conspiracy Section. We want to add a special section. Hasn't even got a name. Headed by . . ."

Wet his right thumb, slid the org chart off, showing a large color photo.

"Jordan Kligerman. TPD up-and-comer. Tough man. An accountant, except he doesn't know jack about computer hacking. He's already got a staff of three people. You'd report as a civilian. Contracted, paid off the books, but equivalent pay of top detective. Sixty, seventy thousand."

He knew the money was not why I'd consider the offer.

"What's this guy like?"

"Between you and me, Kligerman is a pogue. A desk cowboy. Never rode patrol, never worked a crime scene. Strictly an accountant, but somebody you'd never want to underestimate. If you do this."

"Bob, why *would* I do this?"

"A lot of street people are dying. For every gangbanger involved in drugs, these *maras* are killing three, four, hell, whole families of civilians."

"How many?"

"Laura. This is totally off the record. So far, near's we can figure, the *maras* have killed almost one hundred twenty-five people. But that's really not the worst thing of all."

Underneath Kligerman's file, a white envelope stuffed with pictures. Gates started to pull out a few snaps, but I laid my hand over the envelope.

"Not here, Bob."

"They're not dead," he said.

"Just tell me who they are. I don't care, right now, I don't care about what they look like."

"They're children."

"Children?"

"Teenagers, mostly," he said. "Being used as drug mules."

"Carrying?"

"Swallowing."

"Good God," I said.

"They're conditioned to swallow twenty, thirty . . . a

whole lot of small balloons of heroin. They cross over alone or with rental parents. Once in a while, a balloon breaks. We're talking almost pure heroin. Right from Afghanistan, suppliers of at least ninety percent of the world's heroin. It's so pure, if a balloon breaks inside somebody's intestine, no way they live."

"Jesus," I said. "Bob, I mean, where's the dotted line here? Between teenage drug mules and a bad cop?"

"No dotted line. Just a guess. An *educated* guess. Special drug raids, kept secret from all but top planners, some of these raids go sour. Somebody's tipped off. We set a sting, a fake raid. Somebody talked."

"Somebody inside TPD?"

"Yes."

"But you don't know who."

"No."

"And you want me to . . . *what*, Bob?

Gates hesitated, shoved the snapshots back into his briefcase. Laid the Glock in front of me, closed the case lid, and snapped it shut.

"Do you ever hear any of these names? Rogelio González Pizaña, known as El Kelín? Osiel Cárdenas Guillén? A gang of assassins called *Zetas*?"

"No. What's in the other folder, Bob?"

"Our first break," he said. "In the gangbanger hoods, people are afraid to talk. This woman is completely different."

Opened the other folder. No picture, just a single sheet of paper with a name and a phone number, below it a long résumé:

birth date
job history
married, now widowed

"This woman called three days ago. Asked for me only."

"Mary . . . Em . . . *itch*?" I said.

"Pronounced *Em*-ick. Spelled with the *h* at the end. German name. She's the director of Visitor Services at Tohono Chul."

"The park?"

"Yeah. I've never been there. You?"

I nodded, not going to tell him the story of Tigger and the deaf pharmacist, my first murder case after moving to Tucson. Five long years ago.

"What's the connection?" I said.

"This Emich woman, she claims she's got a computer lead to the *maras*."

"What lead?"

"Won't tell TPD unless we send a computer expert to the park. Something about protecting a daughter of hers. I called the number she gave us, she's a real person, didn't want to talk on the phone. I thought about pitching this idea to Kligerman . . . since he wants you on his team, I figured you'd be perfect to talk to the woman. But I decided to keep this woman just between you and me."

"How complete's her résumé?"

He chuckled. "Got it off the Internet."

"How solid is her information?"

"Totally off the record?"

"Okay."

"An ex-cop works at the park. Director of all the volunteers. He's a good friend of Mary Emich, he's a longtime good friend of mine. Ken Charvoz."

Pronounced like a French name. *Char*veau.

"Undercover detective, retired with heavy medical disabilities. Emich saw something on his computer, she asked him what to do. Ken called me personally. Nobody else knows about it. But I trust Ken's instincts. I want it checked out by the best person I can find. That's you."

I heard voices below, went to the roof's edge and saw Spider, lifting Sarah Katherine out of her stroller. Nathan knelt beside them, rubbed Sarah Katherine's

cheek as he stared up at me. Spider carried her baby to
the small pool downhill from the house, lowering the
baby's legs into the water, up to the knees. Sarah Katherine shrieked with delight. Spider jerked off her sandals,
sat poolside, their legs wiggling together in the clear blue
water.

Spider turned on a boombox, cranked up Ruben
Blades and Willie Colon doing *Siembra*. She lifted Sarah
Katherine and began a dance routine.

"My God," Gates said. "What is she doing?"

"Dancing. Salsa."

"She's really *good*," Gates said.

"Well, she teaches."

"Teaches . . . what?"

"Dancing."

Spider's hips rotated in her own blend of salsa and
merengue.

"I hear it from car CD players. Never knew what it
was."

"She dances, she teaches, she practices . . . right now,
she's tuned out most of the world except for her baby
and salsa."

"Good-looking baby," Gates said.

"I'll fix you some lunch," I said, "but I don't have
much time."

"Nope. Can't stay. Section meeting in an hour, they'll
want to know about you. Whether you'll come on
board."

"All legal claims dropped, I keep my PI license?" He
nodded. "I couldn't care less about the gun. I've got another gun. It's not licensed. You'll square that?" Nodded
again. "Okay. I'll talk to this Emich woman. If there's an
honest lead, you turn it over to TPD staff and at that
point, I'm clear. Out of it, altogether."

"Sounds like a start."

"No, Bob. That'll be the end."

"Can I ask . . . why?"

I left him alone at the table for at least three or four

minutes. Thinking about the job. Watching Spider and Sarah Katherine dunking their heads into the pool, Spider demonstrating how to flick her head around and spin off water beads. Sarah Katherine, almost two, insisted on spinning her whole body.

"I'm not . . . I guess the word would be, I guess I'm unsympathetic."

"Just a computer job. Just what you love to do."

"Bob. I don't know if I'm that passionate about computers anymore. Besides, anything that starts with drugs and cartels and gangs will get messy. Right now, life is messy enough. I love my house, I love the people in my life, I *don't* much enjoy the outside world anymore. Down here, near the border, it's only going to get worse."

Bob watched Spider dangle Sarah Katherine's feet in the pool.

"This Mary Emich," he said. "She's got a daughter. You've got a daughter. The teenage drug mules that die, they're somebody's daughter."

"You goddamn *bas*tard," I said. "You son of a *bitch*. Drugs and daughters, that's just, that's just *low*."

"Ah, Laura. I'm really, I didn't mean it that way. I'm so sorry I said that, I really didn't mean to say, to make a connection with your daughter."

But I knew he really did say that intentionally. Truth to tell, I *do* have a daughter. I can't imagine her in harm's way, I can't imagine what I'd do, living with any threat of harm.

"Let me get this straight," I said. "You've got a bad cop. A traitor, somewhere inside TPD. You want me to be . . . what, a spy? What do they call it, you want me to be a mole?"

"Yes."

"And who would know what I'm doing?"

"A very few, a very small, select, and trusted group of people."

"But I'd be at risk."

"No risk. You'd be hired in a bogus position. To advise TPD in setting up a Computer Crimes Department."

"But if the wrong person found out what I was doing?"

"Wouldn't happen," Bob said.

"Oh, yeah. Sure. Just like you wouldn't have a bad cop working with teenage drug mules and Mexican crime cartels."

"The risk would be remote," Bob said. "We'd set up firewalls."

"Remote," I said.

"Nothing personally connected with you."

"That's like lying in the sun with the remote chance of getting skin cancer."

"Well, okay," he said. "Fair enough. These *maras* have a fixed rule. Death to anybody who talks. Death to all witnesses."

"Death to cops?"

"Not directly, no. The threat is for people who'll rat them out. Got a picture of some woman called *La Bruja*. With a slogan. *No me jodas*."

"Meaning?"

"Don't fuck with me."

"Great."

"It's really a remote thing, Laura. You're not going to be on the street, dealing directly with anybody."

"Do you *like* what you're doing to me?"

"You're the only source I've got that I'd trust, Laura."

He spread his hands, a supplication, a gesture of honesty and appeal.

"Plus," he said. "You'll get your PI license back. Guaranteed."

"Who's doing the guaranteeing?"

"Me."

"You'd put your honesty on the line? Knowing the hell I'd unleash if TPD overruled you, if TPD went against your promise?"

"Yes, Laura."

"Okay," I said. "So. I talk to this Emich woman, you get my PI license reinstated. Deal?"

"Deal. But. Look also over Kligerman's data. So you can up or down, yes or no, you'll at least listen to his proposition. He's not married, either, got no kids. Just so you know, if it gets that far."

"It won't. Last thing I need is another man I've got to deal with."

"Another thing. Between you and me. Kligerman hates Charvoz. Some deal went bad, Charvoz nearly tore Kligerman's head off in the squad changing room. Nobody knows why. Not important, just keep that to yourself."

Shielding his eyes, studying the southern horizon.

"You could see both ends of a rainbow," he said. I smiled, nodding. "You ever see a double?"

"From up here, double rainbows are common. You ever see a triple?"

"Never."

He folded his jacket over a forearm, swung the brief-case into his hand, and without another word went down the stairway and out the back door.

Nathan moved quickly to the driveway, but Gates had already three-pointed his car around the driveway and I caught a quick glance of him driving down the hill. Nathan back to look up at me.

And our troubles continued.

2

Nine in the morning, floating naked in the pool.

Morning sun crispy on my body, feeling burned, feeling burned as I ran through the options of what I'd say to Nathan.

My body loosened after twenty laps of backstroke and twenty more freestyle. Loosened, but not relaxed.

Had so few options, had only one that made sense to me.

Tried to rehearse what to say when Nathan came between me and the sun, his silhouette black and unreadable. I paddled sideways, until his shape and colors came into focus. Soft white cotton tee, sleeves ripped off. Cammo shorts left over from Nam. Nathan wore clothes until they rotted off his body, or until I threw them out.

Held one hand behind him, hiding something.

"What did he want?" he said finally.

"I told him to leave me the hell alone."

"And?"

"Nathan. Sweetie. He's got a deal for me. A guarantee that I keep my PI license."

"In exchange for?"

I paddled toward him, hung on the edge of the pool.

"Please sit down," I said.

He moved again, the sun behind him. You can take the boy off the rez, you can't shuck the rez off the Indian.

"In exchange for?" he asked again.

"One little job," I said. "Nathan. Sweetie. All I've got to do is go talk to a woman at Tohono Chul Park."

"Talk to a woman."

"That's it."

"Talk about what?"

"A computer glitch."

"Guy was a cop, right?"

"Yes. TPD. But he only came because a friend of his, another cop, well, an ex-cop, medical retirement, anyway, this friend . . ."

"Some cop is going to reinstate your PI license if you talk to his friend."

"Yes."

"And this?"

Nathan withdrew the hand behind his back, laid my Glock on the deck tiling. "What's that for?" he said. Pursed his lips, nodded toward it with a kissing gesture. Navajo's rarely pointed a finger directly. He tossed my Glock into the pool. I let it sink to the bottom, the dull black matte blurred by the water motion.

"He found it in TPD evidence storage. Thought I'd want it back. Nathan. I've got three handguns locked up in our safe. I don't need another one."

"You don't need *any* of them."

Guns. One of the elephants in our living room.

I never felt safe without carrying my unlicensed Beretta. Nathan despaired of ever having to kill again, despaired of guns and weapons, despaired of violence.

He knelt beside me, stroked my nose, my ears, circled a thumb and forefinger around my hair to squeeze out the water.

"So the trip's off," he said.

"What trip?"

"Tomorrow. You and me, up to the rez. Adopting the boy? You forgot."

"Oh, Nathan. I didn't forget the trip. Can't we just wait a day, can't we just . . . like, go the day after tomorrow?"

"The boy's clans are gathering tomorrow. They're

coming from all over the rez, just to meet me. And meet you."

"Just call them. Tell them to wait a day. It's only a day."

"There was an agreement that we'd meet tomorrow. I can't go back on that. With or without you, I *won't* go back on my word."

"Nathan."

I grabbed his arms, slid down to hold his hands.

"I'll do everything I can to finish this up quickly. So we can leave."

"Promise?"

"Nathan. I love you. I'll tell TPD I can't take their job. I'll have a quick talk with this woman, I'll blow her off this afternoon. I'll go over there right now. Don't leave without me, please."

"We'll talk on it tonight," he said.

Picked up his trimming clippers and went around the side of the house.

"No," I said, dripping from the pool, clinging to his arm as he walked away, the arm behind him, I wouldn't let it go. "Why are you leaving me?"

His coal-black eyes on me, buttons with no shine, no crinkle of a smile.

"I can't live this life anymore," he said finally.

"This is a *good* life."

"This is not a good city, these are not good people here."

"I'm here," I said. "My business is here."

"Your business," he said shortly. "You find things, you find people."

"Yes. I do."

"But what if people don't want to be found? Not bad people, not criminals. Just people who want a simpler life. Who don't have telephones because there's no phone line. Who don't want computers because there's no electricity."

"Where's this all coming from?"

"You have the smell of violence on you," he said after a long, long time. "I can no longer abide that
smell."

"Abide? Abide? What kind of word is that?"

"I need . . . I need . . . I want to live with my family."

"Nathan, I *am* your family."

"You have been good for me."

"Good *for* you?"

"Come with me," he said. "Come be part of my family on the rez."

"That's it?" I said. "That's it? That's it?"

"The only life we have together is up there, up on
Dinehtah."

"This is a good life here. I am a good woman to you.
My daughter, her daughter, we are good people to you."

"I have to choose," he said. His voice so calm, so void
of emotion, so much a slap in the heart. "My people, or
you. I've made the choice, you can come with me, you
can be with my family."

"How can you make this so quick? How can you
choose so suddenly?"

"I have been choosing for months," Nathan said.
"You've just now heard the truth of it."

"Truth?"

"We've always promised we'd tell each other the
truth," he said.

"And what's so fucking great about your *truth*? Why
can't you just try lying, just for a change? It's the way
lovers survive."

"The truth is," he said, "the truth, the truth about you
is the smell of violence and accommodation about you. I
cannot live down here. You can. You love this house,
this . . . this palace. I'd be happy in a *hoghan*."

"If I promise to follow you tomorrow," I said, "will
that work?"

"Laura," he said, "I truly don't know."

"Then I promise to follow you. Tomorrow. Just one
day."

He pressed his forehead against mine, I felt tears on his face.

"Maybe," he said finally. "I just can't make a promise of my own."

Except I didn't know how to tell him that I'd break *my* promise. Only for a day, I thought. My PI license has to matter to my lover. What *I* want, what I *need*, has to matter to my lover. What other more basic trust can there be with a partner?

I wanted to talk to him, to convince him. Instead, when it came time to talk that night, I found him naked in our bed, still wet from a shower.

There are many ways to make love without saying anything, many ways to make love slow and gentle or over-the-top wild, can't wait to finish and start all over again. And somewhere on the edges of however you do it, there are those times when you couple together and one person is totally, completely, sensually lost in the moment and the other person participates wholly with the body and yet in the corner of the mind is the active, disturbing realization that your lovemaking is the same as it's always been or something's changed, you'd crossed a boundary, and you didn't know if it was possible to look back.

And the worst part of those thoughts, before you stuff them far down into the unconscious so you won't dwell on them, is you don't know if you're continuing what *is* or beginning what *was*.

Thinking about change. About what I'd said to Bob Gates, about crossing boundaries, going back to work with the agreement my PI license would be reinstated. I wondered if I'd hyped my answers, if they sounded slick, contrived, flippant, or facetious.

That night, with Nathan, something had changed.

After the sex, my head on his stomach, next to the old,

puckered bullet scars from Nam, he kept silent. I'd promised to talk.

He waited.

I couldn't tell him the truth about not joining him on the rez, but I couldn't lie about it, either. He stroked my body in all the familiar ways, wanting to make love again and feeling my response. Entered me. And I felt a change settle between us. Like he knew I wouldn't come.

Like he knew I'd changed.

When changes happen to me, they rush through my entire being without thought, there's a before and an after. Sometimes, I'd get this, I don't know, a shiver flooding across my body, *every*where on my body, then the sensations vanished.

In the earlier days, when change smacked me without warning, I'd not even realize I'd changed for days, occasionally weeks, until a moment when I just knew things were different. Now I know immediately. At first . . . it's not something a word describes, my body . . . okay, my body vibrates. And I know. Change has come upon me.

Of course, the real work is figuring out what's changed.

In my Ritalin days, when I really popped a lot of Ritalin, I'd do a lot of crazy things. One of my favorite personal dares was to get close to the railroad track when a train came barreling down toward me. I'd stand so close the ground vibrated and my bones vibrated, I'd stand as close as I'd dare, depending on how much Ritalin I'd popped.

I got the idea from an old William Holden and Mickey Rooney movie, I think it was about Korea, I think the name involved some bridges with an Asian name like Tokoriko. But somebody in that movie would stand on back of the aircraft carrier right near the spot where the plane launch piston would slam to a halt. I can't even remember how the piston worked, but when a jet was launched, this piston propelled it off the carrier deck, and this guy, it might have been William Holden, but I don't remember, anyway, he had things figured out to the inch of where that piston would come to a complete stop. And the guy would stand there, he'd scratched a long metal marking on the deck, he'd put his boot toes right up against that marking and wait for the piston to *whoooooooshBAM* and stop just in front of him.

I never felt responsible for what I did when I was on a Ritalin high.

At least, not until I met a woman who took fifteen times as much Ritalin as I did, she'd grind it up into a powder in a blender shake with pineapple, mangoes, and half a Snickers bar.

And then drink the whole thing. Do that four times a day.

"I've got to do this," Nathan said later. Tearing one-inch strips of a penny-saver newspaper, crinkling them between his fingers. "Go back to the rez. Take in this boy, he's got no family. Nobody wants him."

"Why are you doing this to me?" I said.

"To you? I'm not doing anything to *you*, I'm helping a boy."

"Bring him here," I said. "We'll raise him here."

"Made a promise."

"You've promised me, Nathan. You promised you'd live here. With me."

"Promised my elder aunt Sophie I'd take care of the boy. In the traditional ways, that's my word to Sophie."

"You've given *me* your word. To live here. Live with me."

"Boy's got problems."

"I've got a problem."

"You kicked your drug habit," Nathan said. "I've promised Sophie I'd raise the boy in traditional ways."

"Please stop shredding the newspaper."

He looked at his hands, he'd not even realized what he was doing. Dropped the newspaper, picked up a thick rubber band, and started twisting it between his fingers, stretching his hands over a foot apart as though he thought he could make a cat's cradle from the rubber band.

"When are you leaving?" I said finally.

"Oh." He folded the rubber band around his left wrist, twisted and folded it two more times. "I guess. . . . I guess I was waiting until I told you."

"How long has it taken you to say that?"

He shrugged.

"Okay," I said. "You've told me. I still don't want you to go. Don't you care about that? What will people think?"

"People?"

"Spider. She loves you. What will she think, if you leave me like this?"

"I'm not responsible for what other people think."

"And me? I *love* you, Nathan."

Rubber band so tight around his wrist, veins popping on the back of his hand. I didn't speak.

"Then I'm headed out tomorrow," he said. "I guess it's best."

He stared at his hand, watched it swell and darken from the trapped blood.

"I just wanted you to be all right with this, Laura."

"Well, I'm not . . . it's *not* all right, Nathan."

"You're not going with me tomorrow, are you," he said later.

It both was and wasn't a question.

"I'll be there the next day," I said.

We'd both pretended to fall asleep for a while. My declaration lying between us like a bundling board. But you can't fool anybody with that, not somebody who knows you well, like a

partner
lover
friend

Got up, went to my stash of cell phones and acces-
sories, programmed one of them to auto-dial my private
line.

"You take this," I said. Smoothed the rumpled sheet
beside him, laid down the cell. "And here's a charger.
You plug this into the wall, this end snaps into the cell
here. Like this. This is a car charger. Your lighter
socket."

I folded them into his hands. His entire body immov-
able. A statue.

"I'll be there the next day," I said. "Is that so bad?"

He sat unmoving, eyes on me, eyes cutting from my
face to my hands, he dropped the cell and the charger,
took my hands in his so that my thumb lay against his
wrist and I felt his pulse as his eyes moved back up to
mine.

"What's wrong?" I said.

Holding my hands, he lay back slowly, eyes never
leaving mine.

"You know about my past," I said. "More than anybody alive, you know about my past. You know I've been
arrested, I've done jail time when I was younger and
wilder. You know there were federal arrest warrants out
on me for years, even I cleared them up. You know that
Laura Winslow is not even my birth name. I made that
name up, Nathan. You know that. You know all these
things. But the bureaucrats in charge of renewing my PI
license, *they* don't know all that stuff. If they did, I'd
probably never get the license renewed. So here I've got
an offer, no questions asked, my PI license renewed if I
just take a few hours to help the Tucson police department. I've got to take this opportunity, I've got to do
this. Please, *please*, don't ask me to just drop this part of
my life."

His black eyes flickering around, studying me so intently it was much more than a stare, as though he'd sent out his spirit to talk to mine, but the line had been busy.

"Forget the Glock. Okay? I don't need that, but I *do* need my PI license. I may never use it again, Nathan. But *I'm* the one to make that decision, not some bureaucracy."

"Not the guns," he said. "Just the senselessness of it all. Life is falling apart down here, near the border. You talk about needs? *I* need another world. If you're not part of that world, I don't much care anymore."

"That's so simplistic, Nathan. One day can't make a difference."

But he'd already digested my declaration, probably had chewed on it all day and knew what the answer would be, because when I raised my head to kiss him, he'd fallen sound asleep, the cell phone pieces still clutched in his hands.

3

I never used to dream.

Or, at least, I never remembered a dream.

Color, black and white, whatever they might be, those dreams stayed way down there in my head, down in that part of my subconscious where nothing surfaces while I'm awake, and yet . . . and yet,

  later that night
  three dreams

If this part of my story seems to drift off, if you get bored, if you want really just to hear my story without side trips, move on.

I got up to go to the bathroom at two in the morning. Nathan lay asleep, his eyelids twitching, just how people say what happens when you're dreaming, and pa*pow*, there was this dream of mine came flooding back.

I'm staying in a very, very large hotel suite, somewhere in a large city, but just that hotel room was important, not the city or even the name of the hotel. Nor can I remember why I was staying in a hotel suite, but I was far from home.

The rooms were endless:

kitchens
living rooms
TV rooms
bedrooms

I wander into the farthest bedroom and as if the fourth
wall didn't exist, there I am inside the next hotel suite,
among people I've never seen before.

Okay. I wake up. This dream I know, not so hard to
figure out. Nathan wants me to move with him to the
Navajo reservation.

I sat on the toilet, lost in considering the dream.

Went back to bed, couldn't sleep, got the folders that
Bob Gates left, and went back to sit in the bathroom and
read.

Mary Emich.

She meant nothing, I mean, nothing, nothing at all . . .
except . . .

I'd have my PI license reinstated.

That's no small thing, to have a part of your identity
denied. Your livelihood, your business reputation. I'd
spent too many years doing illegal computer hacking, I
wouldn't, I *couldn't* return to that.

I called Bob Gates.

"Um," he said. Coughing, clearing his throat and his
head. "Yeah?"

"Bob. It's Laura. Laura Winslow."

"Yeah?"

"Promise me, if I visit Mary Emich tomorrow, promise that it might end there, for me, I might not have to do
anything else."

"Mmmmm." A deep sniff, a cough, but clarity now.
"I promise."

"Bob," I said. "Why should I do this?"

His phone put down while he blew his nose, coughed,
blew his nose again.

"Sorry," he said. "Bad post-nasal drip. You need an answer right now?"

"Yes."

"If getting your PI license back isn't good enough, I don't know what to say."

"These . . . the *maras*. Why should I get involved with them?"

"You shouldn't. You won't."

"But if I did," I said. "Why?"

"Are you asking again, is there a risk?"

"Yes. Not to myself."

He blew his nose again and again. I couldn't tell if he really had to do that, or if he was working out an answer.

"You ever hear of Rage In The Cage?" he said.

"No."

"Extreme fighting. Up Phoenix way, a few years back, some people wanted to make fake wrestling even more violent. Instead of a ring, they built a cage. Bars twenty feet high, chainlink fencing material all the way around. The *maras* took to the idea big time. Except without rules. Without time rounds or referees or corner men to deal with cuts and blood. Was like that Mel Gibson movie. Except, and I only know this from rumor, with the *maras,* the loser was lucky to stay alive."

"That doesn't help me much," I said.

"It helps me," Gates said. "It helps a lot of us taking down these skels. You . . . well, you decide."

"I'll call you tomorrow."

"That's it?"

"Sorry to bother you. I just had to know."

I hung up. Still sitting on the toilet, I must have laid my head back against the wall and fallen asleep.

Another dream came into my head.

This time, I'm staying in a very large home, a huge home of a friendly couple, I'm taking care of this home and all the plants. There's a large kitchen preparation area next to the living room which is decorated as though it's tropical, vines, trees in tubs and planters, all of which I'm responsible for. In one corner is a Christmas tree, still decorated although I myself don't celebrate Christmas, and as I'm looking at it, the tree, in its planter tub (it's a live tree, I discover), starts to tip over and the entire root ball comes out of the planter and the tree ends up on the floor.

A heavy wind rises, the room is now open on one wall to the outside, I'm thinking it's like a lanai, I'm standing next to another tree in another planter tub when the force of the wind actually snaps the trunk of this tree, completely severing the top half, which blows across the room and outside.

Suddenly my friends are there and I'm explaining, I didn't really break these trees, it just happened. The woman reassures me that it's okay, the man—I have no real sense that they're husband and wife, just a couple, I'm not even sure they're friends.

Anyway, I tried to reset the Christmas tree into its planter, and at that moment there were half a dozen people in the large kitchen preparation area, it's like something out of *The Great Gatsby*, people milling around at individual workstations. One woman is kneading bread, and my woman friend who owns the house is working at something, maybe a salad, and she continues to reassure me that the tree damage is not at all my fault, when the man becomes Sylvester Stallone and begins to threaten me because I broke his trees.

Another senseless violent dream.

Okay, I woke up just as that dream ended, okay, sure, I'm breaking up a home, or . . . Nathan is breaking up a home. Smashing the furniture, just as he'd smashed all of Leon Begay's property a year before, destroying Leon's possessions after his murder, making Leon's house *chindi*.

Naked, I went outside, dove into the swimming pool. The Glock still lay on the bottom. I'd retrieved it three times, but Nathan kept throwing it back.

Took the Glock into the kitchen. Dreams will do that to you, push you toward protection from what's in the dreams. Didn't even bother turning on a light, I'd stripped the Glock down so many times. I laid everything out on the black granite countertop, pieces of the Glock.

Lost somewhere after I played with the slide mechanism for ten minutes or so, and I turned on the kitchen TV, flipped through channels, and came across a scene from *Bambi,* my god, I hadn't seen that movie in years.

Distracted after a while, not really caring about Thumper on the ice, I got Mary Emich's file again, read through it, looking for any reason to just blow her off. She still meant nothing to me, except . . .

I wanted my PI license.

That's what it came down to, so I made that choice. I'd let Nathan leave without me, I'd do the minimal amount of work to satisfy Bob Gates, I'd rejoin Nathan and make things right again between us.

I could control anything, I believed.

Without realizing what he'd done, Bob Gates stuck me in a bad place. If I took his offer, Nathan might leave me for keeps. If I went with Nathan, not only might I not get my PI license back, but the state licensing bureau might look into my past arrest record that I'd never revealed when applying for the license.

Stuck with conflicts between three new cases.

Case file: I investigate bad cop in TPD.

Case file: I investigate my love for Nathan, willingness to compromise same.

Case file: I consider hacking into state PI licensing bureau files, and whatever other databases were involved, to wipe out digital records of my past.

I didn't like my choices.

What PI investigates herself?

I was losing control of my life.

*   *   *

I went back into the bedroom and laid beside Nathan.
Snuggled my head onto his naked belly and *Jesus
Christ,* I don't believe it, I swear I'm sleeping but I'm
aware, I am lucidly aware of walking through another
dream.

At last, a dream where I'm actually going to visit
somebody I know, except . . . I haven't seen these people
for thirty years.

My dearest of dear old friends. Anna Jean and Tom
Jacqua, and their three daughters. They live on a large
farm somewhere in mountain foothills, more than a
farm, could even be a commune?

I get inside and nobody's home. Nobody. Am I in the
wrong house? Suddenly a car pulls up. I run to the front
bay window, thinking it's Anna Jean and Tom, but it's an
ancient Cadillac, the kind with huge fins, rust all along
the bottoms and sides and wheel wells, left rear fender
covered over with rust inhibitor and a primer coat, a dull
purple while the rest of the caddy is hibiscus red.

Four men get out and immediately see me in the bay
window and begin firing shotguns. I run from room to
room, it's like one of those vast hotel suites, the men
tromping around and blasting everything with the shotguns before they round a corner after me until one man
with a huge Fu Manchu mustache says, *Christ, it's them,*
and everybody leaves, the Caddy pealing rubber. Anna
Jean and Tom must be home, again I'm in the bay window, it's still all glass, I thought the shotguns had pulver-
ized it, and outside is a brand-new Dodge Ram full-size
double cab, pulling a large, trailered powerboat. Another
four men get out and they've also got shotguns and blast
away, except this time, I find a portable telephone and
dial 911 and the police tell me the squad cars are already
on the way.

Ten or twelve people fill the living room, Anna Jean is
hugging me fiercely, Tom comes in, he's almost bald, a
round elfish face, he can't wait to hug me so the three of

us dance in a circle and all the others join in, one of those dances they do at weddings where people hold hands and swell out to the full extent of the ring and then, with raised held hands, bunch in toward the middle.

A detective is looking at marks all over the walls, *Shotguns, all right,* he says, except no slugs have penetrated the wall, the plaster has dimpled patterns, and Anna Jean says, *We did that two years ago, want to see our horses?* three horses are stabled in a room inside the house, everybody's drinking Almaden wine, those jugs shaped like the bottom of an hourglass, everybody's cooking some kind of dinner, we're all incredibly connected as friends.

C'mon out back, a cop says. Leads me through a grove of sycamores to an eight-sided stone house, the doorway facing east. *They're all waiting,* the cop says. *Inside, they're waiting.* We enter a large room, the stone house is really just one big room, essentially an eating place and a kitchen with a propane refrigerator and a fifty-gallon drum cut down to function as a wood-burning stove. Part of the room was sectioned off by hanging sheepskins and rugs. The cop held one of the rugs aside and motioned me through.

Nathan stood in the middle of a large group of people. *You're not from my mother's or father's clan,* Nathan said. *Now there are no taboos against us, now we can get married.*

But where's the swimming pool? I said.

It's out back, the cop said. *Want to see it?*

Out back, nothing but desert for miles and miles. The cop held a pistol on me. *You weren't supposed to find me,* he said. *It was a bad mistake, your friend Bob Gates hiring you. You weren't even supposed to come looking for me.*

But I didn't want to find you, I said. *I just wanted to get married.*

Marry this, he said. Raising his pistol.

And he killed me.

* * *

Ultimately, a violent dream. My life, as Nathan saw my life, the violence that Nathan rejected as though I deliberately chose violence, rather than having it wash over my life.

When your lover says goodbye, when your lover or your partner or your spouse says it's over, your way of life is not what I choose, you can renounce it or join me or I will renounce you.

Whoever figures on being dumped?

What are the odds, when you don't see it coming?

And what are the odds of my life of serenity disappearing into the world of random, senseless violence where assassins killed with no more emotional involvement than *no me jodas*?

Those dreams really freaked me out.

I cuddled and nested, touching my nose all over his chest and arms.

Then I really fell asleep. Like a proverbial log, like a baby, like a lover after a picnic on a hot day, the chicken and potato salad gone, the wine bottle empty, naked on a blanket after making love.

When I awoke, Nathan was gone.

I ran through the house, looking. Saw his pickup was also gone.

And the world turned. It's a shock, it's a crossing over, you're in this place, then *whop,* you're in that one with gates closed behind you.

4

All righty then, I thought next morning. Let's look at the odds of my dilemma. I mean, what are the odds that one chosen path is better than another? Have you ever noticed, while driving, that some days you hit nothing but green lights, and on other days, all lights are red?

What are the odds?

I mean, is it random, like flipping a coin, heads come up half the time? Is it your karma? Your mood? Distractions from your too-spicy Thai food lunch?

I never saw it coming.

That he'd actually leave without me.

That he'd actually *leave* me.

Like all unsuspecting lovers, in hindsight, I should have seen the signs.

He'd kept his own house, he'd lived in his own time zone. He'd appear to spend a week or a month with me, then he'd just leave.

What I always expected to happen, what I'd really wanted, really dared to *hope* would happen, was that one day I'd have Nathan permanently at my side, arms around each other, eating at Kingfisher or Ric's or Janos or Cuvee or Hacienda del Sol or Nonie or the Arizona Inn. The two of us seeing movies, hands across adjoining stadium seats at some mall cineplex. Okay, so I loved Robert De Niro and he liked *Finding Nemo*, so what, I'd see anything.

Of course, it never really happened that way.

In truth, Nathan Brittles, my two-year lover, my partner, he didn't care for movies or fine restaurants at all. I might watch or eat anything. He didn't. He'd said more than a few hundred times how he'd rather be back up on the rez. How he wanted to be *dineh* again.

Indian.

Navajo.

One who returned and lived the old ways.

Let's not dwell on this, I thought. *I'll go see this Emich woman, then I'll drive up to the rez. Just one step at a time.* I heard that in a black church one day, in Yakima I think, back in my wild days. Had no meaning for me then.

I snugged into my oldest swim suit, black, with a racer back and the embroidered Speedo logo. Chlorine-resistant, but old enough that the chemicals had degraded the polyester. I snapped it against my butt and breasts, my nipples erect under the fabric, we used to call them high beams. The suit a size too small, but this morning it protected my heart, squeezed my heart inside so I didn't have to deal with it.

I slid into my pool, dove through layers of heated water toward the bottom and cooler water. Breath almost gone, I surfaced like a small whale and crashed back into the water. Without thought, I swam idle laps, easing into a backstroke. Overhead, a red-tailed hawk dipped and dived, riding a thermal, surveying me and my property for

rodents
snakes
birds
anything small enough to eat.

I powered into a freestyle sprint for four laps, focusing my body and focusing my thoughts.

I *needed* my private investigator license back. I'd do whatever it took. I'd always run my life that way:

   set a goal
   move undistracted to that goal
   find another goal
   one step at a time

This morning I fixed the most important goal in my life.

I'd accept that Nathan had just left, unannounced, as he'd done many times. And that he'd come back to me.

That was my goal.

I'd meet Mary Emich later in the morning, I'd shuck her off quickly, I'd report to Bob Gates that I'd done my absolute best, but I really needed to get up to the Navajo rez today.

Goal fixed.

Head clear with determination.

And so I'd go running, then I'd see my Reiki master and psychic.

When I came back, Nathan might even be home.

Or not. I'd face that if I had to.

Later, I sat in the kitchen, munching celery stalks, still wearing the wet swim suit.

Yesterday, sure, there were problems in my life, but when I went along with Nathan to the reservation, after he'd adopted that boy into his family, then I figured we'd just work out who lived where and how much time we should spend together. Check that. How much time *I* should spend on the reservation to keep Nathan happy.

And today, everything's so . . . so complicated, which is to say, I no longer felt serenely confident in working out problems, in fact, I didn't believe there *was* a serious problem. I'd naively believe that my days as a licensed, working PI were over, my involvement with violence reduced to occasional random computer searches that no longer bore any resemblance to the illegal hacking I'd done.

I stared at the television where I'd watched *Bambi* the night before.

Bambi, the innocent.

Today, I felt more like the hunter that killed Bambi's mother, I felt . . . I felt as though . . . I felt as though I was destroying my love for Nathan, but I felt powerless to make the choice of love, to join Nathan and leave police work behind, I felt impelled to get back my PI license and in that, my dear friends, I felt more like the hunter than the innocent deer.

Decision. Enough soul-searching, second-guessing, emotional games.

Eventually even Bambi has to grow up.

5

"So what's wrong?" Sandy said.

After she'd laid Reiki hands on me. After I'd cried for fifteen minutes.

She knew, even before I jogged into her yard and lay on her massage table, she knew something was wrong. But Sandy never probed and pressured, never asked too many questions unless you gave her permission. If you've never been to an astrologer or a psychic, my friend, if you've never given yourself over to tarot readings or to Reiki, don't jump to a quick dismissal.

Sandy was my new Reiki master, after Georgia Roan told me that she'd not work with me unless I left my Beretta at home. Not wanting to do that, not wanting to feel less vulnerable without the Beretta, our relationship ended suddenly and it took me quite a while to find Sandy.

Sandy places her palms on my shoulders. I lie on her massage table, but I could equally sit in a chair, or, and this is totally unfathomable to nonbelievers, I can be *any*where in the world and Sandy can connect.

Reiki is not like a massage, where you fall asleep. Reiki attunements send you to such deep relaxation that your body sags, warmth spreads from the Reiki master's touch, warmth radiates from the spot of physical contact.

Sandy was my priestess, I was her altar.

Or to come down from that soap opera feely-touchy

way of talking, quite simply, Sandy had a power. Sandy had *the* power to give you relaxation. She also did traditional massage.

This morning, I needed every kind of relaxation.

Massage is a bond between giver and taker. If you don't really communicate stress to your masseuse, you never get maximum relief. It's as simple as that. Massage is also about pressure. Physical pressure, sure. Like you feel physical discomfort and the masseuse presses and pokes your body until it hurts good.

A time of pure pleasure, a banishment of pain.

But of course it's only temporary.

My cell rang. Thinking, believing that Nathan would call, I'd violated one of Sandy's basic rules. Turn the cell phones *off*.

"Nathan?" I said. Sandy frowned, shook her head.

"No. It's Bob Gates."

"Sorry," I said. "Sorry, Bob."

"Something's just gone down," he said.

"I can't deal with you now. Not right now."

"There's a crime scene," he said.

"Abso*lute*ly no way."

"We'll need to talk. Once I get some input, we'll at least need to talk."

"When?"

"Keep your cell on."

I disconnected.

"You want to tell me what's going on here?" Sandy said. "Damn! Laura, your body just went ballistic. You, Laura, what's wrong? Laura, just cry, sweetie, just cry it out."

She swiveled her body to cuddle behind me, her head sideways on my sweaty back, one hand stroking my forehead. We lay there together for so long I wondered if I was dreaming.

"I don't want to talk about it," I said finally.

"Do you want to talk at all?"

"I've got four hours to change my life," I said.

"Geez laweez. That's kinda . . . kinda cosmic. You ever cross over? From one way of life to something different, something you'd not even imagined was out there?"

"No. But. I've got to leave. I'm going over to Tohono Chul Park."

"I've got two clients there!"

"Do you know Mary Emich?"

"What are the odds?" Sandy said. "That I'd know both of you. So. What's the story, is Mary Emich a friend?"

"Never met her."

"Why are you seeing her?"

"I don't really know."

"Okay," Sandy said. "Guess she's not a friend of yours."

"Just somebody that needs help," I said.

Sandy gently laid her hands on my shoulders again.

Relaxed, almost asleep. Wishing I hadn't even mentioned Emich's name. It's the stress, my friend, the body wants to release its secrets in order to heal.

"Help with what?"

"Computers. Something. I don't know, really, what she wants. Listen, Sandy. Actually, I don't want any more clients right now."

"She comes here. Friend of hers from the park brought her. Peggy Hazard. Both of them lay out on the same table as you. So. Mary needs some help?"

"I don't want another client."

"All right."

"But I *need* another client."

"Laura, you're so irrational today. We're not going to solve anything, just let me tell you some things about Mary, then you decide what to do. You know Tohono Chul Park?"

"You'll see her, okay?"

"Uhhh," I said.

"You just lied," Sandy said. "I felt the aura."

"What's she like? This Mary Emich."

"Just call the park. Ask for the director of Visitor Services."

"What's she like?" I said again.

"First, listen to her voice," Sandy said. "Then you'll know. But I've done her chart. I can tell you what I think."

Chart, meaning astrology chart.

What a way to run a business, depending on the stars to tell you if a client is good or . . . or whatever.

"Whatever use is that?" I said.

"She's a very complex, a very bright woman," Sandy said.

Launching into Mary Emich's chart without blinking.

"She's got a hop-scotch mind and loves to engage in ping-pong conversations. Why do I say this? She's a Libra, that's an air sign, with her moon in Gemini. Another air sign."

I sat up on the table.

"That's gibberish," I said.

"Listen, just take it in, just . . . for god's sakes, Laura. Just turn off your head for a while. Okay?"

"I survive because of my head."

"Oh, pule*eze*," she said. "You survive because you analyze with your head, you draw up an agenda of choices with your head, and your gut tells you the right choice. The only thing really private about your investigating is that you make your decisions, you keep your life bottled up inside, and you keep insisting that your head is what's making the choices. Survival is *here*." Thumping my gut, my heart. "Thinking is up here." She laid a hand on my head. "It's not up to me if you go see Mary Emich. You've got a whole lot more than another client on your mind. But I know Mary. Maybe you can help her."

I rummaged around in the clothes I'd removed, got the Beretta, laid it on the massage table.

"What do you think about this?" I said.

"It's a gun."

"You look at it. Do you see protection? Violence? What?"

"I see a tool," Sandy said. "Shane said that. In the movie, he's teaching little Joey how to quick-draw, and Joey's mother tells Shane she doesn't want guns. Shane says a gun is just another tool. I saw that movie when I was twelve years old. I talked about it with my dad, he said Shane was right. I loved my dad. So that's what I thought then, that's what I think now."

"Sandy. I'm going to see this woman, but I'm going to blow her off. Okay? Then I'm driving up north to find Nathan."

"Oops," Sandy said. "Whoa! Major stress. Lover leaves you."

"Please. I won't, I can't talk about that right now."

"Okay. Mary Emich. Ascendant in Virgo, earth sign." Determined to make me hear her out.

"Libra and Gemini are what they call dual signs. Libra's symbol, the scales of justice. Always seeking what is fair and balanced. Gemini. Twins. Off in two directions. Gathering information. So right off the bat, you have four people going in different directions. I'll bet she never met a conversation she didn't like but oh so charming. Next, let's add the fact that both Gemini and Virgo are ruled by Mercury, the fastest-moving planet in the Zodiac."

"Stop," I said. "You want me to see her? I'll see her."

"Just let me add that Virgo Ascendant means she loves being helpful, also, when there is an abundance of Mercury in the chart, she could be awash in nervous energy always on the move both physically and mentally."

"This is exhausting me," I said.

"That's because it's *you* writ all over."

"Me?"

"Let. Me. State. This. Very. Plainly. No way are either

of you ever, ever, *ever* going to make a snap decision. It just isn't in your makeup."

"You talking to me?" My Robert De Niro impression.

"The need to weigh everything," Sandy said. "Every *single* thing. About a dozen times, and even then you might change your mind."

"Listen," I said. "Where do you get this stuff?"

"Birthdays."

"If I give you somebody's birthday, you can . . . what do you call it?"

"An astrology chart. Yes. You want advice about somebody?"

"Maybe," I said. Fishing in my bag, I handed her Kligerman's info sheet.

"Hey. What a hunk. This guy married?"

"Nope. But he's a cop."

"Okay. I'll make up his chart. If. If you'll promise not to blow off Mary until you talk to her."

"It's a deal," Sandy said. "Now get back on the table."

But after the massage, after I said goodbye, she held me with both arms. Not a hug, but hands on my upper arms, her arms extended, her eyes searching my face.

"When you're ready to do the work," she said. "Call me any time."

"I'll spend an hour with Mary Emich," I said. "Then I'm done."

"Not with Mary. With yourself."

"I'll do my own work," I said shortly.

"Ummm," Sandy said. "You're a private investigator. Out in the world, I have no idea whose privates you investigate. But if I'm wrong, and forgive me if I'm wrong, but I'm getting this aura from you about trouble with Nathan. If you ever need me, come by. If you ever need just to vent, I'm open twenty-four seven."

"I've got to go," I said.

Tohono Chul.

An island of serenity inside a state of chaos.

Where art and nature connect.

I went there whenever I really *really* needed to be serene.

I Googled the Park website.

Director of Visitor Services.
Mary Emich.
Marketing

Using one of my untraceable cell phones, I called the park's central answering system, got switched to her voice mail.

"Hi. Thanks for calling Mary Emich, the director of Visitor Services at Tohono Chul Park."

I waited through the rest of her message.

A distinctive, clear, happy voice. Careful enunciation, more than a hint of an Irish lilt. I left a message, I'd be there later in the day, meet me in the grotto.

I loved the grotto.

I started to hang up, but a woman answered.

"Who is this?" Mary Emich said.

"A friend of Bob Gates."

"Yes, but . . . who *are* you?"

"My name?" I said, the conversation going in a strange spiral.

"I need to make sure," Mary said. "I need to know you're . . ." Sound of papers rustling. "Laura Winslow?"

"Yes."

"You'll be here today?"

"Yes. But . . . what is this about?"

"I can't talk on the phone."

"Does it involve your daughter?" I said.

A long, I mean, a really long silence.

"She's not my daughter," Mary said finally. "But yes, it's about a young girl. I want you to help me."

"Help you how?"

"Keep us both alive."

"I don't, what are you saying, what does that mean?

.

Help keep you alive? I work in computers. That's all I do."

Another call. The Cosmic ring, a triad that moved down a full note and then up and up. C. B. C. D. I'd set it to ring Cosmic for Bob Gates.

"Wait," I said to Mary, and disconnected. "Bob?"

"You want to know about the *maras*?"

"No. I do not want to know more."

"It's an official request from TPD. You specifically. You've been requested."

"By who? For what?"

He gave me an address.

"Jordan Kligerman wants you to help us out."

"Help with *what*?"

"Some men at a crime scene. They have, I don't know what they're called, some kind of computer phones. Plus all of our CSI photographers are at other scenes, so bring your Nikon."

"Bob. What's this got to do with a bad cop? You know, what you came to see me about?"

"For your ears only. One of the dead people was an undercover cop. The only person we've got inside the *maras*. Three years and change, he's been working his way up the cartel as one of their money launderers."

"A white-collar guy?"

"No. Another drone. Born in Guatemala, parents killed by the right-wing death squads. This guy's one of the *maras* contacts with financial institutions. All done by computers, I don't know, stuff bounces around the world, you can move millions without making eye contact."

"But if he's dead, why me?"

"They're not all dead," Bob said. "And there's some kind of cell phone gadget, our people at the scene don't know what to do with it."

"A cell phone gadget," I said. Shaking my head.

"Will you come?"

Flip a coin
Run the odds

Make a decision
I looked at the address

"Meet you there in twenty," I said.

"Not me. Lead detective's a friend. And listen. You don't have to give an answer about joining TPD, but I'd like just to introduce you to Kligerman."

"I'm leaving today."

"Tonight. Late evening. Just for a drink."

"Is it a bad crime scene?"

"You'll need a drink afterwards," he said finally, and disconnected.

6

"They came in front and back," Renteria said.

Wanting some of the Cuervo Gold on the table beside him.

A crime scene tech had already coated the bottle with black fingerprint powder and lifted off the prints. Renteria, stretching out shaking fingers, reaching for the bottle, got some of the powder on his hand and jerked the hand away, trying to rub off the blackness.

"Been printed before," the lead detective said to me. "He knows what it's all about." A very patient man, somewhere in his fifties.

We waited.

Renteria sat on the white plastic patio chair. Knees clamped together, trying to stop his thighs shaking, head in hands.

"They came in front and back," Renteria said again.

"So you told us," lead detective said.

"Excuse me," I said to the detective. "I don't know your name."

He thumbed a card from a gold case, handed it to me.

"Christopher Kyle. Numbers at the precinct. And my pager."

"Chris," I said. Took the card.

"Christopher."

Skin wattles drooping along his neck, like he'd lost at

least fifty pounds in recent months. Saw me eying his canes.

"Hip replacements," he said. "They offered me retirement, but I said I was too old to retire."

Wraaaaaack. Wraaaaaack.

Cactus wrens chattering on the roofing tiles above us, but otherwise it was quiet out here on the patio.

No bodies out here, no blood.

"These GPS units?"

"I'm not telling you anything," Renteria said.

Meant to be a curse, or a scream, instead came out just a whisper, he'd gone past his defense positions.

We knew it. He knew it.

We just sat there, waiting.

"This lady here," Kyle said. Cut his chin toward me. "She knows all about computers. And things like that."

"Why is she taking my picture?"

Clatter from the wrens, two of them on the aluminum rain gutters.

"Well, she does that, too. She does forensics, she takes pictures, she looks at anything we think is a computer."

"It's just a cell," Renteria said. "Just a cell phone."

"With a cloned chip." Kyle scrunched his head at me.

"Phony," I said to him. I'd taken the back off, ran a diagnostic with my laptop. "Stolen number. Untraceable."

"Ain't mine," Renteria said. "They didn't give me one."

"Is that why you're still alive? Because you didn't have a cell phone?"

"Shit, man, I hear that front door crash open, I crawl under the sink."

"A GPS unit," I said. "Global Positioning Satellite."

"*What the hell is that?*"

"C'mon. Ramon?" Kyle said. "That's right? Ramon Renteria? That's the name you gave us?" Didn't wait for an answer. "Ramon. That his woman and kid in there? Your friend's woman? Their child?"

"I don't know them, man."

"How old's the child? That baby child?"

"Don't know."

"I'd say, four years old. Tops. And the woman?"

"Not his woman, okay? Not his kid, okay?"

"So. Ramon. You know the guy well enough, you know it's not his woman or his four-year-old child?" Renteria said nothing. "Are they just hired out from Rent-A-Family?" Head still down, Renteria's eyes cut to Kyle for an instant.

"Drug couriers," Kyle said to me. "Women and kids, they sell space in their bodies for a day. Drug mules. Swallow balloons of heroin, bring a kid along to look like a family. I go into the bathroom, Ramon, I'm gonna find some laxatives? Well, I'm here for drug smuggling. You're a suspect for a triple, Ramon. Three people dead. Your friend in there. His jacket's probably *loooong* and *thick*. Once we got him all ID'd, multiple multiple drug busts. Jail time, county time, prison, his friends, their jackets also an inch thick. Soon as we find out your real name, we'll know that you've got a jacket."

"It's a cell phone, okay?" Renteria said. "It ain't mine. I don't even know how to use it."

"Back to whoever came in. Front and back."

"*Pendejo!*" Renteria said. "I've told you about that a dozen times, I'm not telling you again."

Wraaaack wraaack.

Wrens, desert trash birds. I hate them, hate their raucousness. The uniform officer standing nearby clanked his baton against the aluminum gutter downspout, but the wrens just went farther up the roof.

"Yeah," Kyle said. "All we want to know, you recognize anybody?"

Renteria shook his head. He wouldn't look up.

"He knows who they were," Kyle said to me.

"*No*, man. I don't know who they were, okay?"

"Did they all have tattoos?"

Renteria's teeth chattered. Kyle offered him the

tequila and Renteria took large, thirsty gulps, tequila dripping onto his clothes.

"Tattoos," Kyle said. A very soft, gentle voice. "They had big tats, right? Especially on their faces? Like a number? You know the kind of people I'm talking about, Ramon."

"*Maras,* sure, okay? They're gonna find out I told you, I'm dead."

"They won't find out." Kyle turned to me. I'd been studying the GPS history on the cell. "Anything useful there?"

"One of the best GPS units around," I said. "A Brunton multi-navigator unit."

"I'm not a techie," Kyle said. "What does it do?"

"Barometer, altimeter, compass. And a twelve-channel parallel receiver."

"So?"

"You know those navigation systems in cars?" I said. "Same thing. This gives a simple, one-button to find your way back home, find your way anywhere. Stores up to ten reversible routes, with stops in between start and finish. It automatically records your trip and stores the data."

"So?" Kyle said again.

"Four different locations," I said.

"Meaning?"

"Just that. I can pinpoint three different places here on the south side. One up somewhere in Tucson."

"Does that thing show addresses?" He leaned over, I turned the tiny screen so he could read it.

"Within a few houses."

"What would we find there?"

"Not my job," I said.

"Nope. Sure not your job. Just write 'em down, I'll send out detectives. This gonzo here. This Ramon. Whaddya think he knows from this GPS thing?"

"Doesn't matter. I've got the locations. Data talks, even if he doesn't."

He waved the uniform over to keep Renteria secure. "You ready to go back in there?"

"Hooo," I said, not meaning to exhale so loud.

"Repellent," Kyle said. "Not pretty. You want to leave, just walk around the outside of the house. You got the GPS stuff, that's most important."

He waited.

"I'm here," I said finally. "Let's do it."

He grabbed the assist canes, levered himself to his feet quickly. Fit the metal support bands around his upper arms and moved easily. Slid back the screen door to the dining room, went inside, and I followed.

One body lay across the kitchen floor, a hand pushed against a carport utility door screen with such force the man had shoved the bottom corner of the door open three inches before he died. The CSU techs weren't finished, so the door stayed open. Flies already swarming inside, feasting on the blood from the stumps where all his fingers had been chopped off. The man's other hand was nailed to the linoleum flooring, the fingers also missing, the arm smashed to bits at the elbow so the forearm protruded at an impossible angle from the body. Impossible if you're alive, I mean. When the tech moved I saw the feet lying flat against the floor, the ankles smashed and both feet also nailed to the floor.

"Different pattern with the fingers," a CSU tech said. "Hand on the door, somebody just whacked it off with one blow. Probably used this." Pointing at a meat cleaver on the Formica countertop. "But this hand . . . first they nailed it down. Roofing nails, I'd say. Zinc heads. Then Joey here—"

"Joey?" I said. "You've got an ID?"

"Tom, Dick, Joey, what's the difference? They started out, they took off one finger at a time. The other two, in the living room, shotgun with no hesitation. Didn't even have weapons, but whoever came in here, they wanted something only from Joey here. Did his teeth first. Then, near as I can tell without running some DNA and blood analysis, this guy's hand? It's been chewed on.

"Chewed?" Kyle said. "He trying to fight off the horror?"

"Nah. He's already nailed down. My guess? A dog."

"A dog," Kyle said. "Jesus. I always think I've heard it all."

The tech placed a latex-gloved finger under the body's jaw, turned it so I could see his mouth.

Bits of teeth and bone.

"Teeth first, or last?" another CSU tech said. "But not random, I'd say."

"Bled out from both hands and mouth, small amount from the feet. They left this guy alive long enough to find what they wanted. Then they put the shotgun against his back, wham. Random?"

"These aren't gangbangers out to get revenge for some *vato* humping another *vato*'s sister. This is deliberate."

"Why are you so sure about that?" I said, done with my digital photographs.

"Well, I'm not. But first off, there's the familiar death card. *La Bruja* warns all snitches and rats and witnesses. *No me jodas*. Plus, in seven years working homicides, I've seen all kinds of mutilations, this just has the smell of deliberate torture, you know what I mean, lady?"

I did.

I went into the living room.

Sensory overload. Not the shotgun pattern. Nine double-ought pellets, bloody holes splattered across each man's shirt. The pattern tight, the shotgun probably no more than five feet away.

Not the pattern, nor the blood. Not the missing fingers. Just every detail of the room:

   cheap mesquite and fake rattan furniture
   overstuffed sofa and matching chair with huge
     cushions

    a dead woman
    a dead young child

The woman and child had been irrelevant to the
killers. I worked extra hard shutting down my gut feelings, shooting one picture after another.

Kyle moved next to me, his mouth to my ear.

"Guy was our inside man. Three years it took to get
him inside. Now he's just toast."

Rental house furniture with a busy tan and rust fabric
that wouldn't show stains, the kind of junk you buy at a
chain discount furniture outlet, no payment for one year,
no interest for two. Five-foot-long faux brass coffee
table, the mirrored top crazed with age. Flat black
assemble-it-yourself entertainment center with expensive
flat-screen TV and surround-sound speakers and DVD
equipment. Biker and car magazines everywhere, stacks
of porn tapes and DVDs.

I shot over a hundred images. Different aperture, different times. Had to mount my flash on the Nikon shoe
for the body in the corner. Enough. I went out to the
front yard, leaned against a TPD car in the driveway,
hands down in front, holding the Nikon while I tried a
mantra, to get the whole sensory data out of my system,
I couldn't leave the crime scene unless I started reclaim-
ing myself before I drove away. I can't do this work
much longer, a thought which had distracted me a lot
these days, distracted me now so that I didn't hear Kyle
until he came beside me.

"You all right?" Kyle said.

"Smiles and cries," I said finally.

"*Cries and Whispers?*" he said.

Out of my mantra, halfway between curious and irri-
tated. He mistook it for confusion. "An Ingmar
Bergman film, right?" he said.

"No. *Training Day*. Denzel takes this new detective,
Ethan Hawke, to Scott Glenn's house, Hawke's over-

loaded with some PCP Denzel made him smoke, but
Hawke says that's what the streets are. Smiles and cries.
How you've got to learn to hide them."

"Don't watch many cop movies. What do you see on
this street?"

Typical South Tucson street. Small stucco bungalows
on small lots, fencing everywhere, all the windows with
wrought-iron bars. Old cars, furniture, discarded toys,
even clothing, strewn around some of the yards. Half a
block away a large Dodge pickup sprawled across a front
lawn, the hood up, the car boom box speakers thundering.

"I don't see any people," I said finally.

"Hiding. They all know that *maras* have been here.
We'll do a house-to-house survey, but nobody'll know
anything, they didn't see or hear anything. They don't
want to be slaughtered, either."

"This gang, these *maras,* are they really that savage?"

"You've been inside, you've seen the slaughter. What
do you think?"

"The death card," I said. "Who's this *La Bruja*?"

"No idea."

"And the threat. *No me jodas.* Where'd *that* come
from?"

"Border slang. My theory? You know that movie
Heat?"

"I thought you didn't watch cop movies."

"The bank shootout. Pure adrenaline, watching that
scene. Anyway, there's this grungy guy who's part of the
early crew that robs the armored truck."

"Waingro," I said.

"Yeah. Well, he's holding a nine mil on the three armored car guys, who are stupefied out of their brains by
the accident and robbery. Waingro, he's pure psycho. He
says to one of the guards, 'Don't fuck with me. You want
to fuck with me?' And kills the guard. These *maras,*
they're like all gangbangers, they've got the director's
cut of movies like *Scarface*. They get off on all the movie

psychos. Anyway. That's my theory about these cards. So what are you doing at this crime scene, anyway?"

"I came here to look for financial records. I mean, that's why I thought I'd been asked. But the CSI techs didn't find any computers, any disks or data CDs, no bank account information, no deposit slips."

"The GPS units?"

"You'll know when your people seal off those locations."

Kyle eyed me carefully. "You know more about this than I do," he said finally. "I'm the lead homicide detective, but you know something more. Right?"

He unsnapped a leather pouch on his belt, his thumbs flying over the cell phone keyboard, sending several text messages, waited for brief replies.

"Listen," he said. "Word is that you're up for some job at TPD. Tracking *maras* computer accounts, bank records? Is that connected to this?"

"Ask Bob Gates," I said. "How'd you know that? About the job?"

"Word's around."

"Bob said that the word was *not* around."

"This is just between you and me."

"And who exactly are you?" I said.

"A cop with thirty-seven years on the force. Passed over for sergeant, some say. Didn't *want* to be sergeant, I say. Normally, I'd be off the street, in my little casita, watching TV and drinking tequila and once in a while thinking about eating my gun. Only on the bad days. They keep me around. I've been on so many homicides, I've always got something they need."

"Sounds to me like you enjoy still being around."

"A word in your ear," he said. "Some of the top suits, they don't want you. Jordan Kligerman. He's a good-looking stud, but he's a pogue. Never rode a mile in a unit, never took down a suspect. He's an accountant, he'll use you up."

"Thanks," I said. "Christopher. Who are these . . . these *maras*?"

He hesitated a long time. Not from wanting to hide things or avoid the discussion, just choosing his words.

"They're the worst of everything," he said finally. "The Colombians, the Russian mafia, these *maras* are the absolute worst of all the ruthless assassins I've ever known. You saw the woman and the kid? Executions. Meant nothing to them. Probably made the man watch before they nailed him down."

"Are drugs that serious a problem in Tucson?"

"Tucson," he said. "I've been here since the old days. Before stretch marks."

"And I should be interested in this . . . why?"

"In the old days, you used to know who did what. Gambling, women, horses and dogs, racing, I mean. The dog track is still here, but now there's a big greyhound rehabilitation group. They'll place a greyhound in your home. Only problem is, especially with the males . . . they're trained to race on the flat, to go after the rabbit. You try to adopt one of these males, they can't go up and down stairs, they can't even jump into your car. They only know what they've been trained to do. They don't know anything else."

"And you? These days, you don't know . . . what?"

"The border is broken, Laura. These days, it's not just your average Jose coming across so he can feed his family. Now, the people coming up from Mexico. Hell. Coming up from Central America. They're different people, different criminals, different values. But mainly, they're criminals."

A low-rider cruised slowly by, subwoofer pumping a salsa beat, the five occupants turning their heads in unison to stare at us while driving by. I flinched.

"Not a drive-by," Kyle said. "They're just curious."

"This violence, it all seems so . . . so random."

"Unpredictable. Seen enough here?"

Again, he sorted through what to say.

"This isn't about the drugs. It's about *control* of those drugs. I can get you a thick file, if you want in on this. I don't know, I'm not high enough in TPD to know why they want to hire you. But if you choose to go with TPD, count on me. I'll watch your back."

"Why would you promise that to somebody you just met?"

"You look like a woman with trouble in her heart, you talk about smiles and cries."

He pivoted his upper body, looking up and down the street, deciding what he wanted to say to me.

"Another word in your ear," he said finally.

"Yes?"

"I don't know anything about this possible job at TPD. But don't do it."

"Why?"

"You see anybody on this street yet?"

"No."

"Most of them are illegals. Or undocumented workers, if you're politically leftish. Most of the men, and they are mostly men, they send money back to Mexico. At Christmas, they all go home and celebrate Three Kings day. Then they find another coyote who'll smuggle them back across the border, so up here they can earn more money to send home. They pay two to five thousand dollars to get smuggled across, with a guide. Most of them haven't got the money, they've given all they earned to their families. So they take out loans to pay for the smuggling. It's all just . . . just, well, it's a system that benefits a few. The border is broken, Laura. People and drugs and all kinds of things flood northward. Whatever hushhush operation TPD wants you for, it's just a waste of time."

"And your advice?" I said.

"More than a few Tucson cops," he said. "They may not be on the take, but their eyes are for sale. They work on the edge, they depend on their CIs, but sometimes they use police secrets, something they've overheard, or an internal document they've seen, they trade off these secrets for CI tips."

"Okay, Bob," I said. "You've warned me, okay. So?"

"Forget it."

"Forget . . . what?"

"Whatever they've offered you."

"Chris."

"Christopher."

"Christopher. Nobody's offered me anything. I'm doing one small thing for them tomorrow. I get a payback, then I'm gone."

"Payback," he said. "Here's my view on payback. My ex drove a Honda Accord. It got stolen and recovered the next day, except the passenger seat was missing. Like they only had time to remove that one thing, and the heat showed around the corner. So a month later, my ex is bitch bitch bitch, get a new seat, so I'm at a junkyard looking for a replacement and I see this seat that looks so familiar, it's so familiar it's . . . it's the stolen seat, it's still got the smiley face decals on the side. That's when payback is just plain sour."

His cynicism enveloped me, overwhelmed me, I turned to my car.

"What small thing?" Kyle said.

"Say what?"

"You said, you're doing one small thing for TPD, then you're done."

"Take *my* advice, Christopher. You don't want to know."

"Fair enough."

"Thanks," I said. "Christopher, tell me. How'd you lose so much weight?"

"Seven hundred calories a day. Three hours on a treadmill. My wife said I'd got to take it off or she'd leave me."

"She must be happy."

"Well. She left me anyway. See you around."

I trudged to my Jeep Cherokee, set the Nikon on the

passenger seat, and drove away, I didn't even put the lens cap on or turn the battery off.

I called Mary Emich, apologized for being delayed, said I'd be there soon.

Headed up I-10 and turned east on Ina, but not really to meet Mary Emich. Just to go to the park and be by myself. In a world where a child's life meant so little, I wanted to spend time in my favorite spot in Tohono Chul.

The grotto, the Riparian area, the soothing watery ripples of the artificial creek bed and the puppyfish. A spot where I'd found serenity five years ago, but where I also set in irrevocable motion the events from which Tigger died.

But that's another story for another time.

7

"Oh, dear," the old woman said. "These aren't the desert pupfish."

Reading the placard beside the stream, listing several different kinds of endangered fish. She'd banged her walker into my serenity, couldn't stay in one position, moving around and around until I gave up.

"Over there," I said. Pointing to the grotto some twenty yards away. "This is the riparian habitat."

"This isn't the grotto? This plaza, this isn't the grotto?" Confused, trying to read her park map while navigating her walker.

"Let me show you," I said. "Just a minute." I dialed Mary Emich's number and she answered immediately. "I'm here. Near the grotto."

"Five minutes," Mary said.

"I appreciate your help," the old woman said. "But look, there are some fish in this little stream, I don't care if they're pupfish. I'm going to sit on the bench, I'm just going to listen to the water, I'm just going to watch these fish."

The bench where I'd been sitting, remembering.

Tohono Chul is a nonprofit Tucson park, dedicated to showing and preserving Sonoran Desert vegetation. Spread out over forty-nine acres, with a completely remodeled parking lot, many looped trails, and a lot of new fencing.

Some years before, the night security guard had been inexplicably shot five times in the head, and the park was now marginally less accessible. Most of the fencing would be easy to get over for anybody determined. Mostly, I realized, the fencing just kept out random night visitors like sexually active teenagers or the stray large dog, but not bobcats or coyotes.

I'd used the park five years before because I could always guarantee privacy when talking to clients. Back then, I rarely met clients face-to-face because I didn't like them seeing me.

I remember being nervous, back then. I remember I couldn't find the water fountain where, bending over to drink from the spray, I'd fingered my belt pouch, wanting to take another Ritalin or two, just to keep me focused.

Sliding the zipper open and closed, open and closed, trying to resist the pills. I did that a lot, back when I was addicted to meth.

But I'd always remember that day when I first met Ana Maria Juarez, which led to Tigger's murder.

I could hit *replay* and run the vivid memory.

Tigger was out of sight as I walked up to the pincushion cactus ramada. The circular roof was interlaced with twigs and branches, woven into a grid of plastic-coated green wire. A semicircular concrete bench provided shelter for those who wanted to escape the hot summer sun. I could hear traffic noises from Oracle and Ina roads, but nobody sat on the bench.

Tigger's real name was Tigist. She was Ethiopian, scarcely five feet tall, with luminous kohl-blackened eyelids and intense ocean-green irises, the eyes set deep over a long, slightly hooked nose in the exact middle of

a thin face. Since few people remembered how to pro-
nounce her name, she'd started calling herself Tigger
after reading a Pooh book to her son. And the name fit,
since both the fictional and the real Tigger were always
nervous, excited, bouncing up and down with relentless
energy.

Tigger was a Fugitive Recovery agent. She tracked
down bail-skippers, arresting them without any help
except assorted stun guns. I'd never met a client without having Tigger look them over first, then staying
out of sight during the meeting so she could track the
client back to a vehicle and make sure it left before I
did. It's part paranoia, I tell you, but when I did
mostly illegal things with computers, I had fixed rules
about security.

And the first rule was to make sure that clients were
exactly who they claimed to be. I still follow that rule.

Another rule was to avoid letting clients know things
about me, which was why I disliked personal meetings.
I'm a lot more social now, but back then few people
knew what I did. I remember when Tigger told me from
her microphone that the women had moved.

I remember what they looked like, the colors, the fingernails, what they wore, and how they spoke.

*I'd walked along curving dirt paths toward guidepost
twenty-six, where a trapezoidal concrete table sat underneath another circular ramada.*

*Two women sat on a concrete bench along one side of
the table. One of them toyed with a folded sheet of paper and a yellow legal pad. Seeing me approach, she
stood up quickly, her eyes darting in all directions to see
if we were alone. She was near my height, but slim and
small-boned, with shoulder-length brown hair pulled
back by twin brown barrettes. She wore yellow spandex
runners' pants and a pale strawberry North Face tank
top, with spaghetti straps over bare arms and shoulders.*

Veins popped along her well developed arms, and her
body looked muscled and taut in that way which only
comes from working out with free weights.

"Laura?" I heard somebody say. "Excuse me?"

This had to be Mary Emich, seeing the old woman,
the walker, confused, mistaking her for me.

"Over here," I said.

A tall blond woman hurried toward me, not running,
but stepping quickly and with purpose. Wearing a
sleeveless cotton pullover, with a small hula girl on the
front, bits of yarn hanging loose for the hula skirt. A
short above-the-knees Madras skirt, the kind you wash
and ring out by hand to dry in the sun. Lightly streaked
and dyed-blond hair bunched loosely and carelessly in
the back with a huge butterfly clip and

> two dangling earrings, wood, parrots
> designer sunglasses
> another pair of sunglasses tucked into her hair
> a tiny patch of green dye, where she parted her
>   hair in front

"I'm Mary." Held out a hand, a huge smile over white
teeth. "And your name is . . . what *is* your name?" She
fumbled through a stack of folders and pads held under
her left arm, trying to be casual, taking off the sunglasses and sticking them up into her hair without realizing she now had two pair up there already. A real or a
feigned casualness, asking me my name. She *knew* who I
was, but I measured her fear in her offhand, seemingly
forgetful question.

"Laura," I said. "Laura Winslow."

A clanking sound, the old woman moving around.

"Let's go to the grotto," Mary said.

A half-moon-shaped pond, set against an unfinished
wall, probably from the original property. Water bub-

bled from uncapped pipes and something intensely blue glittered and disappeared when I looked into the pond.

"Puppyfish," I said to myself. Knelt to look. "I call them puppyfish."

Close up, the pond alive with small, silvery fish, barely two inches long, each banded with half a dozen or more stripes of brilliant blue.

"They don't live very long," Mary said. "But they're so beautiful."

I read the placard aloud. " 'Desert Pupfish develop quickly, sometimes reaching full maturity within two or three months. Although their average life span is short, some survive more than a year.' "

She giggled.

Actually, while reading, I looked sideways as best I could, trying to read Mary Emich and contrasting what I saw with what I'd memorized from her résumé. The giggle stopped, she turned in profile, a strong face, strong profile, somehow reminding me of Crazy Horse, or not really the man, but that big statue being carved in the hills near the four presidents.

"That green spot," I said. "Right above your forehead. Does that glow in the dark, or what?"

"Oh." She touched it, I realized she'd forgotten it was even there.

"A dye stick, supposed to be gold. It'll wash out tonight."

I stood suddenly, faced her directly.

Several inches taller than me, which put her about five-foot-ten. As tall and slim as a Kansas cornstalk with curves. Her smile returned quickly. A brilliant smile, nodding her head as though to some song, both pairs of sunglasses falling from her hair. She picked them up, not at all embarrassed.

"Behind your back," she said. I turned around, confused. "No. Under your shirt. Is that a pistol?" she said.

"Yes."

My shirt must have ridden up in the back when I knelt to look at the puppyfish. So she'd seen my Beretta, so she'd been reading me also.

"Most people don't notice it," I said.

"Nine millimeter," she said. "Glock?"

"Beretta," I said shortly.

"I've fired the 92FS, but that looks totally different. What model Beretta?"

She cocked her head, a combination of seriousness and curiosity.

"A new model," I said. "A Px4 Storm."

"Can I see it?"

"No. No, you can't. I came here about computers, not handguns."

"I shoot a lot," she said. "There's a target range down off Flowing Wells. Inside a gun store. I go there two or three times a week. But I never heard of that model Beretta." I must have looked skeptical. "Even from a few feet away, I can see there's a very different back-strap. What else?"

"Slide stop can be either standard or low profile. Magazine release button comes in different sizes, depending on small or large grip. And I've got this rigged out for constant action, with a spurless hammer."

"Magazine capacity?"

"Seventeen," I said. "But I could extend it to twenty. This is just a little weird, two women talking about pistol tech specs. How come you know guns?"

"I grew up on a farm. Well. My family owned a farm, for a while, but the bank foreclosed, so we all trooped off as seasonal pickers. You name it, we picked it. Everybody had guns of some kind."

"I thought seasonal pickers were, well, from Central America."

"We were poor. Apples, pears, grapes, tomatoes, cherries, walnuts, we traveled all around the circuit. But this is Tucson. Why do you carry a pistol?"

"If you think I'm that kind of PI," I said, "if you think

that I'm available for personal security, or a bodyguard . . . I'm not really the person you need."

She fingered a medal at her throat, dangling from a silver chain. A religious medal of some kind, probably
Catholic. I don't know much about religion.

"No," she said finally. "I don't need a bodyguard
right now. I just need your help."

"For what, Mary?"

"Will you? Help?"

Not begging or pleading, not defensive, just an out-
right question, almost matter-of-fact, her mouth starting
a smile, then just open.

I tell you, she had this . . . honesty? Directness? Open-
ness? For the life of me, I couldn't figure out why I liked
her so immediately.

"You *are* Laura?" she said.

"Yes. I am."

Confirming it to herself, the smile gone, replaced by
lips closed and curved down gracefully, like a sad
clown's smile.

Liked her, yes, I liked her for whatever reason, but I
wasn't in the park to find friends, and that was the
problem.

"Listen. Mary. I have to be clear about something. I'm
seeing you as a favor. For my friend Bob Gates. You
talked to him, he gave you my name. That's pretty much
all you have to know, I mean, know about why I'm here.
But I don't have much time. I should really be driving up
to Window Rock right now."

"Are you Navajo?" she said.

"Hopi," I said. "Half. Please. Don't ask about my going up to the rez."

"I'm Lakota Sioux. Half. But . . . why won't you
help me?"

"Mary," I said. "I don't really know what you want.
Something about *maras*? That's all Bob told me. Something on a computer?"

"Mr. Gates told me that you were a computer expert. I Googled your company." Reaching for one of the hundred stray ends of paper sticking out of the packet of folders and pads. "So you know about . . . hacking?"

"Yes."

"You know, uh, I don't understand computer security that well, you know how people hack into your system? You do that kind of work?"

"Yes."

"Illegal hacking?"

The smile, back again. This time, too bright. She giggled, something I knew a lot about. Giggling around a stranger. When I first started spending a lot more time around strangers, I hung by walls, sat on couches, and giggled because I didn't yet know how to interact. Mary Emich's giggles sounded like she'd laughed all her way through life. *This woman*, I thought, *is wrapped way too tight*.

"Yes," I said shortly. "But I don't do anything illegal."

"But you know people that, what do you call it, um . . . create identities?"

"Fake ID?"

"More than that."

"You mean . . ." I said, understanding where she was going and already backing away from her—in fact I took two steps back and nearly stumbled into the grotto pond—"you mean," I said, "change somebody's identity."

"Yes."

"Whose?"

"There's a girl," Mary said. Shook away the thought of a tear, I wondered if she was wrapped too tight to cry, I sure knew what that was like.

"Your daughter."

"She's not really my daughter. Here." She pulled a teenager's pink diary from inside a folder. "I wrote in this, I couldn't find anything else to write in. This is the girl's story. Somebody almost killed her once. I'm afraid . . . she's Mexican, she's illegal. I'm afraid, with what showed up on one of our computers, Laura, I'm afraid somebody knows about her and wants to hurt me. Hurt her."

She held out the diary.

"Read this," she said.

But I sidestepped away, slung my bag over my shoulder. Ready to leave.

"I can't help you," I said. "I *won't* help you. Not with a fake ID."

"Please," Mary said. Iron in that word, pure steel.

I remembered what Sandy told me about Mary's astrological chart.

Awash in nervous energy always on the move both physically and mentally. No way are either of you ever, ever, ever going to make a snap decision. It just isn't in your makeup.

"At least, okay, I can look at whatever is on your computer," I said. "What is it that makes you so afraid?"

"The *maras*," Mary said. "They're inside the park."

Instinctively, I looked around. She put a hand on my shoulder.

"No. I mean, there's nobody here. No real person. It's on a website."

"*Maras,*" I said. "Until yesterday, I'd never heard of them. Now *every*body wants to tell me about them. Is it a threat, have you been threatened?"

"Not really. No."

"Your daughter, this girl," holding up the pink diary, "has *she* been threatened?"

Ah! I thought.

"How old is she?"

"I'm not sure. Fourteen, fifteen?"

"Was she a heroin mule?"

That staggered her, she reeled against the sign describing the pupfish, she shuffled her papers, she looked everywhere but into my eyes. "How did you know that?" she said.

"A lucky guess."

"Just hearing about you," she said, "just meeting you and your Beretta," she said, "I don't think you make guesses of any kind."

"Another case," I said finally. "And it was really an educated guess. Is that part of why I'm here?"

"No, not really."

"You're kinda hard to pin down, Mary Emich. Was the girl a heroin mule?"

"Yes. Once," she said. "At least once. And I can't let it happen again."

"You asked about whether I could create new identities."

"Yes."

"For your daughter."

"For the girl, yes."

"And?" Stunned at my insight. "You want a new identity for yourself?"

Mary fingered her religious medal, kept her eyes on me, nodding.

"If that's what it takes," she said. "Yes. I'll give up my whole life here. We'll go somewhere, we'll start as a mother and her daughter."

"And if they find you then?"

She stepped off the path, bent down to what looked like a dead twig, thrust in the ground and surrounded by a circle of foot-high chicken wire. The ID tag said NIGHT BLOOMING CEREUS, but soil fragments blurred the Latin name. A few yards away, she knelt beside a little legume vine with half-inch magenta flowers against a background of dark green leaves.

"The flowers will open a bit in the late afternoon," Mary said. "When it cools down. *Galactia wrightii*. The flowers shine brightly, once they open. Our Curator of Plants says . . . this is a great landscaping plant for people who work days, because it is at its best as they return home. The vines will form a low mound or climb if a shrub or trellis is provided to probably four or six feet."

She stood up.

"Mr. Gates told me what you do best. You find people. Is that what you meant? That somebody like you, a scalp hunter, no, a bounty hunter, you'd find me even with a new identity."

"Yes. Eighty percent certain."

"Eighty percent. So you can fail."

"To find somebody?"

"To find somebody, yes."

"With a new identity, a false identity?"

"Yes."

My cell rang. Caller ID showed it was Bob Gates.

"Let me check if Ken Charvoz is here. I'll be right back."

"What?" Mary said, when I disconnected. "What's wrong?"

"You're so emotionally honest," I said finally. "If I wanted to, I'd find you. They, whoever they are . . . they would, too. And what would you do then?"

"Then? If they still find me," she said. "Then I'll get a gun."

"And then?"

"I'd do anything to protect this girl," she said finally. "I'm a complete pacifist. I can't stand senseless violence. But, to protect this girl, I'd do anything."

"Even if you had to shoot somebody?"

"Even if I had to kill somebody. Yes. If that's God's plan. Yes. It would . . . it would be the end of my life, as I know it. But Ana Luisa's life is more important. She's the future."

"I've never met anybody quite like you," I said.

"What do you mean?" Mary said.

"Like I said. You're so . . . so . . . emotionally honest."

"What do you mean?"

"We're not so different," I said. "I'm not sure about

God's part in anything. But you and I, as people, we're really not so different.

"I asked what you would do to protect your child. You said you'd kill."

"If that's truly God's plan," she said. Hand on her religious medal, hiding it between thumb and index finger, I couldn't see what saint she admired, who would protect her, and why God would approve killing.

"Yes," she said. Defiant, sad, determined. "Wouldn't you do the same?"

8

"Did you know?" I shouted into my cell.

"Know?" Gates said.

"Did you know?"

"What? Laura, what are you talking about?"

"The girl."

"Girl? Laura, what? I give up."

"You didn't know about the girl," I said. Trying to calm myself in the old way I'd calmed for years. Deep breath, *one Mississippi*, breath, *two Mississippi*.

"What girl?"

"I just met Mary Emich."

"Her daughter? Is that who you're talking about?"

"Yes, Bob. Her daughter, my daughter, my granddaughter. You played me, Bob, you fucking *played* me."

"Laura, whoa, what, oh, no," he said. "I did *not* play you."

"Yah, sure. The dead girl at the crime scene. You knew about her when you came to see me yesterday."

"Laura. I talked to you yesterday. I first heard about the crime scene not more than twenty minutes before I called you today. Besides. The dead child was a boy. Not a girl."

"You *played* me, Bob. You've known these bastards killed children. You played on that, you knew I'd have a hard time saying no once I knew this *maras* business involved dead children."

"No. I did not." I waited, he'd something more to say. "Kligerman," he said. "He thought, he calculated you'd have more interest. Knowing about the children. I told you, he's an accountant."

"And you want me to meet him later."

"If you can. Yes."

"For drinks."

"Just to introduce you."

"To introduce me."

"He's not all bad, Laura. He's divorced, got a young girl of his own, you know, he thinks about children's safety."

"Children's safety. There's an inside hook there, Bob. He's using you in order to use me. And what's the story with this detective, this Christopher Kyle?"

"The story?"

"He told me, he said there were rumors, whistling down the lane, that I might be working for TPD."

"Laura. He's guessing."

"How would he even know what to guess about? How many people know about me, Bob?"

"Five. Me. Kligerman, and three of his most trusted staff."

"Nobody else?"

"The chief of police originated the idea."

"And Kyle? Is he a suspect?"

"Christopher Kyle? God, no. He's a legend in Homicide. Old school. Excellent at a crime scene, a disaster with new information technologies. Somebody tried to get him to work a computer, he finally pointed the mouse at the screen and clicked."

"I like him," I said. "If I decided to do this work for TPD, and I have *not* decided that at all, but if it happened, could Kyle be assigned to the team?"

"Not my decision. But I'll ask Kligerman."

"Are you on a secure line?" I said.

"Ummm. What does that mean?"

"Find a pay phone and call me back."

"A pay phone," he said. "Geez, do they still exist?"

"Just do it."

"What's the difference?"

"Because I can dump this cell number in a minute, but you're . . . you're not secure, where you're calling from."

He hung up abruptly. My cell rang in seven minutes.

"What does that mean?" Gates said. "That you can dump your cell number?"

"Doesn't matter. I need to ask you a basic question."

"About working for TPD?"

"Yes."

"So ask."

"I'm assuming this whole business with Kligerman is a smoke screen."

Gates laughed into the mouthpiece, a real belly laugh. "I told him you weren't dumb."

"But the real thing is to find some digital trace of this bad cop. Right?"

"Right."

"So give me a direction," I said. "Steer me so I don't waste all kinds of computer time for myself and my staff, looking at records of everybody who works for the Tucson PD."

"Detectives," he said finally.

"Have you got a name?"

"No. Absolutely not."

"How about . . . I looked at the org chart for TPD. There are four basic substations. East, South, West, Midtown."

"Could be somebody in any of those substations."

"Bob," I said. "Narrow the search for me. Please."

"Violent Crimes."

"That's definite?"

"That's a guess. Nothing more. Not even a guess. A hunch."

"You're playing me, Bob."

"No. I won't let my gut instinct steer you. Not yet."

"Okay," I said. "I'll meet Kligerman. I'll play along with him, about whatever I assume he thinks is the *real* reason for TPD wanting my help. Thanks."

I flipped my cell shut, cutting off the call. I started to power the cell down, but it rang.

"I'm in Tuba City," Nathan said. "I'll just wait for you here."

"Tuba City," I said. *Shit, shit shit.* "Umm, well, I'm just about ready to leave."

"It's almost noon, Laura."

"Yes. Noon."

"It'll take you at least four hours to get here."

"Tuba City," I said brightly. "I'll show you where I used to live."

"Well . . . I can't wait here that long."

"Okay," I said. "Okay, where do I go?"

"To meet me?"

"Yes. Where on the rez?"

"You haven't left yet," he said finally.

"Just another half hour, maybe an hour."

"The ceremony is at sundown."

"What ceremony?"

"The boy," Nathan said. His voice drifted in and out, I'd moved around and without knowing was between two different cell towers, the signal weakening. "The born-to and born-for clans are already assembling up near Monument Valley. There'll be many, many people there."

"I'll make it."

"No," he said. The slow, almost toneless cadence of sadness. "No, you won't be here."

"I might be late, but I *will* be there."

"No." A very *very* long pause. "Goodbye, Laura."

"*Nathan!* Wait, what are you telling me, wait, I'll be there. I promise."

"If you'd meant to come," he said, "you'd be here already."

"It's just not that simple."

"Yes. It is."

"I'll find you tonight, no matter how long it takes me to get there, I'll leave in five minutes. Where will you be?"

"I can't tell you."

"You *can't*?"

"I'm sorry, Laura."

"I'll find you."

"That's just not really going to happen."

"No, wait, Nathan, what does this mean?"

"I'm sorry, Laura."

"Sorry? Sorry about *what*?"

Vibrations pulsing through the cell, just a technical thing where digital signals exactly match a resonance point on the cell phone chip, but the vibrations moving up my hand like symptoms of a heart attack.

"I'm driving through a flock of sheep," Nathan said. "They're spilling across the road, probably thirty of them, nobody's watching them, they're just moving to find someplace to eat."

"Fuck the sheep!" I shouted. "Don't do this to me."

"I belong up here," Nathan said. "I'm part of *Dineh-tah*. Someday, you'll figure out where you belong."

"I belong with *you*!"

"Goodbye, Laura."

He disconnected.

Figure out where I belong? Figure out my identity?

I've been working on this forever, I thought I'd finally resolved my life.

Those of you who've known me over these years, those who've read my stories, you all know, my friends, you know I always talk about crossing borders. Drug addiction, yes, I crossed back and forth over that border.

Safe now.

Safe for good.

Computers. I've broken into so many computers illegally, I no longer could even estimate with any certainty how many computers or networks or websites. For several years, I used computers all over the world, against their will, against their owners' lousy security, I'd used those computers as drones. Mostly to hide my digital self from anybody. I rarely left traces.

Now any twelve-year-old boy with the will, the computer, and the impishness or malignancy, anybody could do what I'd done. At night, instead of playing with themselves, boys play with their computers. So I, personally, I no longer did that, I no longer crossed over the border between illegal and legal.

Death.

Now, there's a border.

You either are. Or you're not.

You can kill entire families, just because you can kill.

You can even kill Ena, kill Bambi's mother, with a hunter's bullet. You can also walk up and kick Bambi in the face, but he will grow up. Until he dies. That's the fate, the destiny of loving animals. They live just long enough to break your heart. Of course, people are animals, too.

Love.

I'd thought I'd crossed this border for good, once I'd met Nathan Brittles. And yet . . . and yet, here I am, he's . . . gone?

There's one final border I want to cross.

My name.

Over the years, I've had many names. *Many* names. For the past few years, I have been Laura Winslow.

That is not my real name.

My Hopi name is Kauwanyauma. A Hopi word.

Butterfly Revealing Wings of Beauty.

This is the irony of that last border I want to cross. I am an *ex*pert in tracking people down, in exposing false identities, yes, in creating them as well. At some time in my past, probably in those years of drugs and sex when

I lived in Yakima, I created a whole new identity for a woman named Laura . . . Laura . . . I don't even remember what last name I used at first.

Winslow is a small, decaying town in Arizona. I chose that name one day while looking at a map. I created my whole identified life from the name Laura Winslow. Social Security number. Driver's license, credit cards, even a major-league business in computer forensics.

You see the irony, my old friends? I can track down anybody. Eighty percent minimum. Guaranteed. I'd just been asked to create a new identity for Mary Emich and her girl. I could do that in thirty-six hours, bottom line.

But sometimes, creating new identities works. I'm the proof.

I don't even know my real name.

I was born on the Hopi reservation in a traditional village. I never knew my mother, never knew her name, never knew her life except for the singular fact that she was a prostitute working the southwest rodeo circuit. My father had a name. George Loma. But he left no written records behind that he ever existed. When I knew him, he didn't even carry a wallet or any kind of identification holder. I can distinctly remember when I was twelve, by then I had spent a lot of time in bars in Flagstaff, so I knew about ID cards and driver's licenses and social security cards. When I asked my father about these things, he pulled out an old cigar box filled with newspaper clippings of rodeo events that he'd entered and sometimes won. *Here's my identification,* he said then. *See my name? I circled my name every time.*

But in the dozens of newspaper clippings, the circled name varied from year to year, gradually stabilizing on George Loma. So I don't even know if that was his birth name, nor did he ever reveal his secret Hopi name.

I am nameless, as much as anybody can ever be.

But with my ability to create truly authentic-looking identity papers, I am now named Laura Winslow.

Do you see the irony of my life?

One of the best private investigators in the business, absolutely dynamite at finding people who don't want to be found. But I can't even find my own past!

9

"I love this part of the park," Mary said.

She'd come back to get me, not really paying attention to me, intent on her own purpose and leading, toward that purpose, me along one of the park's paths. I hardly looked at the signposts, scarcely could focus on where I was, on what I was doing.

"God*damn* those sheep," I said.

"What?"

Still within myself, everything outside my emotional shield.

"Fuck those goddam sheep," I said.

"Laura," Mary said. "What sheep?"

"What?"

"You're cursing some sheep."

Looking around, lost just for that instant. Like when you're in your car at a stoplight, foot on the brake, but the car next to you moves ahead and you react in panic that somehow *you* are moving.

The entire heavens shift while you remain static, you're aware that events and people and machines function totally outside your control or awareness.

"I can't stay here," I said.

"What's wrong?"

"Talk to me while I go to my car. That's all the time I've got."

"But . . . Laura. You promised. You said at least you'd look. At the computer. You said you'd help me. Laura?"

"Let's do it really quick," I said.

"Are you sick?"

"Let's get it over with."

"Thank you," she said.

Walking ahead of me, always turning to slow for me trailing behind, lost in my own world, Mary herself very much a person used to walking these paths while dealing with the public, while accommodating other people.

I can't exactly say what I'd seen to like in Mary Emich.

I can't tell you why I felt close to her, but most of all, why I didn't just leave her and drive away, drive up to the rez.

I'm really confused, I thought. *What do I do?*

My offer to help Mary. Something morbid or coincidental, a contrast between the murdered child, Mary's not-quite-a-daughter, and my own girls, Spider and her baby?

Two years, that's how long I've loved Nathan.

Two years.

However does somebody say goodbye, after just two years?

Is it my fault?

These thoughts left me paralyzed, so I had to tamp them way down inside and resolve to come back to them later.

"I love this grotto," Mary said. "I really love the riparian area. Don't you?"

"I've got bad memories of this place."

But lost in her own thoughts and emotions, she ignored me.

"This place, the grotto, it makes me write poetry, it makes me put things into words. In the shade of the

sycamores, in the ramada, the plaza, with its deep blue
Mexican tile work, oh, I try to write haikus about this.
Except I have a hard time keeping myself to the three
lines."

She stopped.

" 'As a gentle breeze wafts the scent of chocolate flowers up into my brain and the *splisssshsplassssh* of the waterfall snarepats my eardrums, there, there, it's okay,
everything's okay, sweetheart.' I wrote that poem, it's really a dreadful poem, but I wrote it for my daughter, for
Ana Luisa. I got a few lines like a haiku. Around the
rock wall, five syllables for the first line, but I kept wanting to write more first lines of five syllables. 'The wild-
flowers in spring. The pingponging penstamens,' no,
that's seven. 'The bowing bluebells, the shimmering
salvia,' well, seven again."

No idea where she was leading me. Not with her poetry. Not with our destination along the caliche pathway.

"The night-blooming cereus of Ron's garden, inter-
twined and climbing up the mesquite trees. You know,
it's hokey. I think of poetry when I look out Mary I's
window, that's one of the women I work with. They call
us Mary E and Mary I. I love watching the baby coyote
pups cool off and splash in the fountain of the vacated
children's garden. And there's this chunky, purple lizard,
he's called Vin. He hangs out near the stone-covered water fountain, he dares to cross my path every day. Maybe
he's telling me to slow down? Someone or something
snatched off his tail the other day. He's not bothered at
all. Life goes on. Here we are. This is what used to be
the Haunted Bookshop. Now it's our education center,
our discovery center."

She swung open a door, held the metal bar with her
left hand. A gold wedding band, a diamond ring, and on
her small finger, a Cladagh ring, the heart turned inward.

I'm taken.

"I didn't know you were married," I said.

"Well, I am, well . . . I'm not, I'm . . . he's dead."

"I'm so sorry."

"A year ago. Fourteen months. Iraq. Are you? Married?"

She'd already scanned my left hand, looking for a ring. Not much got by her.

"No. I have a daughter. And a granddaughter."

"You're old enough to have a granddaughter?" she said. "I'm thirty-six, you don't look much older than me."

"I was really young when I had the baby. Fifteen, I think."

"You were married before . . . ?"

"That was a long time ago," I said. "And I don't talk about my life."

The edge of my sorrow popped out, she smiled, I wondered again, does she cry? Her smile widened even further, she tilted her head slightly, and I felt her sweetness wash over me, so it wasn't just a coincidence that I liked her.

Sometimes, two people just hit it off. Bam. An emotional connection during the first ten minutes.

"Uh . . . let me show you the computer."

"What kind of facial muscles make these dimples?" I said. Held up a finger, reached out to touch the vertical lines above her smiling mouth.

"Actually, it's the lack of muscles. You smile, but your whole face can't smile with you. We've got to go upstairs."

Inside the building, she led me past photographs and exhibits, up a narrow flight of stairs, and past a closed office door.

"Jo's office," she said. "Jo Falls. Director of public programs."

"Mary?"

A man's voice from an alcove overlooking the downstairs exhibits. Mary steered me around a corner into a work area, several computers placed at different stations along three sides of the alcove.

"This is Ken," she said. "Ken Charvoz, Laura Winslow."

Tall, slim, long curly black hair, somewhere along toward handsome but definitely eroded somehow by life, and certainly on the other side of forty. He gave Mary a slight hug as we shook hands.

"Bob mentioned you," I said. "Bob Gates."

"Oh," he said. Now both of his hands on mine. "He just called me. Said you've had a rough morning. A bad crime scene."

"I've seen worse," I said finally. "But never a dead child."

The completely *wrong* thing to say in front of Mary.

"Child?" she said. "Child, what dead child? Who is Bob Gates?"

"Nobody," I said. Quick as I could, smiled a bit, got her automatic smile back. "Just something for the Tucson Police Department."

"For an old friend of mine," Ken said. "A good man. But, Laura. You're not here to talk about TPD. You want to see the website."

He sat at one of the computers, opened the web browser.

"Totally a coincidence," he said. "It's not bookmarked, not obvious. I'd Googled something last weekend, so I went to the browser history file. Found something that shouldn't be there."

Clicked the mouse, waited for a site to load.

Welcome to
ChupaLuck Casino Online

A variety of images loaded slowly.

"Chupa," Ken said. "A small tribe, another Indian casino, my first thought. So I Googled the name. No tribes, at least in this hemisphere. You must be familiar with these sites," he said to me. Page fully loaded, yes, very familiar.

"First off," I said. "The name means nothing to me. It could be real, mostly likely not. Got most of the traditional images for an online casino. Your account name, for logging in. Your password."

"Ken," Mary said. "Show her the other page."

"Just wait," I said. "I've got my routines, I guess. So, by using this casino, you play totally online. You don't download free games, like the legit online casinos offer. All this place wants is that you list a valid credit card or bank account, from which they say they guarantee they'll use to pay out winnings."

"Is it a scam?" Ken said. "Like stealing credit card numbers?"

"Possibly legit. See this image?"

24/7 Customer Service
Toll Free Phone Lines
Live! Chat Room
Email Contact

"Got a registered eight-hundred number phone line. Email address. All this is traditional. They're not out to scam you right away, they just want your money. The downside is how long they'll stay in business. Most of these casino websites are located in Central America or on a Caribbean Island."

"Can *you* find out where?"

"You have to understand, all you're looking at is a web page. On a web server, a computer that could be anywhere in the world. Literally, anywhere. The money transfers take place in a completely separate place, again, anywhere in the world. I can find out where the web server is, I can do that easily. Then it gets hard."

"Show her the page," Mary said.

"Before I do that," Ken said, "you should know what *Chupa* probably means. If you Google the word, it can be a lollipop, somebody's pet dog, somebody's name, or business or a flower. Mostly likely, though, it's short-hand for *el chupacabra*."

"Sounds like a Subway special sandwich," I said.

"No," Ken said. "It means 'the goatsucker.' "

"A vampire bat?"

"No. They're real. I've seen them, deep in Mexico. Eight, nine inches long. They love blood, but they don't suck it out. When they bite into living flesh, usually a cow, a horse, the bat secretes a fluid so the blood won't congeal. Then they lap up the blood. *Chupacabras* are mythical. Stories began in mid-seventies, with dead farm animals in Puerto Rico, funny punctures on their necks. Stories spread in the countryside. Hundreds of animals slaughtered, drained of their blood, mutilated."

"Like the Navajo skinwalker stories," I said.

"Sure. One website report said, 'It was as if all had been sucked out through the eyes. It had empty eye sockets and all the internal organs had disappeared.' The stories spread from Puerto Rico to other Caribbean islands, then jumped across the water to Mexico, Central America, and finally into the southern United States. Florida, Texas, and Arizona. Now," Ken said, "let's go back to the casino. See this menu of items across the bottom of the page?"

Home—About Us—Slots—Games—Tournaments—Help

He clicked on Games. Another web page, listing traditional casino games. Poker. Roulette. Craps. Keno. Anything and everything to take your money. Ken clicked on the item *Tournaments*. A much longer list, listing different payouts to winners, the list scrolling all the way down to the bottom of the page. Ken put on a pair of drugstore reading glasses, their plastic lenses reflecting the web page colors as he peered close and clicked on one item.

ChupaLuck DeLux. Another web page filled the screen slowly, a huge black and white photo of a man's face, the mulatto-skinned face itself partially covered with a large tattoo. *Mara 18.*

"That's it," she said. "Now find the other page."

"Wait," I said. "That's . . . *what*?"

"The tattoo. When I found the young girl—you have to read the diary."

"I will, Mary. I will read it. But how's this tattoo connected to the girl?"

"When I found her," she said. "There were several men, all dead. With the same kind of tattoo, except the number was different. Twenty-seven. Not eighteen. Ken. Show her the other page."

"The *Maras* gangs," Ken said. Clicking through menus, trying to find something. "Tattoos are a gang symbol. I found it, was under the links page to other gambling sites." The top of the page had a small image. Underneath it read simply

**La Bruja Pray for her now
Our mother of the maras**

Mary gasped, fingering the religious medal at her throat. I thought the image was a tarot card, but looking closer I saw it was a postcard image advertising an old Mexican movie. I'd seen many of them a year ago, when the collector and art historian David Schultz showed Vincent Basaraba some full-size posters from 1950s Mexican B films.

LA BRUJA
THE WITCH

I stepped sideways, my foot looking for a chair. I sat down too hard, too focused, a hand already in my bag, concentration on what I was thinking. The chair rolled away from me and I fell heavily to the floor. Mary's stack of papers and folders flooded the room as she instinctively threw up her arms to steady me, Mary on one side and Ken on the other, but I sat on the floor, found the cell phone I wanted, and called Alex.

"Laura," she said. "What up?"

Alex Emerine, my business partner and friend.

"Who's there with you?"

"Sarah B and Sarah C, Stefan, and Kelle Maslyn. The new video woman."

"Stop whatever you're doing. Call up a website named chupaluckcasino.com and work backwards. Find out anything and everything, you know what to do."

"Laura. We're almost done with the phony green card online scam."

"Dump it for now. Call me back, report anything new. Wait. Ken. What happens when you click on that tattoo?"

"Dead end." An almost totally blank page came up, showing only two boxes. One required a user identity, the other a password."

"Who has access to this computer?"

"Practically anybody," he said. "Or, I guess, practically everybody. When either Jo or I are here, we can turn over one of these computers to park staff, interns, maybe even volunteers. If nobody's around during the day, anybody can use this computer, anybody who comes into the building. At night, only the security people."

"These computers are networked," I said. "We don't know who used this computer. Or why. I need permission to look at some key files on your network's main computer."

"I don't think the director would allow that," Mary said.

"Does she have to know?" Ken asked.

"I don't work illegally," I said. "Can the two of you explain it to her? It would be just a onetime thing. I'd go in there to get the log-in data on everybody who's used this computer in the past three days."

"The director's out of town," she said. "Vacation. Somewhere in Hawaii."

"I need somebody's permission."

"It's a one time thing," Ken said. Working it out for himself. Nodding as he ran through each point of his decision. "Somebody's used a park computer for online gambling. It's totally against the ethics, against all the park stands for. You only want one data list. You'll not change or delete any network files. Yes. You have my permission."

"I don't think so," I said.

He'd set it up to take the fall, to assume responsibility and, on the downslope, to assume blame and repercussions if his decision was wrong. He knew Mary was stressed beyond normal, okay, so he wanted to help a good friend, okay, but he also assumed that I was one hundred percent ethically moral.

I'm not.

"Yes," Ken said. "I'll give you access permission. I figure, what you're going to do is hack into our network from outside, right?" I nodded. "And the easier it is to hack in, the easier it would be for *any*body to hack in. Right?"

I nodded again.

"What's the reality of that happening?"

"Of somebody hacking into your system?"

"Yes."

"True odds?" I said. "Within twelve hours, I can upload every one of your files. All your financial and personnel data, all your emails stored on any of the networked computers, all personal stuff on individual computers. Then I'll plant some software where nobody would ever see it on your main network computer, and that software would let me use everything you've got for my own reasons. I could send viruses, spam email, I'd just hijack your computers and you'd never know the difference."

"Is it that bad?" Mary said. "You could really do that?"

"Yes. It's that bad. Total chaos, millions of sheep never see the wolves."

"So we're doing the park a service," Ken said. "We're testing our security, we've probably never thought much about it. Yes. Do it."

I gave instructions on my cell.

"Tohono Chul Park," Alex said. "Is that the client?"

"Yes." Only a small lie, a personal lie.

"And what's the fee?"

"Pro bono." That, I can't lie about with my partners.

"Bottom line?" Alex said. "What do you hope I'll find?"

"Bottom line . . . I don't know. Deep background, a connection, any financial connections with a Central American cartel called *maras*. Evidence of laundering drug money out of the U.S."

"Slim pickings."

"First, get the name of whoever used this computer to log in to the website. Then track the website itself, crack the passwords, tell me what's out there."

"Well. It's not like we're going where nobody's gone before."

"Last, put somebody on a search for anything you can find about a woman, or an old Mexican movie, called *La Bruja*."

"Funky. I can tell you right now there's a mountain bike with that name. And I think a pop singer. But we'll check."

"Contact David Schultz. Ask him about that name. Call in whatever extra help you need."

"Twenty-four seven," Alex said. "We never close."

"Alex. Wait a minute," I said. "Can I replace this computer?"

"What?" Ken said.

"I want to examine the hard drive."

"I've looked at the browser caches," Ken said. "The deleted emails. There's nothing on there of any use."

"If I get you a replacement computer and take this one for my techs, is that okay with the park?"

"Sure," Mary said. "I guess so. For how long?"

"A few days at most."

"Take it."

"Alex," I said. "Courier over a standard PC, hire a geek to set it up however these people want."

"I'd already thought of that. Anything else?"

"No." She disconnected.

"How, what are you, what?" Mary said. "Look. I don't understand this."

"It's a labyrinth," Ken said. "And this woman is going to the center of it."

"I make no promise," I said. "Some of this is untraceable."

"I don't understand what you're going to do," Mary said. "Just do it. I've got to go to a meeting. Laura? You'll help me?"

"Yeah, sure. Yes." For the moment, she didn't want to hear anything else. When she left, I sunk into one of the office chairs, head lowered, shaking my head slowly, overwhelmed with my day.

"What's wrong?" Ken said after a while.

"What exactly do you do here?" I said.

"Coordinate all the volunteers."

"How many of them?"

"Three hundred, give or take, depending on the season."

"Do they trust you?"

"Yeah," he said finally. "Not that I'm Big Daddy or Mr. Wonderful. But yeah, they trust I'll do my best to match up whatever they're seeking with what needs doing at the park. Why?"

"I want to volunteer."

"Whoa, baby," he said. "What are you asking here?"

"I need to trust somebody. I've got a daughter, I've got my own psychic who's also an astrologer and Tarot card reader, I've got myself."

"And you don't trust any of them right now?"

"Not to make decisions. No."

"What decisions are we talking about?" he said.

And so I told him everything from the past day.

Nathan leaving
Photographing a horrible crime scene
Working for TPD to get my PI license back
Helping Mary

"Wow," he said.

After I'd pretty much laid my soul on the table in front of him. He didn't poke away with questions, he just listened. He barely moved, I noticed he'd lay his index finger into that small vertical depression just below the nose, what some people called the touch of God to show humans we're imperfect. We sat in silence for a few minutes, reading each other, nothing like a Vulcan mind meld, but I felt as close to him in those minutes as I'd felt with anybody in a long time. At one point his cell rang, but he fiddled with the menus and turned off the sound.

"Wow," he said again. "That's a real shitload of deciding you've got. You're wrapped way too tight, girl. Here. Have a candy."

"A candy?"

He handed me a peppermint candy. "My ex wife," he said. "Man, she'd roll the candy around in her mouth, show it between her teeth, taunting her girlfriends who didn't have any candy. Me, I crack the thing into bits, I have no patience with candy, I just want to taste the peppermint. You, I'd bet you'll suck on that candy without crunching or showing off, you just enjoy it to the last itty bitty flake while your head crunches away trying to decide something."

"What am I trying to decide?"

"Leaving out the guy?" I nodded. "You're conflicted about working for TPD, that's pretty obvious. You're conflicted about helping Mary, that's pretty obvious. Actually, you're pretty much stuck in a conflicted state of mind, right?"

"Right."

"And you expect me to explain . . . what?"

"What to do."

"And you somehow expect me to know that?" he said. "Somebody you just met? C'mon, get real, Laura."

"Sorry," I said. "This was stupid, even asking, stupid telling you this stuff."

"Hey. I can't explain what to do. But if you need help of any kind, just ask."

"That's really sweet, Ken."

"Turned out okay, didn't it."

"What?"

"Our first date." I stood up abruptly, he stood up, he offered his hand. "But I've got to tell you, I don't sleep with anybody on the first date."

10

"Kyle."

"I have a question," I said.

"Who is this?"

"Laura Winslow."

"Laura, I'm sorry, Laura who?"

"We just met. At that crime scene."

"Oh. I'm sorry. Just woke up."

"No problem."

"What did you want, Miss Winslow?"

"Laura."

"Laura, okay."

"I'm confused about something," I said.

"I'm confused about a *lot* of things."

"The *maras,*" I said. "I've read stories. On the Internet."

"Okay?"

"These are brutal people."

"They're assassins."

"No regard for life?"

"Regard for their own lives," Kyle said. "And even then, if the contract goes out, they'll kill their own children."

"I'm looking for a connection."

"Between?"

"What do they do for fun?"

"You mean, besides killing?"

"Yes," I said. "Enjoyment. Music, drinks, drugs, sex, what else?"

"Sounds like you've got a suggestion?"

"Cockfights."

"Ahhhh," Kyle said. "Oh, yeah. Cockfights, dogfights, anything that kills. I've also heard about rodeos, unsanctioned rodeos, where horses and bulls are spurred and ridden until they die."

"Cockfights," I said. "Right now, just cockfights."

"Why that?"

"I can't tell you."

The faint sound of liquid being poured into a glass, a sip, a gulp.

"Cockfights. It's a Latin thing."

"And betting?" I said.

"Legal betting?"

"Illegal."

"Sure," Kyle said. "Miss Winslow."

"Laura."

"Where are going with this, Laura?"

"I don't know."

"Need some help?"

"Not right now, no."

"Okay. I got a call, earlier. Gates called me. Said he might have a proposition for me. You have any idea what that proposition would be?"

"No," I lied.

"I'm tapping my nose right now," Kyle said. "I'm laying my index finger alongside my nose, I'm tapping it. The insider thing, you know? I smell something, you're on to something. I might be asked to be a part of it."

"Can't really say."

"I've worked hundreds of homicides, Laura. I've got a system, I get hunches, I've got instincts, you know what I'm saying?"

"Really," I said. "I've got nothing to say."

"Just remember this one thing."

"Yes?"

"Today, you saw what these assassins do. They torture people, they slaughter people, their pulse rate hardly goes up at all, they love it. You be careful, Miss Laura Winslow. Whatever you're doing, you be careful."

"I'm a good detective," he said. "I hear things."

"Right now," I said. "All I hear are three morning doves. What else should I be listening for?"

"A rooster?"

"Christopher," I said. "Enough of this cute routine. What do you want to say to me?"

"Maybe I know why TPD wants to hire you. I've been tracking illegal fights for nine months. Cocks, dogs . . . there's even some extreme human fights. Winner gets a guaranteed good-as-gold Green Card. Loser gets hurt. Or dies. I brought it to my lieutenant once, he's trying to cut down homicide statistics. Birds or dogs, he's never been interested. So I've done this on my own."

"What are you saying?"

"Word is that these fights are sanctioned by cops."

"Wait, wait, wait," I said. "What, are you saying, dirty cops?"

"On the pad."

"To protect the people who stage the fights?"

"Protect and serve."

"I don't know anything about that," I said.

"Well, maybe they're hiring you to find out. To find dirty cops."

"Christopher," I said. "I work computers. I work identity theft, illegal Internet scams, money laundering through a dozen banks. That's all I do."

"I just thought, being as how it's TPD showing interest in you, financials about some dirty cops. Just my instincts, just my gut."

"Not my line," I said. Some truth in that, it wasn't *yet* my line, it might never *be* my line. "But thanks, Christopher."

"No problem."

"Anything else?"

"Nope," he said. "I just thought, these are vicious people. You're better off, you stay away from it all."

"I'm going up to Monument Valley tomorrow."

"You're leaving town?"

"Yes. Leaving town."

"Well then, Laura. You sleep good, these nights."

11

The monsoons came early that summer.

Late in June, not at all the typical season, three storms thrashed up from Mexico but never reached Tucson. From Green Valley south, rain fell intermittently for eleven days. Temperatures stayed in the nineties, but the humidity soared beyond forty-five percent, never pleasant in the desert, not popular for those of us who live here because it's both hot and dry.

From my front yard lap pool at my home in the Santa Catalina foothills, all of Tucson stretched below me and I could watch the bands of gray cloud formations drift up from Sonora and veer toward the northwest. I'd lay in the bright sun, clouds covered my usual view of the Santa Ritas thirty miles to the south. Sun so brilliantly blue, layering southward into gray. You didn't want to look directly up, you'd squint your eyelids shut, like when you're on a lake, sailing in the clearest of clear days, or skiing in fresh new powder, the sunlight reflected and refracted until your eyes burned. I rarely wore sunglasses, except for the days like these. Occasional breezes would lick my Palo Verde trees and tall lantana bushes, but the sun always shone, and on June twenty-first, the longest day of the year for sunlight, the temperature slid above one hundred degrees.

In the evenings, the sun slid through the skies and through parts of the color spectrum and just at that moment before it started to dip below the horizon it glowed like a bald, orange head.

I loved to stare at that orange head, I loved watching it disappearing until, if I really focused my senses on watching, at the exact moment the sun disappeared I'd see the green flash.

"Damn," Spider said to me that afternoon as another monsoon passed us to the south. "You think it'll ever rain up here?"

In Tucson, you never really knew about rain. It'd come by surprise, Santa Claus unexpectedly stopping by with water. But she didn't come out of the house to talk about rain. Holding a portable phone in her hand, staring at it with concern.

"Mom. Uh, that was Nathan."

"Why didn't you bring the phone outside?"

"Um. He just wanted to talk to *me*."

"Tell me what he said."

"Well. He called me, he just wanted to say goodbye. That's all. His actual words were, 'I just called you to say goodbye.' What's wrong?"

"He's just gone."

"Well, he'll be back."

"No. Not this time."

"What do you mean?" Now showing alarm and concern.

"He's gone up to the rez."

"So, go up there yourself. Or wait, he'll be back. Won't he?"

"Not this time. He wants to live up there."

"So? Go up yourself."

"I don't want to live on a reservation."

"You don't have to live there. He needs you."

"Not this time."

"You need him."

"I don't even know that for sure," I said finally.

"Oh, Mom." She sat beside me, arm around my

shoulders. I can remember, not that far back, when I'd give the world just for an hour of her touches. "Call him, Mom."

"I gave him a cell phone. But it's turned off."

"So call where he's going. Leave a message."

"He's gone beyond telephones."

Her head flicked around like a lizard, darting just a fraction of an inch to the right, to the left, up and down, just like a lizard uncertain of his territory, uncertain of the dangers.

"Can I help?" she said.

"Just leave me alone."

I dove into the pool, a racing dive, a streamlined dive, crashing into another world to let the water wash all my cares away as I glide along in relative silence, my senses insulated by immersion into water.

In the first lap, I began with a slow kick, blood awakening in an all-body pulsation beginning with the head, the shoulders, the back, the thighs, all the way down to my toes, my entire body undulating into one dolphin kick, the rhythm continued as I lifted my head to breathe, lifted my eyes toward the sky. As my toes broke the surface of the water, *woooooshhhh*, a spurt of energy, thoughts of Nathan fading, not entirely gone, but fading and lessening as I accelerated into the power of the butterfly stroke, grabbing the water, my hands following a circular shape, like entering the top of the keyhole, hands powering around, meeting at my belly, and then the surge at the bottom of the stroke, shaping the triangular base of the stroke, pushing myself ahead and winding my arms around, stretching ahead, my hands pounding into the water, into the next stroke.

Stroke, kick, stroke, kick, a dichotomy of ease and power, my entire body fully into the rhythm, constantly adding power and strength.

Each stroke entering the keyhole, sliding through the gateway into my inner thoughts for now, when I gain this power and strength and shape, the motion and the water and the breathing are all, I'm the sum of these motions, my anxiety gone, I am entirely quiet, immersed in an isolation tank.

It's just me.

Just me fighting the forces of nature.

And gradually becoming one with the flow, one with nature. The two-hundred butterfly, a warm-up. Next, flipping my body over for the backstroke, arching back and over then under the surface, using a butterfly kick until I'm staring straight up into the blue sky, then switching to a motorboat flutter. The alternating windmill arm sweeps and the leaning into each stroke rock me like a baby. I could breathe constantly, but I keep the rhythm. Starting a breaststroke I experiment with the old-fashioned frog kick, but switching into the power of the whip kick which propels me half out of the water with each whip.

Finally, I settle into the old reliable freestyle, the flutter kick constant, quick breaths on alternating sides with every third stroke. Whapping my legs to create a splash at each flipturn.

Fifty laps of a twenty-yard pool is more than half a mile.

I always lose count.

Lost in my own world, fused with all.

I love to swim. I swim fast. I'm physically unable to float, I've got to keep moving or I sink to the bottom. A small peril of being slim with little body fat.

Swimming is, I don't really know, I guess it's just knowing I'm good at something, and then being able to prove I can do it well.

There's something about pushing yourself and trying to get past your physical limitations, then actually getting past that point, past being tired, I feel like I can do anything. Time has no meaning, that's when I start cutting time off and I get the feeling that nothing can hold you back, no rules, no people, no promises to make or break, nothing except my body in the water, everything in that I have complete control over it all.

Until I get out of the pool. The dry Arizona air slaps me back into reality, the world rushes back in, and my peace is gone.

12

My cell rang, an insistence, a startling intrusion.

"Hello?" I said. Answered too quickly, voice too eager. "Hello?"

"Laura. Bob Gates."

"Oh," I said. Sad that it wasn't Nathan.

"Magellan's Steak House. Six. You're meeting me and Jordan Kligerman. For a drink. Just to meet him." He waited. I could hear myself breathing into the cell, held it against my neck for a moment and quickly took it away, afraid my furious pulse rate would vibrate the cell. "He's got your PI license reinstated," Bob said.

"Tell him to put it in the mail."

"He wants to tell you himself. That he's reinstated the license. C'mon, Laura, it's just a quick meeting, okay?"

"Okay. Six."

I stood against the worn oak bar, one hand on a wine glass. Waiting.

Magellan's Steak House. Very elite, very expensive, everything in addition to the steak cost money. And since it was on the north side of River Road, smoking was allowed, the restaurant always plumy with cigarette and cigar smoke. Magellan's, where Tucson power people ate, drank, smoked, and worked out whatever deals, public or private, kept a lot of Tucson running.

Built in the thirties, when few properties existed anywhere near River Road, Magellan's stood on a half acre lot amid a grove of Arizona sycamores. Bricked pathways rambled between these trees and elaborate gardens for those who wanted to eat and drink outside.

Tourists ate outside, seating at the inside tables requiring a lot of connections since the restaurant was always jammed. Realtors mixed with TPD captains and lieutenants, B-list actors and rock stars and big league baseball players during spring training. When stars or ballplayers from the bigs show at Magellan's, all kinds of Barbie babes come dressed to kill, well, actually, dressed to be undressed by somebody famous. Groupies aren't just for rock stars.

On the other hand, few places in Tucson had better food, and nobody had better steaks. Magellan's got beef from the smallest of the Japanese cattle markets, brand names you'd never hear of, where cattle ripened in individual stalls, fed a mathematically and nutritious meal, stoked with beer, given massages, which somehow was supposed to make the meat even tenderer. An eight-ounce steak cost ninety dollars, and that was just the steak.

Waiting for Bob Gates, I catalogued everywhere I'd eaten in Tucson, remembering my early years when I ate at fast-food or inexpensive chains, often getting just takeout because I'd never have to talk to anybody while picking up or eating. Eegees, Fuddruckers, how can there actually be a restaurant with that name, or any of those places in the world like Chuck E. Cheese and Jreck, or "dreck," subs. No name sounds ridiculous anymore.

I must have drifted off somewhere until a waiter clanked clean silverware onto a nearby table. I watched another waiter set places for three around a table in a nook, obviously a special table. The hostess carried over a centerpiece, three different-size crystal flutes bonded together, each flute holding a rose. Three pink roses, each a different pastel hue, all of them perfect.

Four thirtyish women laughed their way past my stool, their arms around each other's power suits, one of them brushing against me and her automatic *I'm sorry* smile quickly beamed at me, but she really wasn't sorry at all, I couldn't have been less significant to her. I felt like one of those crumpled airline magazines stuffed in the seatback, the crossword crudely attempted, shreds of peanuts in the pages and some of the ads ripped out. I caught the bartender's eye on the group of women, his smile blossoming as one looked at him, but once she looked away his face changed, as though he'd seen things in her smile he didn't like. He saw I'd caught his look, my smile small but genuine and he half-cocked his head in thanks and poured me an extra glass of wine, no charge.

Those beautiful young women so, so confident in their youth and beauty, confident in *us*ing their beauty. I once saw three of these women in the dining room of the Arizona Inn. One needed more water. Instead of looking for a waiter, she just held out her glass to the side, kept on talking to her friends until a waiter appeared and filled the glass, and she just kept on talking without acknowledging the waiter's presence.

A wait captain checked the table, straightened a napkin, aligned a knife and fork, and turned to me with a snap of his wine towel and said, "Madame?"

Caught me still partly in that daydream, I must have stood there for another half a minute before I realized he was talking to me. Patient, not moving, saw me snap out of the daydream and with perfect grace said again, "Madame?"

"Yes," I said. "Yes. Yes."

"I'll bring the gentlemen from the cigar rack. May I seat you?"

"Yes."

And a moment later, he returned with Bob Gates.

"You, uh, you a bit nervous about the interview?" Gates said.

"Some," I said. Wanting to be honest because I looked nervous, although it had nothing to do with the interview.

"Bound to be." Smiled at me. "I've read your job history over and over. You've got just what we want."

I'd like to see that job history, I'd like to know what was on it. That's also part of the honesty with a policeman, even one who's somewhat of a friend. You know my past. Lots of things I don't want on a job résumé.

"It's like . . ." I said, "it's like the day before."

"Before what."

"You did sports? Football, baseball, like that?"

"Third base. U of A, starter in my senior year. Thought I had a shot in the bigs, but I didn't have the arm or the bat."

"Had a tryout?"

"Yeah, I . . . ah, I see. Yeah. The day before, right?"

"You wish it was over," I said.

"You wish it was the next evening, everything's over. Well. I wouldn't get too nervous, Laura. You're the person we want. But just a word. This meeting is strictly about drug smuggling. It's a cover, for you. There are half a dozen TPD offers in here, they're already checking you out. Word will spread, quietly, that you're being considered to help investigate computerized financial records of drug money laundering. Don't say anything about your real job."

"The dirty cop."

"And here we are," he said, turning to shepherd me to another man.

"Hi. I'm Jordan Kligerman," he said. "Laura Winslow. Glad to meet you."

A tall handsome guy, with just enough of a tan to let you know he cared about being tanned without seeming over the edge about it. He wore a pale gray Brioni suit with a faint herringbone pattern, easily a fifteen-hundred-dollar suit over a kettle-black mock-turtle sweater. No dress shirt, no tie.

The wait captain sat us at the table. Gates and I plumped down comfortably in the cushion chairs. When Kligerman sat, he carefully adjusted the creases of his Brioni pants as he crossed one leg over the other. Not wearing any socks, just those tasseled loafers that good-looking men consider really cool. With my mock-turtle sweater and these loafers, oh, they're handmade for me in Arezzo. No wedding ring on his left hand, and I caught his casual glance while he put his briefcase on his lap, popped the latches, and swept his eyes over my left hand and then across my waist, quickly but efficiently over my breasts and neck, lingering with a smile on my arms, veins showing because I still did hand weights an hour every day, I had the muscles to show for it, and when meeting men like Jordan, without knowing what I was yet getting into, wearing a sleeveless blouse, tight around my arm so nobody could catch the right angle and look underneath the blouse.

So, while he's checking me out, I'm doing the same with him. Except our motives are different. He wants to know if I'll come out and play. I just want to know if he's good at what he does.

A florid-nosed, heavy-joweled man stopped by the table.

"Jordan," the man said. "The women you hire get better and better looking. Or is this somebody private?"

"Laura Winslow," Kligerman said. "Assistant Chief Django Manouche."

"Pleasure," Manouche said, his eyes all over my body until I realized he really had no interest in who I was at all, he just wanted to appraise my body.

"Django approved my talking to you," Kligerman said.

"Computers aren't my thing, God knows." Manouche laced his fingers together palms outward, cracking his fingers. "Pleasure, Miss Winslow."

He moved away. Kligerman opened his briefcase, took out a sheet of paper. "Your PI license," he said. "Or, sorry, it's just a fax copy. But I had Sacramento take care of your reinstatement this afternoon."

"Thanks," I said. "I really do appreciate this. But I'm not sure what else I can do for you."

"I understand. Bob tells me you may have a link to the *maras*?"

Actually, Bob hadn't told me any such thing. I'd avoided all phone calls since leaving the park earlier. I'd left clear instructions with Alex that our office would not respond to requests. Mary Emich called twice, but I had nothing to tell her yet. Nor had I worked out what I wanted to do.

"There's a third party, yes." I left it at that. "If something develops, you'll know. Otherwise, I'll be leaving tomorrow."

That wasn't what Kligerman wanted to hear. "I thought . . ." he said, "I thought at least you'd visit my department, meet my people, get a briefing on the tools and technology and money we want to throw at this problem."

"Laura," Bob said. "Are you firm about leaving tomorrow? Can't you at least spend an hour or two with us? In the morning?"

"Early is no problem," Kligerman said. "I can assemble the team at six."

Neither Gates or Kligerman pressed me, no urgency in their words, or in their eyes or bodies. They both sat relaxed, open to my not working with them. Trouble was, I really didn't know what to do. The murdered family at the crime scene kept popping into my head at weird moments all afternoon. And I'd promised Mary Emich that I'd follow up on the gambling website, although Alex could easily handle that.

"With all respect," I said to Kligerman, "I'll have to think about it."

"Good. Can't ask for more, at least right now. I'll have the team on standby, ready anytime you say. I'll show you your equipment, your office."

"I'd expect to continue working from home."

"Our networks are internally secure," he said. "Outside access is severely limited. Even I've got to go through five passwords to get through our firewalls."

He knew of me, he knew of my work ethic. I wanted privacy, I wanted my own computers, I guarded my security, I wasn't going to let any data traveler get to my computers.

"With all respect," I said, "the only secure computer is one that's not connected to anything. You want my expertise? Fine. But I don't want your five passwords and your firewall. I trust only what I myself set up and control."

"Surely," Kligerman said, "computer security isn't that much of a problem."

"You're a fool," I said. He clearly didn't like people saying that to him. "Name me *any* institutional database used by *anybody* in this city and I guarantee you I will get inside that database and suck out all the information I want. I will change whatever information I want, I will create fictitious identities and alter real ones."

"Well." Kligerman laughed, nudged Gates. "Bob, you sure picked the right girl for us."

"You're a *double* fool," I said. Being called a girl always pumps up my sarcasm. "If *I* can do all of that, so can somebody else. You want me to locate *records*? Sure. I'll locate records. But what*ever* are you listening to when I talk about what I can do? How the *hell* would I ever know if the records I found were genuine? Jesus Christ, Bob. *He doesn't even know what he's talking about.* This is a waste of time."

"Whoa, whoa," Kligerman said. *Oh shit,* I thought. *He's going to take back my PI license.* I smiled, okay, it was a half-hearted smile, but I tried.

"As a minimum," I said. "I've got to work at this from outside your office."

"We might be able to work something out," Gates said. Kligerman's jaw tensed, muscle plates shifted at his temples. He said nothing. Not even aware of the transparency of his thought process, you could see Gates's comment work its way from his head down to his gut and then back up to reason and his back straightened.

"You make computers sound so mysterious," Kligerman said.

"Not so much computers. Data. Looking at somebody *else's* data, being unaware that somebody else is looking at *yours*."

"I don't see why it's not controllable. Why you make it so . . . so mysterious."

I cut my eyes to Bob, he *knew* my frustration, he held out both hands, palms down, the cool-it signal.

"You're right about one thing," I said. "All of this *is* a mystery to me."

"How so?" Kligerman said.

"Life is a mystery," I said. "What you're asking me to do, *that's* a mystery. *Why* you're asking me to do this, that's a mystery?"

"Gee. You sound so cosmic. But fascinating. All right, Laura. I'll honor your paranoia about security. How would you work from outside my office?"

"A VPN," I said. "A virtual private network. I'll set up."

"Now you *are* sounding mysterious."

"You're okay with that, Jordan?" Gates said. "Her working off site?"

"Of course." Kligerman smiled. "Laura. A pleasure. Tomorrow."

Gates stayed long enough to bring his head close to mine.

"You look really pissed off," he said.

"I am."

"So, working with TPD isn't going to happen?"

"That's not why I'm pissed off, Bob." He waited. "Private thing."

"Maybe you'll charge your pissiness tomorrow," he said.

*   *   *

After half an hour of being bustled around by the Magellan's crowd, and after a wonderful steak, I started to get really chilly. The aircon was on frigid, all the men with shirts and suit jackets and warm inside their clothing cocoons, but I'd only worn a short-sleeve cotton blouse, open in front.

Goosebumps on both my arms, I frowned at whatever guy was hitting on me right then and walked to the exit and outside into the hot June weather. Fifteen percent humidity is great for coping with ninety-five-degree heat, but not when the aircon is set to polar and you're wearing shorts, or short sleeves or a tank top.

Two men bumping each other with knuckled fists, laughing and oblivious to me, tried to come inside Magellan's front door just when I was leaving. And they weren't there for the first drink of the day, nor did they have breath mints, just boozy odors, we were jockeying for position at the door, each of them taking one of my arms, *Hey, don't leave, baby, we just got here, give us a shot*. I pushed violently between them, an elbow in each guy's gut, I had to resist kneeing one of them in the balls. Just outside the door at last, the hot monsoon humidity enveloping me with a wonderfully warm hug.

I drove around with the windows down and the moonroof open. Somehow I found myself back at the park, but a chain hung across both entrances. I parked across the street, turned off my engine to watch three gardeners inside the park struggling with an uprooted thirty-year-old mesquite.

During high winds, and frequently during a monsoon, in seconds a tree can be uprooted. It shudders in the wind, but the roots are shallow, and somewhere around forty miles an hour, winds rip the root-ball out of the ground and the weight of the tree pulls it over, toppling to the ground. Sometimes, although not common, the tree can be saved if gardeners work quickly. Usually, the tree lays there until it rots, or somebody chain-saws it to pieces. I used to save stumps, gnarly ones I'd find while out driving, and I'd wrestle together some people who could load the stump into my pickup and then position it somewhere on my property.

One time, I remember this so clearly, a huge blue Palo Verde lay across a hedge of Arizona bird-of-paradise flowers. I sat on the trunk of the Palo Verde, the bark still smooth and rippling with imperfections of a few decades of growth. Nobody else around, so I leaned over to lie, sideways, on the trunk, which, being nearly a foot wide, meant I couldn't lie on my back, but lying on the side was perfect. I put my ear against the tree, looked around to make sure nobody watched me, lay on my chest, and wrapped both arms around the tree.

I heard a woman sob and I sat up quickly.

"Oh, I'm so sorry," the woman said. Tears runneling down both cheeks. "I really, really didn't want to disturb you. That tree, I know that tree so well, my grandfather planted it when I was about eight or nine years old. When we owned the house, back there, it was the only house around at that time. So when I saw you hugging the tree, I had such memories of how we all watched over that tree. I didn't even know it was down. I hardly ever come by here, I live a mile away and I walk every day but usually along another road."

"It's a beautiful tree," I said. "Maybe we can find a gardener or landscaper who's got the equipment to plant it solid."

"Maybe," she said. Took out a cell phone, started to punch in a number. She wiped her tears and gave me a laugh. "I've just got to say, I've been an environmental protection person for years, but, true story, while I'm used to being called a tree hugger, I've never seen anybody hug a tree like you just did."

My cell rang. "You've got to see this," Alex said.

"See what?"

"I can't describe . . . we've never, none of us, we've never seen anything like this before."

"Is it a name? Somebody we know, is it their name?"

"No."

"Someone from the park?"

"From the park, yes. But nobody you know."

"You're talking in codes, Alex."

"Yah. Um, first thing we did, we found who'd used the computer. To look at the online casino. I called, what's his name, Charvoz. Told him the name of the person. He said he'd contact you later. But Laura, you've got to see this now."

"Right now I'm not in the mood to see anything."

"You sound really worked up."

"Whatever."

"Laura." Insistent now. "Laura. You've *really* got to see this."

"Okay. I'm closer to home than the office. Bring it to my house."

"No," she said. "Come here."

"What's so important?"

"Laura," Alex said. "I don't know what's going on here. I don't really know why I'm looking at this, this . . . Laura, is this something personal? This online casino website? Or are we being hired by somebody?"

"Does it matter?"

"I want to put these people down," Alex said. "I want us totally involved in this, I want us to drop just about everything else we've got and work this case."

"We don't need any more clients," I said.

"I don't care if there are clients or not. I'll work this by myself, if you don't want anything to do with it. This really *really* can't be ignored."

"Alex," I said. "I'm not sure who's more worked up tonight."

"Oh, I'm angry," Alex said. "At first it just freaked me out, but now I'm so angry I won't work on anything else."

"Okay. Who's there with you?"

"Kelle's still here, but I've sent everybody else away for the night. You've got to see this in the office, Laura."

"Why?"

"Because you don't want it in your home."

13

What wouldn't I want to see in my own home?

What would be so . . . terrible? Disgusting? Horrible? What would make me walk immediately away from it? And I immediately thought of Nathan, walking away from me. Was *I* disgusting, was I somebody to be shunned, erased from his life?

I clamped down hard on that thought.

What wouldn't I want to see in my own home?

Something on the Internet, that was clear. In ten years, I think I've seen everything possible. Websites displayed anything imaginable:

pornography
war
senseless violence
gambling

Pornography is boring. I've sifted through hundreds of spam emails and websites, I've seen the most grotesque sexual positioning of naked genitals. Pornography is a huge business, generating thirteen billion dollars every year.

War is for television news programs and documentaries on the History Channel. War itself is senseless violence, but violence is all over television and movies. Despite years of rumors about snuff films, filming an actual death no longer seemed *outré,* the Vietnam War changed all that, and cameras in the two Iraq wars perfected battlefield violence.

Gambling. Had to be something involved with gambling. Alex had cracked beyond the entry requirements of the online casino. People gambled for

> money
> excitement
> sex
> anything of value
> things of no value.

The gambling game of choice was whatever suited the gambler.

Online gambling exploded into popularity around the turn of the century, fueled by the increasing number of casinos on Indian lands, state lotteries, and televised poker sessions. Gamblers always wager on the endless number of sports which demanded that somebody win, somebody lose.

You can bet online, but this is passive gambling. You make a bet before the action, you collect or pay out when the game is over.

Gamblers want hands-on action.

Dealing the cards, flinging the dice, staking chips on red or black or number twenty-seven.

For most people, the boringly repetitive routine of activating a slot machine.

Few slots even have a handle these days. You don't pull down the handle, you punch a button. Slots duplicate all kinds of TV game shows. America's top-rated TV game show is no longer for couch potatoes. You could play *Wheel of Fortune* and be your own Pat Sajac, Vanna White, or better yet, be a contestant.

Online casinos have mixed reputations. Some guarantee financial security with recognizable protection programs. Other casinos are like most websites. Here today, gone next month. Reputable and disreputable online casinos are indistinguishable to whatever flies are drawn to the site.

Now there are so many websites that casinos offer bonus chips when you make your initial cash deposit. Up to one hundred dollars if you predeposit a thousand dollars from your credit card or bank statement. Deposit more, get two or three hundred in bonus chips. Not to worry, an online casino isn't basically different in most ways than going to Vegas. They have the odds, they have the edge, and eventually, they'll get your money.

But once again, what had Alex found on an online gambling website that I wouldn't want to see in my own home?

I exited from I-10 Southbound at Congress and turned east, toward our office on the third floor of a 1930s renovated brick and adobe building.

What don't I want to see? Or turn that question on its ear. What wouldn't I want my daughter to see? Spider had seen everything. Like me, she'd been a runaway, a thief, and had served jail time. My granddaughter was too young to really see anything.

Cruising past the downtown park, I almost rammed the Chevy Suburban in front of me at the stoplight. In the park, three women had a man pinned to the ground, kicking and punching him. One of the women picked up a shopping cart and smashed it against the man's knees. The sudden violence caught me by surprise, cars behind me honking and screeching around me when the light turned green.

Violence.

Think video games, okay, sure. All manner of slaughter and destruction. Wreck cars, become a gangbanger, sell drugs, and most of all, the first person-shooter games like Doom, but now involving sophisticated graphic animation of warfare. Save Private Ryan yourself, storm ashore at Normandy.

But the thrill is the destruction, the ultimate rush when you've reached the highest game level by efficiently avoiding your own death by killing everything that's moved. How would you gamble, if you were actually driving the game?

No. That wasn't gambling.

Violence.

I parked in our office underground garage. When I park down there at night, after business hours, I always think of Robert Redford meeting Deep Throat underground in *All the President's Men*. Deep Throat, well, Hal Holbrook, half hidden behind a concrete pillar, clouds of smoke curling around his half-hidden face, and the end of one scene where a car's tires squeal somewhere inside the garage and Redford looks away and looks back to find himself all alone, the scene ending outside the garage as he's running away from . . . running from what?

Violence.

What kind of online casino would let you gamble on violence?

Boxing? Wrestling? Iron-man-to-the-death contests, animated?

What if . . . and then it came to me, what Alex discovered.

It had to be violence.

Real violence now appeared on the Internet in an unpredictable way. A year after declaring victory in the war against Iraq, armed revolutionaries and terrorists still blew themselves and other people apart. Worse, kidnapped innocents were made to appear on grainy home videos, pleading for their lives as they knelt before heavily armed and hooded terrorists.

Most of the world never saw the beheadings. Editors and publishers have moral and ethical standards, any sight too gruesome never makes it through the publication gateways. But the graphic pictures exist on the Internet.

Knives drawn, the terrorists forced Daniel Pearl to repeat, "My father is Jewish. My mother is Jewish. I am Jewish," and then he was decapitated. Many of the executions captured on video were reproduced on inexpensive CDs, including the final beheadings, and sold by the thousands on the Arab street.

This gruesome entertainment, and it does entertain those with violent political beliefs, probably started with the Chechens and Iraqi terrorist groups like Abu Musab al-Zarqawi's Tawhid and Jihad. Zarqawi realized the awesome power of images, probably influenced greatly by the Abu Ghraib photographs of U.S. jailers humiliating Muslim prisoners. Zarqawi and others quickly and correctly estimated the power of the image, so the most logical step has a terrorist becoming a video director, despite the amateurish posing of the terrified victim on the ground in front of five hooded and armed men, one of whom reads out the death sentence.

American film ratings dilute this violence with an R-rating:

> Restricted—Contains mature themes (usually sex and/or violence). Children under 17 not admitted without an adult

Violence. The videotaped executions weren't so much political statements as recruiting videos for more terrorists. Whatever Alex had found, it had to be something violent on which people would gamble.

Nobody gambles on war. There are too many sure profits to be made on war.

I swung my legs and bag out of the car, headed for the elevator, looking around me and moving faster. Thinking of Margaret Hassan, one of the last people to be kidnapped before the U.S. forces moved to destroy terrorists in Falluja. Hassan's body was found in the rubble, a bullet in her mutilated body. Hassan, long married to an Iraqi, her videotaped face still in my head, pleading for her life.

A warning to anybody who'd think of cooperating with the devil. I've seen enough evil, but I've never seen an execution video all the way to the end. Now I had a desperate feeling of reaching my limits, of going over the edge, across the border from which . . .

Stop these thoughts, I told myself. *Don't get ahead of yourself.*

And yet I still wasn't prepared. One thing I've always known about myself: When I'm not prepared, no matter what the issue, I'm not yet ready to face it.

Two phone calls.

"Alex," I said. "Give me about half an hour."

"No problem. We'll be working this all night."

"Just half an hour. I need to talk to somebody first. But . . . this website. Just don't tell me it's a snuff film."

"No," Alex said finally. "At least, people aren't being slaughtered."

"Animals?"

"Cockfights," she said. "Not live. Animated. But Kelle believes the animations originated with live birds, live fights. It's just . . . gruesome."

"I'll be there soon, maybe as long as an hour."

"Christopher," I said. "You awake?"

"Nope," Kyle said. "Just watching the *Seinfeld* rerun about shrinkage."

"Meet me for coffee? Right now?"

"Where?" No hesitation at all.

"There's a Starbucks on Grant. A block east of Swan."

"Be there in fifteen."

14

"Violence," I said. "Drug smugglers and violence."

Cup at face level, Kyle blew on his triple espresso, eyes on mine. Waiting.

"You said these people would do *any*thing for entertainment, for fun. Especially if it was violence."

"That's not quite what I said."

"Meaning?"

"Well," he said. "At some level, they're just people. They've got all kinds of people enjoyment. Eat, screw, hang with the brothers, race their hundred-thousand-dollar Honda Civics. But you're not interested in that part of them. Do you love great food?"

"Excuse me?"

"Great food. Do you love great food?"

"Sure," I said.

"Do you cook?"

"Not much."

"So you eat out? Janos, Cuvee, Arizona Inn . . . places like that?"

"Sure," I said. "And your point?"

"You ever think about what gets killed for your supper?"

"No."

"Exactly," Kyle said. "You get a good steak, you don't imagine the cow being slaughtered. Veal, forget about the baby lamb in the cage. Fish, I suppose if you're one

of those people who want the fish prepared with the
eyes, it probably doesn't bother you."

"I ask the kitchen to keep the heads," I said.

"So you don't get attached to the animal. As something alive, the animal is just out there. You're not eating
the animal, you're eating a steak."

"Christopher," I said. "I don't have much time here.
Drug smugglers and violence, I've got questions about
how they connect to each other."

"Be more specific."

"Drug mules," I said. "I never thought drugs came
into this country that way. People swallowing balloons
filled with heroin."

"Sometimes it's condoms. You know how thin they
are, imagine a condom breaking inside some teenager's
stomach, ten grams of pure heroin immediately entering
the bloodstream through the intestine wall."

"I saw this movie," I said. "*Maria Full of Grace*. This
young woman is trained to swallow up to fifty balloons
without gagging."

"And you want to know why people would do that?"

"Money, sure, I understand money. But the people
who pay the smugglers, they don't really care, do they, if
somebody dies?"

"Sure they care."

"Excuse me?" I said.

"Five hundred grams of heroin lost? That's a lot of
money flushing down a toilet. They do *not* care that the
person dies."

"What kind of people are they? These *maras*?"

"Cold. You remember Al Pacino? *Scarface*? He'd do
anything to become king of Miami's cocaine business.
Somebody didn't work out for him, bang, Pacino would
walk away from him in an instant. De Niro in *Heat*.
You've got to disassociate yourself from a problem,
you've got to be able to walk away from it in thirty seconds. The *maras*, you know, they watch these movies.
They idolize Pacino and De Niro and all the other gang-

sters. And in real life, these *maras*, they use people like . . . like that chrome espresso machine behind the counter. It's a tool. A drug mule is only a tool. Sure, they've got to invest time in locating the people, in training them to fight their gag reflexes, whatever. But people are tools. Nothing more. So is this why you wanted to see me?"

"Cockfights," I said.

"Cockfights?" Visibly startled. "Cockfights?"

"As entertainment."

"Wow," he said. "I need another espresso." He started to lever himself up, one of the canes slipping on a wet spot on the floor.

"Let me," I said. Ordered and paid for the espresso, the counterwoman saying she'd bring it to the table. I bought two almond biscottis.

"Sure," Kyle said. "Cockfights? Why not? Birds, dogs, horses, bulls. It's not the sport, well, not that it's a sport, but it's not the actual contests, it's more gambling on them. You ever spend time in Mexico City?"

"No."

"There's a movie, *Amores Perros*. Love's a Bitch. About the kind of people who raise killer dogs, or that's not quite it, they raise dogs to fight."

"Cockfights," I said. "Are there cockfights in Tucson?"

"Everywhere."

"Are they legal?"

"Well. A slap on the wrist, a fine, if the promoters or handlers are caught and charged. You want me to ask around about this?"

"No," I said. "Mostly, I just wanted to know if the *maras* were involved."

"You mean, as gamblers?"

"Would they actually stage cockfights?"

"You're really out there," Kyle said. "What's your interest in this?"

"I can't tell you that."

"Part of why TPD wants to hire you?"

"Not directly."

"Uh-huh," Kyle said. Clearly not accepting my answer, clearly interested. "Can I give you some personal advice?"

"That's why I called you tonight."

"Walk away from all these things."

"Say again?"

"The drug smuggling. Cockfights. Whatever TPD is hiring you to do. It's a bottomless pit, Laura. You can't possibly make a difference. Just walk away."

"I can't do that."

"Why not?"

"Christopher," I said. "Right now, my life is shit. My lover dumped me, he walked away from me. I don't even really know why. But I'm too angry with people who walk away from things."

"Doesn't sound like a great reason to get involved with drug smugglers."

"I may need your help, Christopher."

"Anytime. Just don't ask me to do anything with one of your computers. I'm really dumb about them. You'd think, given I don't get around much, given that I live alone and I watch a lot of TV and movies on DVD, you'd think I'd get interested in computers and the Internet and email."

"You live alone?"

"Married four times. Two died, one just disappeared, the last one divorced me after I lost all that weight, but then, I already told you this story."

"Thanks, Christopher."

"I've got a lot of friends in TPD. You go to work for them, I can push a lot of buttons to bring home favors. A lot of people owe me."

"Thanks. If I need your help, I'll call."

"Bottom line? Walk away from this, Laura."

The waitress moved around us, wiping down tables, adjusting napkin holders. Behind the counter, her partner poured several pounds of coffee into a grinder, the sudden *whirrr* of the grind startling me and I thought of Nathan. I could see Kyle's eyes on me, but I gazed through them, I had the thousand-yard stare, looking at my past with Nathan and I realized he was gone from my life, that wasn't the biggest shock, I realized that I didn't want to follow him, that my goals *were* important to me. I no longer had a lover, a partner, a true best friend.

"You've just seen a ghost," Kyle said.

"Just said goodbye to him."

"Oh," Kyle said. "Ah. Yeah. Been there. I'm sorry."

"So am I. But I'm here. I'm not walking away from this."

Kyle's cheeks blew out, he expelled the breath and his face sagged.

"Well, all right," he said. "All right. That's the way it will be."

15

"I thought I'd seen it all," Alex said.

Only weeks past the legal drinking age, Alex Emerine hardly looked old enough to have seen much of anything. Slim, dishwater blond hair currently cut within half an inch of her scalp, pierced ears but no earrings, usually wearing whatever clothes were handiest when she rolled out of bed to her laptop. Or no clothes at all, depending. Buying expensive flip-flops, her only financial weakness.

The toilet flushed in the nearest bathroom and a short woman came out, rubbing her hands on paper towels.

"I'm Kelle," she said. "Spelled with an *e*, but an Irish Kelly." Without hesitation she came over, thrust out her hand. "I'm the video person, we've never met before."

"Laura," I said.

"Yeah. I know." A true strawberry blonde, ringlets in front, her face a cross between the beauty of Cate Blanchett and the perkiness of a teenage Shirley Temple.

"You've seen something new?" I said.

"New and unusual," Alex said. "At first I thought it was just another online video game. But Kelle—"

"From the top," I said. "Just start with what I know. The log-in screen for the online casino."

"Right."

She popped from her desk chair without hesitation, already prepped, led Kelle and me to the big display room. Thirty-inch Apple display monitors set on a U-shaped ergonomically accessible desk, wireless keyboards and mice, the center workstation facing a huge composite display screen built from twenty individual units, four feet high by seven wide, with software to take any digital input.

"Here's what you last saw," Alex said. Calling up the ChupaLuck Casino special log-in screen. "Pretty simple to crack, took only an hour or so to work through basic password combinations until we got lucky. Most of these places have pretty generic passwords. Once you know the user ID, it's easy."

"And who was the user?"

"Oh, yeah. Cañas. Carlos Cañas. A part-time gardener."

"On the park staff?"

"Yeah. That ex-cop, uh, Charvoz. Said he barely knew the guy. So. I tried different combinations, saw that he'd taken a user ID of CarlosC."

"So we logged in," Kelle said.

"Taking us to . . ." Alex said. "I'd give you a hundred guesses, you wouldn't get it right."

"Just tell me it doesn't involve killing somebody."

"Yeah," Alex said shortly. "I wasn't so eager to answer that question, either. But no. Killing, yes. Humans, no. Would you believe roosters?"

The next web page was startlingly simple. Centered, both vertically and horizontally, a single word.

COCKFIGHTS

Below this, three choices:

SAMPLE GAME, NO BETTING
HOUSE PICKS THE BIRDS
YOU PICK THE BIRDS

"Which do you want, Laura?"

"We've tried them all," Kelle said. "But just because we wanted to puke, you don't have to. I'm not going to tell you what I think this is, but it's best . . . imagined, if that's the word, by choosing the birds."

Alex looked up at me. I nodded, Alex clicked on the third menu option.

A triple column of graphics appeared, each column containing thumbnail images of a different fighting rooster. A blinking red sign at the top.

PICK THE CHAMPION

"To keep this as short as possible," Alex said. She clicked on a picture labeled *El Vuello*. The picture appeared in larger format, with a summary description of the rooster's fighting data. Weight, color, heritage, wins, losses. El Vuello had dark feathered plumage on all of his body, with a white neck and a rooster-arrogant red comb on top of his head.

"Next, we have . . ."

PICK THE CHALLENGER

"There's roughly forty combinations between champion and challenger birds," Alex said. "The betting is really simple, at first. You pick two birds and some computer program gives you gambling odds. Usually favoring the champion, occasionally, though, for the challenger. Gotta give the possibility of upset, otherwise the odds aren't as tantalizing. So I'm just going to pick this guy."

Padron, the data said. Odds, seventeen to one.

"A long shot," Kelle said. "We've run most of the combinations, usual odds are in single figures."

"And that's all there is? To the betting?"

"Not really. Things change. You may go in with fifty

dollars on the challenger at seventeen-to-one odds. But, uh, first, this is what they fight with. The promoters want to make all birds at least equal in terms of weapons. So. Don't ask how we found this out, but roosters have these natural bone spurs that extend perpendicular to their ankles. Yeah, they are called ankles. But not all spurs are created equal. So the handlers shave off the natural bone spur and attach this."

She squinted at her menu choices, called up a picture of a steel spur, about two inches long, ending in a needle-sharp spike.

"They're called gaffs. The birds kick and slash each other until one is dead. And even that isn't absolutely certain. I know you've heard of chickens with their heads chopped off, but running across the barnyard. Sometimes a bird that looks totally immobile will strike and kill. That's enhanced in this online version, I'm sure, to get gamblers to go for the long shots."

She clicked the button declaring

BILL UP THE BIRDS

In strikingly detailed animation, both birds appeared side by side, cradled in human arms, but nothing else much shown of the handlers themselves. The birds were thrust together until they rubbed beaks and their hackles rose.

"So. You ready?"

"For what?" I said.

"You know what," she said.

She clicked on the pulsing red button.

FIGHT!!!

In animation, the birds pulled away from each other to opposite corners of a ring boarded all around, and then brought back to the center, but at ground level.

The handlers let go of their birds, who flew at each

other amid a flurry of wings, feathers, feet moving in blurs. Crowd noise rose higher and higher with each definite strike, highlighted with glowing red gashes, striking and leaping at each other until both birds drooped wearily and another menu button flashed.

TIME OUT—NEW BETS, NEW ODDS

"Best we can figure," Kelle said, "this is part motivation to wager more money, also based on what really happens in a cockfight. One match we worked out earlier had three time-out periods and the odds dropped each time."

"Just start it again," I said. "Just . . . get this graphic violence over with."

"We'll just stop right now," Alex said. The huge screen went to black. "Each fight doesn't take very long. After the face-off, after the billing and cooing, the fight could be over in fifteen seconds or it could go on for two minutes. We haven't found anything that goes beyond two minutes. In real life, who knows how long they last. Most fights have at least one time-out, maybe three or four rounds. Enough to get the maximum money wagered without losing the bettor. It's a lot like any online gambling site. In a real casino, maybe fifteen hands of, say, Texas Hold 'Em per hour. Online, as many as thirty or more."

"So what have we got?" I said.

"To start, we know what the part-time gardener was doing at the computer."

"But," Kelle said, "we also know this isn't some small-time thing. I've worked in computer animation for over ten years, mostly designing arcade games but lately doing bits of coded segments for things on PlayStations. The quality of graphic rendering here is extremely good."

"Graphic rendering," I said. "Wait a minute. Are these just animations?"

"What we see? Sure. But we estimate that over a month, there probably will be over a hundred different combinations available. Maybe two hundred or more different birds. The only way this could be done at speed would be to base the animations on live digital video."

"Real cockfights?" I said.

"No surprise, really. That last Tom Hanks movie. *The Polar Express*. It's pretty much all animation. Hanks wore clothing with all kinds of embedded sensors. He'd prance around in front of a blank screen, the sensors would record his movements, the digital animators would, and could, create just about anything from that. Same here. There are all kinds of cockfights in this state. Illegal, but culture is culture. The season starts at New Year's Day, ends just about now with championship fights. Somewhere, this week, tonight, somebody is out videotaping cockfights and turning the digital masters over to an animator."

"Wow!" I said.

"Yeah, like wow," Alex said. "But Laura, what are we doing here? We're not looking at animated cockfights for fun or education. Who's the client? What does the client want, even if it is pro bono?"

"I don't know."

"You don't go out on limbs anymore, Laura. What's up here?"

"Don't really know. But I have to make a decision tonight."

"Why tonight?"

"I have to decide if I'm leaving tomorrow. Or staying."

"Leaving?" Alex said. "Is it Nathan again? It *is* Nathan."

"Um," Kelle said. "I'm going out to get some Mountain Dew. You guys want anything?" We both shook our heads and Kelle closed the door behind her.

"Nathan's . . . well, he's left for the rez. He wants me to join him."

Alex sagged against the desk, head in hands. She knew

everything there was to know about me and Nathan. Young in body, Alex had grown up with a mother dying of cancer and, as they say, she was older than her years. She waited for me to say something. I called up the video image again, logged in to the screens, and worked halfway through another match.

"I don't really know what to do," I said finally. "But I can't leave yet."

"There's one more surprise in this. Are you, uh, well, no easy way to ask this, are you romantically involved with the client?"

"No," I said.

"But the client is somehow involved with these cock-fights?"

"Somehow, yes." Thinking of the diary, the pink teenager's diary that Mary gave me. "I've got to review something tonight. Talk to the client tomorrow, then maybe I'll know who's involved with what."

" 'Cause if you, or the client, are directly involved, here's the kicker. I traced down the website to its origin, you know how easily we can do that."

"Mexico? Some island, Costa Rica?"

"Tucson," she said. "I've already probed the online casino's web server. Back door, a quick in and out. But I left it at that, I don't know, like, what *is* this about, Laura?"

"I thought it was money laundering."

"Easy to find out where deposits are made to the casino. You know, work back from the credit card numbers, although I'm not sure they're all legit. Bank deposits, I can easily work back from them."

"Follow the money," I said. "That's all we can do for now."

"You want to really think about this one, Laura. I don't know where you are with Nathan, I don't know what's up with that possible job for us with TPD, but take care, Laura. There are really some sick people out there. Don't get personally involved."

"You're the second person in the last hour who's told me to walk away."

"It's good advice, Laura. I don't mean give up, I don't mean that we shouldn't work this job. But . . . you've got this stubbornness, a lot of times you put yourself way out there. Personally, you go beyond computers. This isn't about some white-collar crime, where we find the embezzled money or discover the truth behind fake identities. These are vicious people."

"I'll be careful," I said, "but I'm not walking out."

"Out?"

"Not walking out."

"You just said 'out' not 'away,'" Alex said. "So Nathan's walked out on you? Is *that* what this stubbornness is all about?"

"Out, away, whatever," I said. "But I'm not leaving this alone."

"Don't let personal anger at some guy dictate the job," Alex said. "When we first started working together, when my mom had cancer, you said don't let personal anger get in the way of the job."

"That was then," I said. "This is now."

16

My cell rang at four in the morning. Thickened with sleep, I'd taken two Dolmaines, but jolted awake so fast I remembered I'd been dreaming of Nathan and as much as I wanted to just sleep, I had to answer. It might be him.

"Nathan?" I mumbled. "Sweetie?"

"It's Ken."

"Uhhh?"

"Ken Charvoz."

"Ken?" I mumbled. Not Nathan, only Ken.

"Uh . . . what?"

"About that gardener," he said.

"Gardener?

"The part-time gardener. At the park."

"The gardener?" I said. It's no metaphor, having a voice thick with sleep. I could barely understand my croak.

"Well, ground staff."

"Ken. What the hell are you talking about?"

"When your people looked at my computer so see who was logging into that gambling site. It was a gardener."

"Oh," I said. "Oh. Yeah."

"Except at the park, we call them ground staff. Even if they work on plants, or in the nursery, or whatever, we don't call them gardeners. They're ground staff."

"Yeah, uh . . . yeah?"

"He's been found."

"Okay. I'll talk to him in the morning."

"Laura. He's dead."

"Dead?"

"Murdered."

"So?"

"I thought you'd want to know."

I yawned.

"I thought . . ." Ken said. "Well, I thought you wanted to know, I guess I thought you wanted to be involved."

"I don't want to be involved with you, Ken."

"Are you all right?"

"No."

"You sound . . . are you drunk?"

"No."

"What did you mean, not being involved with me? This isn't about me."

"Uh," I said. "Right. Wrong."

"Look, just forget it, okay?"

"No," I said, fighting up to consciousness, the sleeping pills holding me down, I felt like I was talking underwater, like I had to really concentrate on every word. "No, I'm sorry . . . Ken? I'm sorry. I want to help Mary."

"You really sound like you're drunk."

"Where are you?"

"I'm at the crime scene," Ken said. "It's in a vacant lot. Not far from the park. You should, well, Laura, I really think you should come here."

I turned on the light, read the clock, rubbed gum from my eyes.

He waited through my silence, then gave me directions when I said I'd come to the scene. He hung up without telling me any more and this was it, this was the time to make my decisions.

17

"Bodies," I said to myself. "More bodies."

"Didn't get you here to look at a body," Ken said.

Four TPD patrol units at the scene, turquoise and cherry lights still flashing, two unmarked detective's cars. Several battery-powered lights about fifty feet into the vacant lot, no trees or landscaping, just scrub desert bushes limping low over the hardpan caliche ground. Under the lights, I saw Christopher Kyle maneuvering around on his arm crutches.

"I've seen bodies," I said.

"All right."

Ken ducked under the yellow tape and had me sign the entry log.

"If we're lucky, we'll be out of here before Kligerman arrives."

Crunching along slowly and uncertainly on the desert floor, using the floodlights to illuminate where we walked, we neared what looked like a jerry-rigged bar-beque pit, nothing more than odd stones and a few bricks in a three-foot-wide irregular circle.

Kyle saw us coming, shielded his eyes from the lighting glare, came forward a bit.

"Ken. Laura. This is bad. You really want to see it?"

"Sure," I said.

Several officers were already pouring fixative into molds of shoeprints. All kinds of debris around the bar-

beque pit, plastic wrappers from junk foods, used condoms, a typical lowlife hangout, typical debris belonging
to nobody known.

"Not a chance for a usable footprint," Kyle said. "But
we're taking them all. All we know is that sometime after
two o'clock, somebody brought the vic out here, smashed
his head apart, arranged ignitable materials in the pit,
dragged the vic so his head lay in the pit. Set him on fire."

"After two?" Ken said.

"Teenagers had a party here, they left about that time.
One of them was coming back with a case of beer, he got
delayed, showed up with the guy on fire, was too drunk
to just run, so he dialed nine-one-one. You don't have to
look, Laura. Except, there's something not right."

"After that house yesterday, after that dead child . . ."

I went to the far side of the pit and bent over and almost vomited.

A brutally disfigured body, its face battered beyond
recognition, both arms and legs badly broken, like
drumsticks and chicken wings, and the face and hands
burned in the pit.

"Torture?" Ken said.

"That. Or revenge. We've got some ID," Kyle said,
leaning on his canes, holding up a wallet. "Why I called
you. A green card. Probably phony, made out to Carlos
Cañas. Plus a card saying he was employed by Tohono
Chul Park. Is this the guy? Carlos . . . Carlos Cañas?"

"Jesus," Ken said. "How would I know? His face is
unrecognizable, not that I'd know him anyway. The curator of plants would know. Probably no fingerprints on
file. No known address, but I can get it from park records. You said, something's not right?"

"Burned fingertips, smashed-in dentals," I said. "Almost as though somebody wanted to make sure we
couldn't be really sure who it is."

"Yeah," Kyle said. "A little too funky. But. A dead
end. I've got seven open homicides this month, my captain will never let me work this case."

"Nothing else in the wallet? In his pockets?"

"Front right jeans pocket, a business card of some kind."

Handing the card, in a plastic evidence bag, over to Ken.

agricultural products
horses
cows
animal feed and supplies

"Chicken feed?" I said.

"You mean, this is crap?"

"No. I meant it literally. Do they sell chicken feed?"

"Yeah, I suppose." Saw me biting my upper lip. "What?"

"Nothing," I said.

A little too quickly, both men noticed.

"You're thinking," Kyle said, "you're thinking rooster food? Cockfight stuff, are you on that again?"

"Cockfights?" Ken said.

"That's a dead end, Laura." Kyle snorted, shook his head. "Walk away from this stuff. It's just too random."

"Ken," I said. "We need to talk."

"Hey," Kyle said. "Hey hey hey, don't be a stranger. What have you got?"

"Nothing," I said again. "Really, it's more personal, not related. Can we stay until you wrap the scene?"

"Sure. Okay. Coroner's on his way, meat wagon probably will take the body within the hour. You're sure? You don't have something for me?"

"Just too many bodies," I said. "And too early in the morning. Once I've had coffee, I'll be more alert."

"Got a readable tattoo here," a CSU tech called.

"Readable?" I said.

"Most of them have either been lasered off, like the guy didn't want them to be seen any more. But on his lower back, there's a number. Letter E. Numbers two ten."

"Is that another *maras* tattoo?" I said. Kyle didn't hear me, bending over to look at the tattoo himself, shaking his head. The assistant medical examiner rolled the body over.

"Yo, yes sir," the CSU tech said. "Got a death card here."

"*No me jodas*," Kyle said. He looked at me. "Don't fuck with this, Laura."

Another unmarked unit screeched onto the street, bumped over the curb, and parked adjacent to the scene. Kligerman got out slowly, dressed as though it were nine in the morning instead of five. He walked around the back of the scene, careful not to intrude without permission.

"Anything?" he called to Kyle.

"I'll brief you."

Kligerman approached the back side of the scene, and Kyle ran quickly down what he knew.

"Laura," Kligerman said. Came around the pit, not getting close to the body. "Seeing you here, I'm enthused that maybe you'll join the department?"

"I haven't decided yet," I said.

"Well. I've called the team together for tomorrow afternoon. If you can spare us an hour, even less. I'll run through the personnel, show you the routines, outline what we need you to teach us."

"Don't push her," Ken said.

"And you are? Oh, my *god*. It's *Charv*oz. You've been retired, Charvoz. You've got no business at a TPD crime scene."

"I invited him," Kyle said. "The vic works for him."

"Meaning?"

"I manage the part-time volunteers at Tohono Chul Park," Ken said. "This vic has a name. Carlos Cañas was a staff member. Part-time, actually."

"A staff member. At the park."

"Ground staff. I've personally met the man two, three times."

"And you brought *Char*voz along, Laura?"

"Actually, he called me," I said.

"Quite a happy family. All right. I've got to leave, but Laura? See you tomorrow, I hope?" Smiling, not smiling, he went back to his car and sat in the front seat, flipping through a yellow pad.

"What was that?" Kyle said. "See you tomorrow, he said."

"In his dreams," Ken said. "Want some coffee?"

"What happens next?" I said. "I mean, what happens here?"

"Not much. They'll run the guy's name through databases, check with TPD narc detectives, check with DEA and NCIC. They won't find anything."

"Let me buy you breakfast," I said.

"Can't leave right now," Kyle said. Knowing I'd asked Ken, not him.

"Okay," Ken said. "I'm riding that Harley, the one with the red tank and fenders. This would be the weekend I put my pickup on blocks. A Dodge crew cab. Diesel, a rod is loose and clanging a bit. I need to get the engine out, do an overhaul, but don't have spare time."

"What's wrong?" I said. "Why are you telling me about a truck engine?"

He thrust out his right hand, the fingers trembling. "I thought I'd left all this behind, Laura. I haven't been to a crime scene in years, haven't seen a dead man in years. I don't know what this is all about, but one look at your face right now, I know it's something really hairy. I don't know if I want breakfast or a drink, I don't drink in the mornings at all, but this . . . this . . ."

"Let's have breakfast," I said. Wrapped his trembling fingers in mine.

"Yeah. Yeah. Okay, yeah, just follow me."

"Where we going?"

"Chuy's," he said. "On Ina, near OldFather. My treat."

18

Chuy's. A lower-end Mexican food restaurant chain. I'd never been to a Chuy's, couldn't imagine a place like this already crowded with people stacked up in three lines at the order counter.

"You want coffee? Or some breakfast?" Ken said.

"Sure. Why not? Get me, whatever."

"I'll get you the usual."

"Usual what?"

"What I have, three, four mornings a week. Here's an empty booth."

We slid into the booth just as the waitress flung a damp rag across the laminated counter, mainly wiping up spills and sweeping bits and crusts of food into a black plastic trash bag. Ken went off to order and I looked at where the other half ate.

The Chuy's on Ina had a very tall, vaulted ceiling, where all kinds of surfing and water stuff hung between fishnets and other water stuff. To order, you stood around a curved central order station, you got your beer or soft drinks or coffee there, but when you placed an order, the order-taker handed you this inflated sea creature. We got a whale, but I saw a porpoise and a shark and half a dozen other unrecognizable inflatables.

Ken slid gingerly into the booth, trying to find a comfortable position. Our booth had totally flat-back wooden benches, no curves of any kind.

"Bad back," he said. "Bad, bad back."

"That why you retired?"

"Didn't retire so much as they booted me out with a medical disability. My back locked up, one night. It's quite a story, but I knew the next week I'd seen the last of being a detective."

"What happened?"

"You really want to know?"

"Yeah. Unless the food's coming right away."

Ken studied the action in what we could see of the kitchen.

"My guess, since I'm a regular and know the process, we've got at least fifteen minutes."

He knew I didn't want to talk about anything remotely personal, anything at all about reality. Nor did he. Small talk. First order of the day, before breakfast.

"How do they serve food here?"

"When your order is ready, the waitron just looks around the room for the inflatable, they're all about two feet long, like this guy sitting right here on our table. When the order comes over, the waitron takes away the inflatable. And here's Angelina with coffee and water."

"You don't want to hear cop stories," Ken said to me. After Angelina set down two heavy china mugs and plastic glasses of water with straws.

"Try me."

"Okay," he said. "Most of my really good cop stories are about one of two things. My body, or my gun. So. There was this Russian immigrant nutcase. He'd been tortured by the secret police, whatever alphabet-soup secret police were around in Moscow. This guy, he also liked to abuse kids. Not just slapping, but, like, kicking them. Dennise was my partner at the time. She's also my longtime friend and cohort, now, you *really* want to hear stories about me, she could tell you things I've forgotten. Anyway. This Russian guy. We went to arrest him and he tried to slam the door on us. Dennise blocked it with her foot, and when he looked around the door to see what was blocking it, I stuck a can of pepper spray in his face and soaked him down. He was a little startled by that, judging from the scream, and he backed away enough for us to knock the door open and get in. We were there because of a call about his nine-year-old son. Dennise kept trying to get the kid out of the house, and to keep him out, but the fight was on between him and me, with Dennise helping when she could. We were all gagging, snotting, and crying from the pepper spray. That stuff gets everywhere. Anyway, I slugged it out with him, breaking his nose, closing one eye, and finally knocking some teeth out. When he got a little woozy for a second, we managed to get cuffs on him. We were all covered with blood and sweat and goo. It didn't take long for him to recover. The backup units that came ended up having to suitcase him. That's when you tie the feet together, lay them on their stomach, and tie the feet to the handcuffs behind the back. It's also how a few suspects have developed serious and fatal breathing problems after the extreme exertion and stress."

"That's it?" I said. "You got a bad back from too much Mace?"

"Uhhhh, well, not really. So. I went to get some stuff out of my trunk. I could barely see and thought my face was on fire, so I wasn't paying much attention to this little Russian dude. Except, like, he's handcuffed behind his back, he throws off the officers, who can't stop him from storming down the sidewalk, dragging one of the backup officers behind him. That's when *I* got the Samsonite treatment, he's on top of me, a backup officer is below me, I'm jammed up totally. My back was never right again. Almost totally wack because of that Russian. But not totally."

"You can still do . . . uh . . ."

"Yeah," he said. "Sex is good for me. Anyway. Some time later, after physical therapy and I'm finally getting back to the street, I had to tackle another guy, a loser who hit a woman's car and took off. We stopped him and as I was standing next to his driver's window, he decided to leave. I grabbed his keys from the ignition, he shoved the door open and took off running. I knocked him down twice, finally cuffed him. A little while later, at the station, my back locked up completely. I mean, I could barely breathe. It was the last day I ever spent on the street. I gotta go to the john. Sorry."

Waiting for our order, watching people crowding in the front door. I saw a "Golden Tee" golf pinball machine against a back wall, more like a video game. It couldn't be very popular, since across the top electronic message board, those things where words flow from right to left describing the wonder of the experience you'd enjoy if only you popped money into the slot, at the end of this message it read, "Last updated on 12-11-2002." I guess golf isn't too popular, probably because kids can't shoot and kill a host of video monsters.

Ken came back and sat down just as our order arrived and the waitron took away our whale.

"What is this?" I said.

"Fish tacos. They're great."

"For breakfast?"

"Hey, I read that the favorite food for undergrad college kids and Wall Street yuppies is the same thing. Cereal. Sugar-sweetened cold cereal. Let 'em have their regulation breakfast. I'll eat these."

While I ate the fish tacos, Ken insisting between mouthfuls they were excellent, I kept hearing a hissing sound behind me, so when I finally looked I saw it was a helium tank and balloons were being filled for kids of all ages.

I picked at the food, ignored the truly weird tortillas under the fish, ate the salad and some rice and beans. Finished, Ken scrunched this way and that, trying to ease the pains of all his police-related injuries, and finally he just said, "I'm dying here. You done?"

"Yes," I said. "What now?"

"Don't think I'm an alcoholic. I'm not. But I've not

seen a mutilated body for years, and I'm kinda freaked by that guy in the barbeque pit."

"I just saw mutilated bodies this week, but I'm still freaked out."

"Okay. If we're going to talk about it, I really need a drink."

"More coffee?"

"Margaritas."

"If that's what you need," I said. "Where we going, who serves alcohol so early in the morning?"

"There's this bar a few blocks away, you just sink into these leather booths. Or naugahyde, you know, it's like sitting on an air mattress that cuddles your body."

The booths were comfortable. It wasn't leather. "Don't you wonder," I said, "how many naugas died just for this one booth?"

He didn't get the joke, but it wasn't worth explaining and I didn't feel hilarious anyway, I couldn't even giggle.

"I saw you eying that business card," he said.

Licking some salt from the lip of the margarita glass, not finding enough salt so he curled his left fingers as though they were holding a beer bottle, poured salt into the small valley between thumb and index finger. Licked it, finished the margarita, and ordered another.

"Agricultural supplies?"

"Yeah. Want to tell me why you were curious?" he said.

"You ever been to a cockfight?" I said. Nursing my iced tea.

"A few. When I worked undercover."

"Ever play a video game?"

"Where you going with this?"

I told him everything I knew.

Mary Emich's fear of the *maras*.

Her diary entry, which I'd not read yet.

Her adopted girl, and the dead child from the murder house.

The online gambling site, with the animated cockfights.

"It's a stretch," he said finally. "Connecting the gardener with cockfights, just because of a business card for a place selling agricultural products. Connecting what looks like a random computer visit to the casino with *maras*."

"I'm stretching it so hard it'll break, snap in my face. It's instinct."

"Yeah. Instinct. Twelve years in undercover, I got the nose for instinct. Saved my partner's life once. But I don't see where you'd go with this."

"How well do you know Mary?"

Salt, lots of salt, smiling into his fist while his tongue dabbed at the salt.

"She's a very close friend," Ken said finally. "One time, I thought I was in love with her. Probably was. But she was still married, really happily married."

"What happened?"

"Husband died in Iraq, killed by friendly fire. Sometimes Mary says she lost her husband years before that, lost him to the army. They were high school sweethearts who married very young, had no children."

"What was his name?"

"Jim. Jim Coyne. Helluva nice guy. Anyway, Jim wanted a career in the Army, after fourteen years of it had been away from home three times as long as he was with Mary. He rose to the rank of captain in the Army Nursing Corps, was in civvies helping wounded Iraqis, and during a heavy night firefight was killed by a young sniper. An American Marine. Broke the Marine's heart, he never could pull a trigger again. Broke Mary's spirit for a whole year."

"She seems happy now. She laughs, she smiles a lot."

"Yeah. Her smile, yeah. It's beautiful, but sometimes . . . she smiles on the outside, it's just a physical thing. You know? She's beautiful. You're beautiful,

Laura. But she's got honor. I'd say it was honor. To protect her girl, this girl, and I've gotta tell you, I have *no* idea where this girl came from. She just showed up one day. Mary brought her to work, didn't want to let her out of her sight for about three months. Mary would do anything to protect the girl."

"She said she'd kill if she had to."

"Yeah. She'd kill. Knowing the penalties, religious, personal, yeah, she'd kill. To protect that girl. As a cop, I guess, I'd kill if I had to protect myself. Protect somebody. I don't know, it never really got that far. But to save a child? I ask myself, would I kill to protect something? Somebody?"

I didn't know what he wanted me to say. Said nothing.

"You don't know her well."

"Well enough," I said. "For a client."

"A client."

"A client. As a client, she's direct, she's self-confident, honest."

"Honest?"

"Yes. Honest. She said she'd do anything to protect her child."

"Mary is profoundly against violence. She's a pacifist, she can't stomach violence, senseless violence. She can't fathom it. But what a profound thing, that this woman would kill to protect her daughter. Do you truly realize what a profound thing that would be?"

"Can I ask you a personal question?" I said.

"Sure. Just do it quick." He'd finished the second margarita, ordered a third, and sat with his head lowered, eyes flicking up to me and down to the glass.

"What happened to *your* marriage?"

His eyes moved instantly to a pale band of flesh on his left ring finger, the rest of the hand deeply tanned.

"Cop's life. She couldn't take it. Her second marriage. My third."

"You watch a lot of movies?" Ken asked. Changing the subject.

"Yeah," I said. What I *was*n't going to say was that I felt that Ken was becoming something more than a movie trailer, more than a coming attraction, it almost felt like the first time I believed that a man's true love was the main feature.

"So? I catch a movie whenever I can. What do you like?"

"Easier if you just tell me what you last saw."

"The second Charlie's Angels movie? *Kill Bill, volume two*, but I liked the first one better. What?" he said. I pretended to stick four fingers down my throat.

"I like *good* movies," I said.

"Okay, how about music?"

"Sure. But let me guess. Country Western?"

"Dixie Chicks, sure. But I like this weird stuff. I listen to this program from San Francisco. Music From the Hearts of Space. Before there was 'new age' music, this program had the best. Terry Reilly, Phillip Glass, Tangerine Dream, Eno. They were also one of the live broadcasts of the group hum."

"The . . . hum? Humming in a group?"

"A few NPR stations across the country," Ken said. "They fill an auditorium, they schedule everybody on the air at the same time. They strike a specific note. People hum."

"You mean, like, a song?"

"No. Just a note."

"They hum a note? On the radio?"

"It sounds weird," Ken said. "When I was a kid, living in some Yaqui village somewhere, I don't even know where, for different reasons there were different songs."

"Like the Navajo singers," I said. "Like a Blessing Way."

"But now, the closest I get is to take part in a group hum."

"How many people?"

"You're a detective," Ken said. "Work out some figures."

"A few hundred?" He snorted. "A few thousand?" He growled, shook his head. "I'll guess, six thousand, three hundred and forty-nine hummers."

"Last group hum, something like fifty thousand."

"No way."

"Way," he said. "Course that doesn't count everybody humming alone at home. So. Music. Who do you like?"

"I used to have some raps," I said. "But tell me, what did your wife hate so much that she left you?"

"Some years ago," Ken said, "I really loved margaritas to the point where I'd have a few every day. To forget about the violence of my work. Then I got to having a few at lunch and more with dinner. I never thought I might be an alcoholic, until my ex listed margarita as one of the reasons she was leaving me. I was in such denial about drinking that for a while I thought she was referring to another woman, a Latina named Margarita."

"Ken," I said. Reached out to touch his hand on the table.

"Laura," he said.

"Ken," I said. I almost felt like flirting, except I couldn't quite remember that dance and anyway I didn't care enough about him to flirt. Liked him, yes, but flirting raises the temperature when you're least ready to get hot.

"So. What do you want to be when you grow up?"

"Hell, that's easy," Ken said. "Either a cop or a jet pilot. And you?"

He laughed at his answer. I'm used to asking people that question. Not answering it myself.

"To be loved," I said.

"Mary used to ask me this question. If heaven exists, what would you like to hear God say when you arrive at the Pearly Gates? My answer? Here's directions to the margarita bar. And you?"

"I've been so far away from God, for so long . . . I don't know, I really don't know. Listen. Here's what I'm going to do. First I'll read Mary's diary. You can ask her if she'll let you read it also, I'm sure it's the story of where she found the girl. Then I'm going to spend time with Jordan Kligerman and consider his offer of working with TPD."

"You just decided that," Ken said. It wasn't a question.

"Yes."

"All right. Here's what I'll do. I don't know how it fits together with everything else, but I do know that this weekend is the finale of the local cockfighting contests. The champions go on to the state finals. So there's bound to be cocks fighting all day long, probably already gearing up for the first match. Let me work some of my sources, find out where we could see one tonight. Would you go?"

"Yes."

"All right. I usually ride a Harley Fat Boy. You rig yourself out like a biker chick, I'll pick you up between eleven and midnight. You really up for this? It'll be . . . you'll have a hard time watching."

"I'll be ready," I said. Gave him my private cell number. "For whatever."

"Weird things do happen. I worked in Texas for a while, before I joined TPD. One day, I'm going to work, I've got this new convertible, at a stoplight, *wham*, this pickup broadsides me from the left. Not much damage to either vehicle, both of us jump out to see if the other person's all right. And guess what? The other driver I recognized. Thirty years before, when my parents had a pecan orchard, this girl would come over with her family to harvest the pecans. The same girl, same me, everything else is random. What are the odds of that?"

"So what are the odds?" I said. "Of us meeting like this?"

"A long shot. But, as Mary would say, there's got to be a meaning."

"Or just a coincidence."

"To us, maybe. To Mary? She'd say, God doesn't roll dice." Eying me over the salted rim of his glass. "You're a kinda fascinating person yourself, Laura Winslow."

"That's the booze talking," I said.

"There's no need to be sarcastic."

"I wasn't, I mean, I hardly know you. What am I supposed to say?"

"Not my purpose," Ken said, "to put words in somebody else's mouth. So what are you going to do about this . . . about . . . this is bad shit going down. You should just walk away from it, Laura."

"Now, that's the third time I've heard that. This morning, I'm going to the park and talk to Mary. Later, I'm doing a command performance for some cops."

"And tonight?"

"Let's get this really clear," I said. "I don't have patience for another man in my life. Not after being dumped by my partner."

"I'm so sorry."

"So am I."

"None of my business," Ken said. "But, this just happened?"

"He made me an offer he said I couldn't refuse."

Ken held up a hand to the bartender, thought better of it.

"I got dumped by email," he said.

"Email?"

"Not even face-to-face."

"Email?"

"What's the difference? A note on the kitchen table, a letter overseas, an email message. When they're gonna leave, they're gonna leave."

"And *why*?"

"Because it's time," Ken said. "For them, it's just over."

19

Following Mary's directions to her office, I bypassed the main entrance to the park and drove slowly up the service road, all the way to a chain-link fence bordering the staff parking lot. Past a short patch of ground, I went up three steps and opened the back door to the gift shop.

"Hello," a tall woman said. "Can I help you?"

"I'm here to see Mary Emich."

"Go through the gift shop, turn left, and go through the two gallery rooms. At the far end, you'll see a swinging door, go through that and turn quick left and quick right. I think she's the only staff person back there today."

I walked away without saying anything, took several steps, realized what I'd done again. I have a hard time with some social things, like, when I'm done talking to somebody, on the phone or in person, I'll just leave without saying goodbye.

"Thanks," I said. The woman smiled.

The first and smallest of the galleries had fascinating pottery called Green Feelies by a woman named Rose Cabot. One had that clear, distinct green that immediately reminds you of broccoli, another the exact faded yellow of a summer squash. In the main gallery I didn't stop to look, pushed on the swing door, and worked my way back to Mary's office.

"Welcome to the vortex," she said. Moving piles of

paper from the guest chair, looking around with no hope, finally stacking the papers on top of other papers. Her entire office awash with paper, cardboard, signs, calendars, event brochures, books, computer disks, and software manuals.

Pinned to a wall, a dozen balloons, all different colors, but limp, exhausted, nearly flat, and still tied tightly at the neck and all of them joined by a yellow ribbon.

"I keep them," Mary said, "because they've still got some of my dead husband Jim's breath inside."

When I sat down I kicked an empty water bottle.

"Sorry," Mary said. "I usually throw that bottle to get somebody's attention. The rest of the staff keeps the debris from flooding the hallway, sometimes my stuff wanders by itself out to Kim's desk."

Lighthearted, chatty, giggling, smiling, and wrapped very tight.

"I'll help you," I said immediately.

"Oh. God. Bless you." Fingering the religious medal.

"What is that?" I said.

"Oh." She reached behind her neck, opened a clasp, folded the medal in my hands. "Mother Teresa medal."

About an inch round, made of silver, hung on a silver chain. A somewhat familiar Mother Teresa in three-quarter profile. On the back, a flattened reddish irregular object, either a bone or a stone, probably a garnet.

I handed the medal back.

"I didn't know she was a saint."

"She's not. But she's who I pray for. That stone on the back, I don't really know what it's supposed to be. They call it a third-class relic, but I don't think it's a bit of her bones."

Giggled, refastened the medal around her neck.

"Plus she went to an Irish convent. I'm part Irish. Did you know that when Mother Teresa died, India gave her a state funeral in Calcutta? Her body was carried through the streets on the same gun carriage that bore the bodies of Gandhi and Nehru. Are you Catholic?"

"No," I said.

"Sorry I'm rambling here. I'm sorry."

"Please," I said. "Don't apologize for your beliefs."

"So you have news?"

"Other than that I'll help you, not really. It's early days. There's something, but it's so intangible, I don't want to tell you about it yet."

"Something you got from that website? The online casino?"

"Do you know the man who visited the website?"

"Yes. Ken told me. One of our part-time staff, I didn't know him."

"He was murdered this morning."

Both hands flew to her chest, a finger touching the medal, her breath drawn in so long and held forever I thought she'd turn blue.

"You didn't know?" I said. She shook her head. "Don't be frightened. As far as we know, it's just coincidence."

Her control returned in degrees, face and throat muscles gradually relaxing. I looked carefully away during all of this, studied her walls, the odd mixture of things spread around the office. A black rubber mouse, four inches long, his whiskers and red eyes peering around the doorway. A baseball cap with the traditional 9/11 letters FDNY. A reproduction of Van Gogh's *Starry Night* painting. A card with a black and white photo of what looked like an old man, bent against the wind and age, walking beside a wall. I stood up to look at the card closely, and the man's shadow projected on the wall showed he was playing a saxophone. The caption read: Some things have to be imagined to be seen.

"Believed," I said to myself.

"What?"

"I think the actual quote reads, 'Some things have to be believed to be seen.' A psychic friend of mine said the writer believed in ESP. I don't really know."

"Belief, imagination," she said. "They're not so far apart. Wishes. Prayers."

"If wishes were horses," I said, "lovers could ride."

"Psychics," Mary said. "I've always wanted to learn more about alternative belief systems. Look out this window. Over there is the old children's garden. Some days, if I'm here early enough, I watch this family of coyotes, mom, dad, five pups."

"Mary?" A woman's voice from down the hall.

"Kim," Mary said. A cheerful blonde poked her head in the doorway. "Kim Miller, this is a friend. Laura Winslow."

"Welcome to the park," Kim said.

"I've been coming here for ten years," I said.

"Are you a member?"

"No."

"You should sign up. I'm the membership coordinator. Well. You two look busy, I just stopped by for something I forgot last night. See you both. Mary, give her a membership packet, get her to sign up."

"She's great," Mary said. Kim was gone. "I hate lying to her about you, I know it's just a small lie. I'm really uncomfortable with lies."

"I'm not," I said. "If I have to tell a white lie, even a black one, I'll do it."

Mary considered that, but just shrugged.

"Whatever works," she said. "Everybody here is great, it's a wonderful place to work. So you've come here for ten years? Is this a personal thing, or do you come with your girlfriends?"

"Girlfriends?"

"Like, who do you hang with?"

"My daughter. My . . ." Trying to get some word out about Nathan, unable to talk about him. "And you? So you've got a lot of girlfriends."

"Yes," Mary said. "Well. Actually, I don't have many really close friends. Two, maybe. Or three. But I know a lot of people. I call them friends, even though I don't see many of them often. My Christmas card list is about three hundred names long. But close friends? I mean,

like, soul-sharing friends? Heart-baring friends? Only
two of those. But what I'd call a girlfriend? Lots of
them."

"Where do you and your girlfriends hang out?"

The question dangled between us, not the thing either
of us really wanted to talk about, but then neither of us
wanted to talk about violence.

"First off," Mary said, "it's a matter of your time
schedule. You've only got half an hour, so you'll go to
one place. Second consideration, money. Your wallet's
feeling kinda slim, you go to another place where the
drinks are less expensive. So, say we want a quick drink.
We'll go to Basil's, or Wildflower, a few blocks from the
park. Or maybe Risky Business, if there's more than two
or three of us, so we can sit out on the patio, same as
Old Pueblo Grill on Ina."

Cocked her head. Closed lips turned down at the edges,
two small vertical lines popping up a bit between her eyes.

"How long have you lived here?"

"In Tucson?"

"Yes," Mary said.

"Three, four years."

"You don't have . . ." She didn't quite know which
word to use. "Girlfriends?"

"No."

"You don't have friends to . . . like we're doing here,
you don't have friends to talk things over? With? You
don't?"

Whoa, I thought. *This woman doesn't hesitate boring
into my soul.* "I've had girlfriends." Thinking of Meg
Arizana, thinking of . . . I couldn't really think of another woman friend. "Do men count?"

"Sure men count," Mary said. "But . . . they've got
their own stuff, sports, how are the Cardinals doing,
who's the next best NFL quarterback . . . the women in
their lives. I don't believe this," she said. "You really, I
mean, honestly, truly, you don't have a bunch of girlfriends you hang with?"

She saw my face shutting down, realized I'd shuttered off talk about emotions, about my personal life, and she made a quick decision and that glorious smile bloomed across her face as she extended her right hand to me.

"You want to be *my* girlfriend?" she said.

Whoa. Nothing else to do but take her hand and shake it and nod. She wouldn't let go of my hand, she put her left hand out, held my single hand with both of hers. "It's not a blood oath," she said. "But I would like to be your friend."

However can you say no to somebody like that?

"I'm gonna say something really, really dumb here," I said to her.

Gave a slight tug on my hand, but she wasn't going to let it go. Not yet.

"I don't know how to do this."

"Do what?"

"Be a girlfriend."

"Oh, pooh," she said. "Listen. Tonight I'm calling a few women, okay? We're going to make a date, okay?"

"Uh," I said. "Sure. This is an even stupider question. What should I wear?"

Mary laughed and laughed, not an insult or an insider joke or anything but sheer delight. "Whatever," she said. "I mean, I've got this huge, huge bucket of margaritas in my freezer. We'll go somewhere outside, I know, we'll go to Ric's. Not far from you, actually. You live at Sunset and Swann?" I nodded. "Perfect. We'll grab an outside table, we'll get there late enough so we'll pay for one drink and eat something, and then, here's the thing, when the wait staff sees you're not going to leave, they close up the restaurant and just leave you there. And then I go to my car, I get the margaritas, which by this time have melted just enough so they're still cold but they're not frozen. And we sit around and drink 'em all. Deal?"

"Deal," I said. "But I've got to make sure my daughter's okay if I leave her."

"Get a babysitter."

"She's twenty-three."

For the first time, Mary looked totally puzzled, her mouth opening and closing like a guppy, I could sense a thousand questions trying to work their way from her brain to her mouth, but she finally just pumped my hand, flashed that smile, and nodded.

"I'll call you," she said. "I'll see who wants to come. Cathe for sure, maybe . . . so I'll call you, maybe, no, let's say, definite for tomorrow night."

"Tomorrow night," I said. "Sure."

But I didn't know if I really meant it, or more honestly, what excuse I could come up with so when she called I'd say, I'd already figured out what I'd say, I might as well say it right now.

"Gee. Mary. I'm so sorry, I totally forgot. There's this client, he wants me to turn in a project by midnight tomorrow. I don't think, probably I'm not going to be able to make it tomorrow."

"Laura Winslow," Mary said. "About this client, and about the job and the deadline and I think, I'm not trying to judge here, and I could be all wrong, but the truth? About your tomorrow night, it sounds like, I'd bet my best hat, and I've got fifty hats, that what you just told me was one outrageous awesome lie."

And yeah. She was right.

Embarrassed, I looked at a picture of a man in civvies sitting beside her computer monitor, a black and white photograph in a silver frame.

"Ken told me about your husband," I said.

"Ken is sweet."

She held the frame, turned it so I could see the picture.

"A fishing boat," I said. "San Carlos, right? Down near Guaymas?"

"We'd scuba down there," Mary said. "When he had leave, he'd always come directly to me, wherever I was, he'd wrap his passion for me around my soul. In San Carlos, I'd gone there with Cathe, she's my best girlfriend, we wanted a weekend to ourselves, and Jim ran down to the dock just when Cathe and I boarded the dive boat, and just like that, he jumped into the boat, hugs and kisses, wow, could that man hug. As the boat pulled away from the dock he'd already shucked his clothes, standing there in his boxer shorts, not his military issue, a special pair of shorts he'd bought in some airport just to wear for me in San Carlos, lots of fish swimming around, and with no hesitation flung himself into the water and launched into his powerful sidestroke, swimming alongside the boat and laughing up at me. Oh, my good sweet mother of Christ, I loved that man so."

She carefully placed the framed photo next to her monitor, beside a Zuni fetish of a mountain lion, carved from Baltic amber.

"You've been to San Carlos?" she said.

"Yes. It wasn't, for me, it wasn't peaceful. This park," I said. "This place is a conundrum to me," I said. "Why do we talk about violence in such a peaceful place?"

"Peaceful, yes, serene, yes," Mary said. "But violence is out there in the world. Those coyote pups? At one time there were eight. Now there's only five."

"And how do you stay serene, with all that?"

"The park," she said. "My Catholicism, and Ana Luisa. My adopted child. What are you doing later this afternoon?"

"I don't know, but I think I'll pass on the bucket of margaritas."

"Do you swim?" she said.

"Yes."

"Where?"

"I have my own pool."

"Your own pool? How *fan*tastic. You can get out of bed and run down there, dive right in even before you're awake?"

"Sure."

"At four this afternoon, come to Ana Luisa's swim meet."

"I didn't realize she was in school here," I said, fumbling.

"She's not. It's a private swim club. Just for girls who have learning disabilities. A special needs high school. Today, our team has a swim meet with a Catholic high school. Please come."

"I think I can," I said.

"Here's a map. Here's the pool. We'll see you at four."

20

"Captain?" Kligerman asked. "You want to start off?"

Bob Gates chuckled.

"She could tell me my computer was directly connected to the moon and I wouldn't have any idea if it was true or not. It's your show, Jordan."

Now there's a verbal tell.

Gates was playing the executive manager role, although not like some chiefs might play it, as a bumpkin who knew nothing about computers. Gates might know a whole lot about computers, but that wasn't his issue here. Gates wanted to see how Kligerman dealt with me, which told me, here's the real tell, Gates hadn't really made up his mind that Kligerman was actually going to be promoted to captain.

"So, Laura," Kligerman said. "May I call you Laura?"

I nodded.

"Your résumé, mmm, I guess this twenty-two-page document you sent us is a few streets ahead of being a résumé. You've been working with computer crimes for about ten years? Give or take?"

"You could see it that way," I said. "But since computer crimes have morphed so quickly, especially in the past four years, you'd be better informed if you didn't try to fit things into a time frame, but into categories."

"Such as?" Kligerman said. Rifling through his papers. "Credit card theft, for example? Or what? That's the key to this preliminary interview. How would you organize these new criminal activities?"

And in that instant I just *knew* how little Kligerman actually understood about computer crimes. I cut my eyes to Gates just in time to see him cutting *his* eyes back and forth between me and Kligerman.

"Starting with credit cards," I said. "Most people don't bother with that anymore unless they're hacking into a major database and stealing thousands, probably tens of thousands of credit card numbers. But the truth about credit cards is that some people, some really clever people, don't even need to steal card numbers. They steal information. Computer crimes is all about stealing and dealing information."

Kligerman started to uncap his Mont Blanc pen to make a note, but caught himself and fiddled with the pen, a distraction as he thought through a question.

"Yes, of course, Laura. We know that. Like all law enforcement agencies, we have all kinds of databases. Our own, for Pima County. The sheriff's department has theirs. And a lot of other people."

"The G," I said.

"The G?" Kligerman said. "Oh, you mean, The Man. Like what we call the feebs, chief," he said to Gates. "Except some people don't say The Man, it's just the G these days."

"We're our own G," Gates said to me.

"Of course," I said. "But on the largest scale possible, the Homeland Security mess, there are so many federal databases that partially duplicate information, or don't even talk to other databases. I have a friend who works for U.S. Customs, down in Nogales. She tells me stories. . . ."

But I didn't want to share her down-to-earth curses about Homeland Security.

"So," Kligerman said. "When the city of Tucson authorized us to create a special Computer Crimes Division—"

"Department," Gates said. "Not a whole division."

"Of course. Department, it doesn't really matter what we call it, though. Right? Anyway"—rifling his papers—"we've looked at a few hundred resumes, contacted Private Investigators in Phoenix, Los Angeles, a few other cities, trying to get a handle on what we'd need to set up. Laura, did you know that a lot of MBAs are hiring out to PI firms?"

"Because these young MBA kids know a lot about computers," I said. "And about computer searches and coding."

"Yes. Well. When we looked here, in Tucson, almost everybody we talked to gave us the name of the best person for the job. For our job. You. Some people tell us, you're one of the very first Tucsonans with a PI license who uses the term Computer Forensics? Not crime scene forensics, or post mortems, although I understand that you've also been hired from time to time to shoot crime scene videos. But Computer Forensics. We hadn't even thought of calling our department anything but Computer Crimes. Computer Forensics, now, that puts us on some kind of cutting edge technology."

"It's just a language thing," I said. "You could just as easily call it digital monkey business."

Gates laughed, a mouth-wide-open laugh. Kligerman smiled and nodded.

"I have a question," I said.

"Go ahead."

"Do you have names of suspected drug smugglers?"

"Yes. That will be supplied to you, along with a list of suspect bank accounts, both here and offshore."

"No," I said. "Do you have names of anybody who employs drug mules?"

"That's just a detail," Kligerman said.

"Anybody who uses teenagers as drug mules."

His body stiffened, even Gates sat up straighter in his chair.

"Where are we going with this?"

"Something personal," I said.

"Well. Not many teenagers have bank accounts. And our plan is to have you tracing financial records."

"You *don't* have these names?" I said.

"Jordan doesn't work the streets," Gates said. "But I'll have somebody look into teenage drug mules. If that's what it will take to get you working for us."

"Yes. It *will* take that."

"Deal."

"Sure," Kligerman said. "I'll get a list of TPD personnel for that."

"I want somebody specific."

"Who?"

"Christopher Kyle."

"I don't see why not," Kligerman said finally. "Bob?"

"No problem. I'll get Chris on board today."

Another tell. Without any body language or verbal inflection, Gates just told me that even Kligerman didn't know I'd been hired to find a bad cop.

"Thank you," I said.

"So. If I've got this right, Laura," Kligerman said, "you don't limit evidence-searching to crime scenes or autopsy rooms. You look on the Internet."

"Actually," I said, "I start by looking inside computers. All kinds of things are saved on hard drives. Even when people think they've deleted something, it rarely occurs to them that all the information still exists on the hard drive."

"Whoa," Gates said. "I delete all my email. I clean out my browser cache regularly. Once a week I bounce all the cookies I've accumulated that I don't want. But do I understand you right? I've deleted them, but actually I haven't?"

"No, you haven't," Kligerman said.

"Explain that to me."

"Well," Kligerman said, "there are these traces. On your hard drive."

"So?"

"People can look at these traces, they can read them. Not the whole deleted email message, say, but most of it. Laura? That's pretty much it, right?"

I stood up. Surprised them both, they stood up also, maybe they thought I was going to do some visual aids. *But,* I thought, *this asshole in his fifteen-hundred-dollar suit would be my boss and he doesn't even know what he's talking about.* I thought about saying goodbye, caught a crinkle in Gates's eyes. Cocked his head, an inch to the left, nodding to himself, and then *he actually winked at me.*

I sat down.

"Think of it this way," I said to Gates. Kligerman moving his chair, so it appeared I was actually talking more to him. I didn't care. "Any digital file is like a long, long bracelet, say you've got a thousand beads strung one after another on a piece of wire."

"That's the best damn analogy I've ever heard, Laura. Good. Really good."

"Except," I said, "when you think you've deleted that whole string of beads, you've probably just deleted or moved the very first bead on the string. And the first bead is like an index page at the back of the book. Except here, it's the first thing in the file. And it tells me exactly what's in the rest of the bracelet, which is usually almost one hundred percent recoverable. Just a matter of having the right software to look at the hard drive."

"And we'll buy that software," Kligerman said. "When I set up the department, my budget will have money to buy all the software we need."

What crap, I thought.

I don't need this job. I don't need this guy who thinks that computer hard drive decoding software is something you go down to find at Office Max or CompUSA. These are the moments where I'm not good with people, I'm just not good with social smiling when I'm seething inside. But I'd worked hard at just doing my old mantra, taking deep breaths, counting to myself until I tamped the anger back into its box. Usually, the anger came out of something unconnected, now I'd learned how to focus on my goals.

"Okay," I said. "I'm in."

"You'd probably like to see the facility space," Kligerman said. "There's not much in the space yet, we're just setting up the cubicles. I've barely moved into the corner office. But you could choose where you'd like to sit."

"No," I said. Calm as I could be. "My first condition is that I work in my own space. With my own people."

"Not a problem," Kligerman said. "Give us a list of names, we'll check."

"When you hire me, you hire my reputation. Who I hire is none of your business. I'm a licensed private investigator. I specialize in computer forensics. I have four full-time staff, any number of part-timers. It all depends on the contract."

"Oh, yes, salary."

"I don't work for wages. We'll draw up a contract. You tell me what you want done, I give you the price."

"What's your normal fee?" Gates kept his hand on Kligerman's dollars.

"Depends. All I know so far, you want me to investigate bank records. Usually, a job like that ranges up into high five or low six figures."

"You get over one hundred thousand dollars for one job?" Kligerman was somewhere between incredulous and seriously impressed. "You rock, girl."

"If the job takes a week, you pay the fee. If it takes two years, same fee, unless we renegotiate. I don't guarantee that I, personally, will do all the work. But I'll be your contact for anything. But. I will *not* be on salary. Deal?"

"Deal," Kligerman said. Without hesitation, his deep brown eyes sparkling, his lower jaw shifting forward and backward, small muscles rippling at his temples, like tectonic plates, as though he'd seen the future and it was an earthquake of personal publicity. We shook hands.

"Come meet three of my people," he said. Pressed a button on an intercom, didn't say anything, just beeped, I could hear the target phone system beep somewhere in another room. A door opened and three young people entered.

"Folks," he said, "this is Laura Winslow."

A young couple immediately stepped forward, right to the edge of my chair, thrust their hands out to me.

"I'm Heather Celli," the woman said. "I'm Casey Celli," the guy said, "geez, we've heard so much about you, this is a privilege, Miss Winslow."

"Thanks," I said. Wondering how such nice kids knew my reputation. "Just call me Laura. Please. Just Laura."

"Yes, Miss Winslow." Like Bobbsey twins, a matched pair. They actually curtsied. "Yes, Laura."

"Just back from their honeymoon," Kligerman said. "They're my two data miners. Whatever you can teach them, you can see their enthusiasm. And this is Lauren Militi." The third person came forward, nodded with a smile, a quick, hard handshake. Older than the Cellis, very beautiful, very tiny, I'd seen a lot of Veronica Lake movies, Lauren even had the same long hair, falling over her left eye, except her hair was a deep, lustrous black. Her hands flew in sign language, reminding me for the second time in two days about Tigger.

"Lauren's a mute," Kligerman said. "She's got an astonishing memory, like a photographic memory, except she stores whatever she's seen on a computer screen."

I signed *Hi, nice to meet you,* back to her and her smile broadened.

"Two more things," I said to Kligerman. "First. I've got a personal interest in these assassins. These *maras*. Understand me on this, I have other clients. All but one of them, I'll hire part-time staff to complete those contracts. But one client is still very important to me. I can't and I won't tell you anything about this client."

"What's his name?" Kligerman said.

"Not even a name. I promise you, right now, your interests are mine. Second. That murder, this morning, the man tortured and burned. Carlos Cañas. Use whatever law enforcement database you access, see if there's any background info."

"This related to what we're contracting for? Or your mystery client?"

"Both. You draw up exactly what you want me to start with, I'll give you a fee, we'll sign a contract. This is probably a first for both of us. PIs don't usually work under contract for the police department."

"Done!" Kligerman said. He beeped somebody else on the intercom, I thought he'd be bringing in champagne next for us to toast our togetherness. I left soon afterward, no champagne, somebody photocopied my driver's license and took down some personal details.

Outside TPD headquarters, I wandered briefly through all the half-truths and lies I'd promised. To get to the end, you do whatever it takes. Even the police lied.

"Yo," Ken said. On our cell phones. "You still want to go to a cockfight?"

"Yes."

"We're on. I'll pick you up around eleven tonight."

21

Swimming my way through my anger and confusion and depression, I couldn't get behind the realization that I'd been abandoned, left behind, deserted, and dumped.

I realize that women get dumped all the time. Everywhere in the world, every day, every hour. Men also get dumped, if that's even the right word.

Stroking through my swimming pool, I tried to sort out what I was feeling, but one thing was certain. My anger at Nathan's leaving, my depression, my confusion, my uncertainties—all of these feelings I powered to keep under control, knifing through the water, thinking of men in my life, try to do the working out of men in my life, going back through all the men in my life.

Nathan Brittles
Rich Thompson
Rey Villaneuva
Kimo Biakeddy
Ben . . . Ben Yazzie.
Lots of somebodys, one-night stands, meth connections
Jonathan Begay, once my husband
And George Loma, my father

Swimming, I focused on doing The Work. Turning a thought on its head, as I was taught to do by Monica

Tilley and Delilah and Carolyn, my friends in Arivaca, the sudden thought hitting me that *yes* I *did* have a few girlfriends, I'd have to tell Mary.

Turning my *anger* on its head.

I *hate* Nathan because he left me.

Was that true? Two laps of the pool later, I forced myself to realize that he'd not left me, I just didn't go with him. But that gave me little comfort.

All kinds of things flooded my head.

If I'm swimming, how do I know if I'm crying?
If I want a life of my own, how do I know I'm not being selfish?
If I hurt, why don't I want to hurt him back?
If the sun is shining, why does it feel like a rainy day?

I *hate* Nathan for not moving into my house, for not living with me all the time. Total irrational thoughts, like, do I want to kill him for doing that, for never really moving into my life? That he should love me enough to be aware of my need to have him close by, all the time?

Getting left behind really sucks. But who would I be if I actually wasn't left behind, if instead I'd been given insight and invitation to a different way of life?

Nathan was a good person. He just couldn't live without being on his reservation, with his own people. He didn't cheat on me with another woman, he didn't threaten or abuse me, he didn't give me the "I'm glad it's ended" speech.

What's the first thing I should feel an overwhelming compulsion to do?

Sex?
Sob into my pillow?
Forget emotions, force myself into my work?

* * *

Or is this something really basic about the kind of person I am? What if I really was selfish enough to believe that *my* life was so fundamentally more important, that actually, by not following Nathan when he needed me, I was dumping *him*?

Still swimming, my stroke and pace settled into a near-constant rhythm. So was I reacting to Nathan's selfish wishes, that he didn't want to live with me all the time? Or was I reacting to my own anger that he would not do so? And why did I *need* him to live with me all the time?

Secondary impression, my life is a soap opera.

So my pain, when I turn Nathan's own decision on its head, my pain is not that he was a total shit for not living with me, I was condemning him for the moments he wasn't nearby, but not delighting in those times his body lay next to mine or we talked or he played one of his native flutes.

Turn that on its head.

Nathan survived Vietnam. Nathan survived the brutal murder of his oldest, closest friend, Leon Begay. Nathan had already too much brutality and death in his life, Nathan wanted, Nathan's soul *needed* time on the *dineh* reservation to regenerate his soul's urge to love life.

Turn that on its head.

Nathan needed time with his people to learn how to love me.

Ah, that's a sticky unanswerable dilemma. But it is what it is.

Fleeting thought. People *watch* soap operas because, they're usually about somebody being dumped for somebody else, about the constant quest for true love, never mind that on TV this turns into the need for another hot body in bed.

Spider watched a lot of TV. One of our real differences. I liked movies, she liked TV. I liked complexity and subtext, she liked *Desperate Housewives* and *Fear Factor* and *Survivor*. Spider loved brand names. I cared less about brand names, as a rule. But these differences didn't affect our love for each other, it just affected what we shared in conversation.

One last piece of doing The Work.

What if I didn't love him anymore? Is there even a right answer to that question? A wrong answer? Is that true, that I don't love him anymore? This is the moment of truth, when doing The Work. Turn that last question on its head. What if I just drop any thoughts about whether or not I still loved him. Or actually, is there some major answer to this question that neither angers or stresses or depresses me?

Turn *that* on its head.

Why does my self-esteem depend on Nathan loving me? What actually did Nathan have to do with my unhappiness with him not constantly sharing my life, living with me, living in my house and not just living in my heart?

This is the power of The Work. Who knows, maybe even the power of soap operas. I felt I needed him to be with me constantly. In truth, he angered me with his need that I be with *him* constantly, wherever or in whatever world that took place. So I should have the freedom of love to be able to tell him to join his people, join his clans, that I would, in my own time, be with him and his people and his clans, but that I had a life outside of his.

Mostly, I thought, toweling myself off beside the pool, mostly it's what I've come to expect from relationships with men. I always seem to pick men who leave me, I felt like an idiot, running through these thoughts as though I were embarking on the five stages of accepting that I had cancer. I called Mary and got directions for the swim meet. Then I called Christopher Kyle and told him to meet me at the pool.

22

Sixty or seventy high school boys and girls clustered around an eight-lane outdoor swimming pool. Skinny freshmen through well-built seniors, powerful thigh muscles standing next to legs like beanstalks, girls flat-chested face-to-face grinning with large-breasted seniors. No makeup, no pretense at all in dress codes and jewelry and body piercings and everything else that teenagers use to identify with a clique and separate themselves from other cliques.

The pool itself surrounded by a ten-foot wrought-iron fence, with fifteen feet of concrete between the fence and the pool, hardly any empty space, parents and families with coolers and portable folding chairs gathered inside the fence while outside the latecomers peered through the iron staves.

Mary waved me to an empty chair, gave me a bottle of water, dragged a large cooler into the middle of a group of girls in reddish swimsuits. The other team wore blue-and-gold-striped suits, sheer fabric completely revealing body sizes, a few of the older girls already with high-beamed nipples standing out against the suits, boys with their sex clearly outlined through swimming briefs.

"Sit here," Mary said. "I'm one of the timers, so I can't much explain to you what's going on. But quickly, the real competitors will swim the middle lanes. Beginners or just warm-up swimmers in the two outer lanes, 'cause when these kids start power-stroking they send waves across the pool to bounce off the ends. Since this isn't an official swim meet, there'll be about ten individual events for girls and another ten for boys, plus half a dozen for relay races. Who is that man?"

Kyle moved slowly to the outside of the fence, bracing himself with one arm and waving at me with the other. I waved at him.

"Who is that?" Mary said.

"A homicide detective," I said. "I want you to meet him later."

"Does he know?"

"Yes," I said.

"Do you trust him?"

"Yes."

"All right."

The Catholic girls' team banded together, arms raised to touch hands in the middle for their school cheer.

"Not quite fair," I said. "Jesus has gotta be on both sides."

"It's just a pep cheer," Mary said.

For an hour, I watched individual races, a few of the boys and girls clearly much better than the rest. Mary and the other timers roamed the far edge of the pool, taking down names, taking times, recording the results. Only later I realized Mary'd not introduced me to Ana Luisa.

Later, when the families disbanded and few people were left, Mary met me at an outdoor table where I sat with Kyle. Again, I saw that Ana Luisa wasn't present, but I didn't ask why.

"I'm not sure why you brought me here," Kyle said.

"To see these teenagers," I said.

"And why?"

"These kids will never have to be drug smugglers," Mary said. "But some of them do take drugs."

"Drug smuggling," Kyle said. Talking to me, but

studying Mary. "Is that what this is about? Why TPD wants to hire you?"

"Yes," I lied. Not a complete lie.

"The *maras*," he said. "They're . . . they're unstoppable, you know. And they're not even the main drug smugglers."

"And who would that be?" Mary said.

"Heroin comes from Afghanistan. Almost the entire world supply comes from new poppy fields. The government is helpless, since warlords control the opium regions. And the warlords work with the Taliban. You cannot stop it."

"So what's practicable?" I said.

"Nothing's practicable."

"I've got to go," Mary said. A quick nod at Kyle, a frown to me before she walked to the parking lot.

"That lady really didn't want to meet me," Kyle said.

"No, maybe not. But unless she saw you with me, she'd never trust you."

"So. Laura. Is this where you get really honest with me?"

"About what?"

"What kind of work are you doing for TPD?"

"To tell you the truth, Christopher, I don't really know. And I don't even know that I want to work with them."

"And what are you doing for your friend?"

"Mary?"

"Since I know you're working with Ken Charvoz, I just get the feeling that something happened at that park, where the two of them work."

"Remember me asking about cockfights?" I said.

"Sure."

"Well, somehow, cockfighting is connected to drug smuggling."

"That's a stretch," he said. "I told you, those guys go to cockfights for fun. No money in it, no drug cartel would spend time running cockfights, the financial return just isn't there."

"Maybe not," I said.

"So I'm asking you again. What are you really doing?"

"Bob Gates told me, Bob said that his worst nightmare is not just having his kids use drugs. It's imagining them in the business, in the *drug* business. And his absolute worst horror is just the thought of some kid, the same age as his boy, that kid being a drug mule."

"Huh," Kyle said. "Huh, imagine that."

"You've got kids?"

"Nope. You?"

"A daughter. And a granddaughter."

"Huh," he said again. "I just don't see that I can help you."

"I may need a good friend."

"You mean, a friend inside the police department."

"No, Christopher, I just meant . . . a friend."

"That's really sweet," he said. "But you, computers, I'm useless. I'm just an old homicide dick. I don't even carry a piece anymore. You do, though."

"My Beretta and me," I said. "Sounds like a cheap movie."

"I haven't owned a piece in years. Can't even remember the last time I fired one. So. Okay. Hope I didn't freak out your friend. Hope I've not disappointed you."

"Not yet."

"So what're you doing now? How about an early dinner?"

"Actually," I said, "tonight, I'm going to a cockfight."

"Laura," he said. "Give this up."

"I can't."

"Walk away from this ugly business."

"Thanks for meeting me, Christopher. And thanks for meeting Mary."

"These *maras,* they're assassins. You go after them, they'll take you down. It's all just business to them. Your

name comes, you get in the way, your name goes on a
contract and make no mistake, you will die."

"Chris," I said.

"Christopher."

"I'm going to trust you with something."

"Be careful who you trust," he said. But he was eager
to hear me.

"I'm not on the TPD payroll."

"Okay."

"But I'm working a special contract for TPD."

"Okay."

"Sometime really soon, word will get out that I'm
hired to look at financial records of drug trafficking,
smuggling . . . all kinds of things."

"Waste of time," Kyle said.

"But that's not really what my contract is for."

"Ahhh."

"TPD suspects they've got a dirty cop."

"Nothing new there."

"No, Christopher. A very *special* dirty cop."

"Involved in what?" Kyle said.

"In drug trafficking. Smuggling. Everything we've
been talking about. For all I know, even cockfights."

"That's a real stretch," he said finally.

"They know it's happening."

"And they know this . . . how?"

"Leaked special ops," I said. "But really meant to be a
sting."

"Well. Doesn't that figure," he said. Disgust on his
face, his eyes behind me, his shoulders rising and falling
and whole tectonic plates of muscles shifting on his face.
"So you've been contracted to . . . what?"

"Look over personnel records. Hack into bank accounts."

"I don't understand why you're telling me this."

"Because I need to trust somebody," I said. "Somebody inside."

"Who gave you the contract?"

"Jordan Kligerman."

"No. I mean, who first came to you with this."

"Bob Gates. Will you help me?"

"Laura. You overestimate my capability. I'm an old homicide dick. They keep me on because of sympathy, well, okay, they keep me on partially because I really know how to work a murder book. But what you're talking about, if it's not homicide, I'm useless to you."

"Unless you hear something," I said. "Just keep me in mind. If you hear something, give me a call. That's all I'm asking."

"You're asking a lot more than that, lady."

23

"Mom," Spider said.

"Yes?"

"Is Nathan gone for good?"

"Spider." I steadied myself, I'd almost hugged her, I saw her eyes open in surprise when my arms went out toward her, but she couldn't hug because my granddaughter, Sarah Katherine, had just started her first steps, and she could stand upright only as long as Spider held one tiny hand.

"I'm sorry, sweetie. I don't know if he's coming back."

"Mom. He's hardly been here the last few months. What's happened?"

"A rough spot."

"Oh, Mom. He didn't, God, don't tell me he beat you?"

"No no no no no. Nathan would never do that."

"What *would* he do?"

"He wants to adopt a boy," I said. "An orphan, nobody else in his born-to or born-from clans wants the boy. Nathan wanted me to go with him, wanted me to meet the boy, welcome him into the family."

Spider drew Sarah Katherine up in her arms, balanced her on one hip, and put her other arm around my shoulders.

"Hug gammy," Spider said to the baby. Sarah Kather-

ine put out both hands to swat at my chin and nose until
Spider pressed the three of us together.

How many years have I waited for this?

Almost all my life.

"So, Mom," Spider said, letting me go. "We need to
talk about that sweat lodge Nathan built down below.
Look at my arm. Up here, near the elbow. That's a bee
sting."

A reddish circle, half an inch around and swelling
vividly at the center.

"Killer bees," she said.

"Killer bees?" I started to laugh.

"Nathan hasn't lit a fire in that sweat lodge for weeks.
Pack rats are in there, but worse, I think there's a nest of
killer bees."

"What a concept," I said.

Couldn't stop laughing. A swarm of killer bees, near
my house? What a concept, that I'm not dealing with
real people, it's just killer bees.

"Mom. It's no joke. There's a swarm in the sweat
lodge."

Leave it to nature, it always kicks you in the butt
when you're feeling low. I couldn't stop laughing, after
all I'd been through in the past forty-eight hours.

"Mom. These are Africanized bees. They're very aggressive. If they swarmed on my baby, she'd die from
shock. This is serious, Mom."

"Yes. You're right." Tried and failed to suppress a giggle. "We'll call the exterminator. We'll kill those killer
bees. We'll rip down the sweat lodge."

"You don't have to do that."

"Yes, I do," I said to myself.

And like that, things seemed lighter, less serious. I
staggered slightly, grasped a mesquite bush to steady
myself.

"Rip it down?" Spider said. "So he's really gone?"

"It is what it is," I said.

"So he's really gone."

It wasn't a question, despite my facile answer.

Killer bees. Not much of a unique metaphor, but I'd already seen four bodies, the results of aggressive assaults and torture by the *maras*. If that's who did the killing, so be it. Killer bees, killers of any kind.

"Let's call an exterminator right now," I said. "And a trash remover, to tear down the sweat lodge."

"Mom." Concern veins rippling blue in her temples, a long wiggly vertical vein down the center of her forehead. "Do you know what you're doing?"

"No," I said. "But I've got to do this quick or I'll talk myself out of it. And when he comes back, *if* he comes back, he can build another one."

Over the next four hours, Spider dealt with the exterminator and the man who came with his son to rip apart the sweat lodge and truck it away. I called Nathan's cell number fifteen times, it rang and rang and rang, and nobody answered.

Around eleven at night, Spider gave me some of her Mexican clothes to wear to the cockfights. Latinas dressed with panache. A lot of skin, a lot of fake long fingernails and eyelashes, too much black or purple or pink eye shadow, we settled for pink. Spider's leather pants fit me like a glove, not so bad at all, looking at myself sideways in a full-length mirror. No tummy, no tree-trunk thighs despite my long miles of swimming every day. And no panty lines, Spider emphasized this, made me take off my cotton panties and pull the leather pants tight, being careful of the zipper. A leather halter top without a bra, I couldn't fill it out to Spider's breast size, but it worked. And four-inch platform heels, amazing myself I could walk in them.

"So who's the guy that's taking you out?" Spider said.

Clothes approved, guy not yet checked out.

"Ken. Ken Charvoz. Used to be an undercover cop. Now he's coordinator of all the volunteers at Tohono Chul Park. And he's not taking me out."

"And you know him . . . how?"

"Spider," I said. "It's not a date. It's for a client. I don't want to tell you about it, I don't want you to know."

"Hey, cool. And here he comes."

The *blahtblaht* of a Harley, downshifting to crawl up our driveway. We went down the back stairway to the parking area, Ken revving the Harley a few times before he switched off the engine.

"It's a Fat Boy," Spider said.

"Come on," I said. "He's in good shape."

"Mom," Spider said. "That's the bike. A Harley-Davidson Fat Boy."

Ken removed his helmet, neck-length black hair spilling out over his face and he shook his head like a dog to free the hair. "Ken," he said.

"Spider. Cool ride."

"Well," he said, "Laura. Look at you." Spider shot me a smile, climbed onto the saddle, trying the clutch pedal, leaning forward slightly to grasp the handlebars. "Mom," she said. "This is one nasty bike, this is so cool. Just like the battle cruiser Arnold rode in *Terminator 2*."

"One more thing to do," I said. "Come up. See the view. I'll be out in five."

Back in my office, I carefully fitted a miniature video camera into the leather halter, wincing at the small hole I cut with fingernail scissors in the left cup. After securing the camera with surgical tape, I fitted a five-hundred-and-twelve-megabyte memory stick into the right halter cup, linked it to the camera. In front of the mirror, I adjusted the halter, turned to three-quarters profile, decided everything would stay put as long as nobody groped me.

"This is incredible," Ken said. An amazingly clear night sky, all of Tucson laid out below us as far as we could see. "This is your house?"

"Yes," I said.

"I mean, you own this place?"

"Yes."

"I'm in the wrong business," he said. "Nonprofits don't pay this well."

"Just a client. Nine months' work, a team of five people. He paid off his debts by deeding the house over to me."

"You mean"—he couldn't quite grasp what I'd said—"it's all paid for?"

"Yes."

"I could work nine years, I still wouldn't be able to afford this."

His cell burped twice, not the insistently obnoxious ring tones you hear in malls and airports and even restaurants, just two short burps, then two again. He answered and just listened, then snapped the cell shut.

"We've got some time," he said. "Can I just enjoy the view?"

"Come up to the roof."

"Oh, man," Ken said.

We emerged from the narrow stairway onto the dark roof, the only lighting from the full moon. Stars glittered over half the sky, dimmed only over the street-lit portions of Tucson, a city built to be dark for the many observatories on peaks rimming the southern basins. Once our eyes adjusted to the moonlight, I led Ken to the wooden chairs, pulling aside the broken chair used by Bob Gates two mornings ago. Ken turned his chair around, sat backward, leaning on the carved wooden backrest, a broad grin on his face as he looked everywhere.

"Oh, my," he said. "Oh, my, my, my."

"I come up here to watch monsoon lightning. Tried to photograph it a hundred times, but lightning is tricky to capture. I'd just rather watch."

We sat in silence until his cell burped again. Opening it, he read a text message.

"Ten minutes, we'll leave," he said. "So I hear you met with Gates and Kligerman today. You going to work for them?"

"A contract, yes."

"I hope you know what you're doing."

"I don't."

"Be realistic here," Ken said. "Be honest with your limited knowledge of the power politics within the Tucson Police Department. They want you at a midlevel position. You've not met the chief of police, not met the movers and shakers out of headquarters. The guys who move in political circles inside and outside TPD."

"I like Gates," I said. "I probably trust him a lot."

"He's a fair man. But Kligerman is the next wave of TPD politics. You'll never, *ever* really know why decisions are made, why people are hired or motivated or fired. When I retired, I was a Detective Level One. I ran a whole squad, I made calls, I controlled crime scenes. But once something became political, I'm just the guy who follows parading elephants with a broom and a shovel. Well. That's not fair.

"Kligerman never wore a uniform. Went right from the academy into administration. They knew, back then, they knew he'd move up really fast and nobody wanted to get in his way. So he never strapped on the gear, he never rode a sector car. There's good men in admin. Gates, he's a good man. Eight years in a unit, never wanted undercover but they made him detective. He knows."

"Knows what?" I said.

"Most of us out there in the units, uniforms and undercover . . . you ever see a neighborhood sweep?"

"I don't know what you mean."

"It's night, it's after midnight. Say you're driving down Grant, you've had this great meal at Kingfisher and you're headed east to your home, up here, your palace away from the streets. But along Grant you see the bubblegum lights a few blocks ahead of you. Cherry and sapphire, 'round and 'round. You get closer, you see a unit blocking off side streets. And uniforms are humping over fences, Maglites bobbing around backyards,

every uniform's got his duty piece out, they're all yelling,
clearing out one backyard after another. Sometimes it's
all just . . . somebody heard a noise, saw a shadow,
punched nine-one-one. *Guy's got a gun,* somebody says
to the nine-one-one operator. Out we go. Do the sweep.
Jump up to clear a six-foot fence, you got *no* idea what's
on the other side until you put your Maglite on the yard.
Adrenaline pumps big-time, this sounds like a movie,
like a TV reality show. But it's really what it is. Some
guys . . . after clearing a dozen fences, sweeping a dozen
yards, maybe they find a perp, maybe he's got a gun,
maybe it's a coyote eating somebody's garbage, or somebody's little dog, it's all melodrama, you've seen in a
hundred movies, a thousand TV shows. But those
movies, that TV, you never *smell* what it's like those
times when shit really goes down. Listen to me, I'm talking like Al Pacino. But that's what movies don't give you.
Blood, how it smells, coppery, metallic. Some guy's puk-
ing his guts out, if the scene's really bad. What an old
cliché, that you can smell fear. But you *can*."

"And Kligerman?" I said.

"Never."

"But that doesn't make him any less good at what he
does."

Ken looked at me a long time. A sad look. Shrugged.
"Yes," he said finally. "Yes, it does make a difference.
He's done a lot for the department, but he's still an equal
opportunity asshole. You ready?"

"I'm ready."

"Where you guys going?" Spider said. Ken climbed onto
the bike, helped me get seated behind him.

"Can't say."

"Okay, Mom. I guess you're old enough."

"She's nowhere too old for me," Ken said.

"Where's my helmet?" I said.

"Honey Bunny," Ken said. Just a term he used, like

baby or *dear,* I didn't take it personally. "Where we're going, a helmet would be like the only dog in the mall. Tie your hair in this bandanna." He kick-started the bike. "And away we go."

24

Beyond Tucson, heading north, I-10 stretches past Marana and what used to be mostly desert and old ranches, now heavily populated with subdevelopments, industrial parks, and fast-food strip malls. With a full moon, in the distance you see Picacho Peak looming dark against the skyline.

Ken wove the Harley in and out of thinning traffic, exiting at Tangerine and then north on a state farm road. We passed through a few small towns, not even towns so much as gatherings of trailers and houses surrounded by abandoned vehicles and all manner of junk dropped randomly on the desert floor. Some of these little places had a gas station and a store or two, occasionally a bar which might be a double-wide trailer or some ancient cinder-block building with the adobe facing pretty much worn off by the wind and the dust.

Ten miles and three cattle guards later, the paved road disintegrated into loosely graveled dirt ruts and, not far past that, a clump of a few dozen trailers. Oddly enough, the rutted road came back to a paved surface, an old two-lane road with a yellow center line so old it barely registered in the bright sunlight. Power poles jagged into the place from the southeast and ran off across the road into the desert. Power cables sagged down to most of the trailers, a few cables so old they hung just a few feet off the ground, you could see the bare aluminum wires and you knew they were hot.

Ken pulled over at a four-way stop, but motioned me to stay on the bike as he straddled the tank and anchored both boots on the shoulder of the road. He checked his cell phone, read off three text messages.

"We're looking for a barn," he said. "You watch the left, I'll watch the right, it's supposed to be set back a hundred yards from the road. Probably a dirt track to the barn, past a single-story, flat-roofed house."

"Wait," I said. "Before we get there. I don't know what to expect."

"Expect the worst," he said finally.

Two miles later, I grabbed his shoulder, pointed to the house. Light sparkled in the distance, some of it from vehicle headlights. Passing the house in low gear, it looked typical of neighborhood houses in South Tucson, well landscaped and maintained over the forty or fifty years since it was built. No derelict cars or stuffed furniture baby toys lying haphazardly on a sandy front yard. Not that that's typical of poorer neighborhoods, but I'd passed a lot of that random style of living while driving through South Tucson.

The house was surrounded by tall and well-tended trees of all kinds. Palo verde, hackberry, a few mesquite, the house itself partially shadowed from the road by ten-foot-high oleander bushes. Sixty yards ahead, we saw the barn. An ancient RED MAN TOBACCO sign painted on the front side, almost erased by decades of wind and rain. Ken stopped the bike between a Mercedes and a Beemer, let me get off, and parked.

Rusted pickups, a dozen motorcycles, two RV vans, five travel trailers, lots of brand-new SUVs of all makes, many expensive.

"I thought this was a redneck thing," I said.

"Lots of money wagered in there, by all kinds of people. Just getting inside is expensive. The handlers usually pay three to five hundred dollars for each cock they enter."

"How do they figure odds? For gambling?"

"No odds. You'll hear people shouting out their bets, before the cocks are let loose and all through the match, sometimes people switch their money over to the cock they think is winning. Whoever is promoting this fight is the banker, all bets are with him, he's the 'house.' I'll follow the money, you shoot video of whatever you think best."

"Not the cocks," I said. "I can't watch one animal killing another."

"One thing," he said to me. "Remember this one thing. Follow whatever I do. We're acting, you've got to be exactly who you're supposed to be. We're at a cockfight, okay? Ever seen a cockfight?"

"No."

"You're *not* going to like it. *But you can't look away.*"

"Damn," I said. "This is going to be hard."

"Just remember the only rule in there. You're acting, you *love* cockfights. Okay? You geared up?"

"Once we get to the door, I'll start the camera, but it won't run continuously. I'll have to start and stop for what I think's most important. I've got enough memory and battery power for about twenty minutes of video. Just the picture, I can do a small zoom, but not much. So get us seated as close as possible. So we can video whoever is running the fights."

"You ready to start?"

He wrapped one arm around my waist, high, started the two of us walking to the front doorway where a huge Indian collected money. When the Indian's eyes turned to us, Ken moved his hand higher to cup my breast and he turned his face to me, lips out, and I kissed him.

"We're on," he said.

*   *   *

Two men just inside the doorway, wearing headsets.
They ran flashlights up and down our faces, just a random thing but enough to terrify me, each man with one
hand on his flashlight and the other holding a pistol
down at his side. Not at all apologetic, one took out a
metal detector and hand-wanded each of us, then looked
in my bag, probably checking for cameras or recording
devices.

Ken paid fifty dollars apiece to get us inside. The barn
was huge, more of a warehouse, full of cars, pickups,
and bikes parked all around the walls, about three vehicles deep. At the center, a rectangle of bleachers, eight
rows high, surrounded a cock pit boarded off on all
sides by three-foot-high sheets of plywood. The crowd
roared, seated and standing on eight rows of graduated
aluminum planking. I finally wedged between Ken and a
biker wearing a blue denim vest and jeans so worn and
faded they were almost white. Laundered, I saw. Ironed
and pressed, creases on the sleeves and down each side of
the front, the jeans six inches too long and folded back
up like John Wayne used to wear them in his westerns.
The biker smiled at me, dipped his longneck beer bottle
at Ken just as two more fighting cocks were released in
the ring.

"Give us all they got!" he shouted at the ring, settling
the bottle at his feet before he stood and yelled, even
with the other people yelling and screaming the biker's
voice slicing through the intense noise. "Give us all they
got!"

People in front of me stood up just as I triggered the
videocam button, but instead of standing I tried to wiggle sideways to shoot video between the people.

"Stand *up*, Laura!" Ken said. Elbow in my ribs. "This
is not a tennis match. If you act polite here, you'll just
stick out."

Blood squirted straight up from one of the cocks,
staining the white feather around his neck. The other

cock slashed again, so quickly I didn't even see the
wound, but the bloody cock flew sideways, head mostly
severed from the body, feet moving for another twenty
seconds. When the fight ended, the winning cock hoisted
by his handler, the loser, dead, was carried off unceremo-
niously. I tried to look away, but Ken jabbed me with his
elbow and I shouted and applauded. At one corner of the
cockpit, I saw that the fights were being recorded by a
digital video camera mounted on a tripod. Diametrically
across the pit, another camera. While waiting for the
next bout, the two cameras made periodic sweeps of the
audience and I saw the camera's zoom lenses working.

"The video game," I said in Ken's ear. "Here's where
they shoot the digital video that gets processed for the
animated video games."

I saw one videographer give directions to the other via
a headset. Ken nudged me as the promoter of the fight
gave directions to the next pair of cock handlers and the
videographers.

"*Hoyo,*" the promoter shouted to the next pair of
men that swiveled themselves over the boards, both men
bringing cocks to the center of the pit, allowing the two
cocks to swipe beaks against each other. Two other men
came into the pit, holding the steel gaffs, even from my
seat in the top row I could see the gaffs were nearly four
inches long, ending in a sharp steel point. Gaffs were attached to the bone spurs of each cock, and everybody except the handlers left the ring. They knelt to the sandy
floor, held out the cocks toward each other, and released
them with a flurry of wings and feathers, each bird kicking out, dodging, slicing, pecking once in a while but
keeping their strikes moving toward the other cock until
one scored a direct blow to the head, instantly killing the
other cock. The victor was carried off over his handler's
head, the body of the loser disappearing with his handler
to behind the stands.

"*Ésta es la primera lucha semifinal,*" the promoter
shouted.

"The first of the semifinal fights," Ken said to me.

"De Nogales, el campeón, luchas de Renaldo Roo. Veintiséis como ganador, él les mató todos. Y de Yuma, el desafiador, Arnold el asesino. Diecinueve matanzas."

"Champion, twenty-six kills. Challenger, nineteen," Ken said. "That promoter isn't speaking very good Spanish. I'm watching him, so get him on video and then record whatever you want."

"Para ambos gamecocks. Celebre su fuerza y salude su honor," the promoter shouted, circling his arms to bring the two cocks and their handlers to the center of the ring. The crowd stood and cheered.

"Fuerza y honor!" the crowd shouted. The biker beside me shouted, "Strength and honor. Strength and honor."

"Las maquinillas de afeitar!" the promoter shouted.

For this match, the needle-pointed spurs weren't held up. Instead, I saw what looked like knives, like razors, being strapped to the cocks. I grabbed Ken's arm, tried to stop biting my lower lip, tried to look enthusiastic at the bloody spectacle of a fight that lasted almost nine minutes, the crowd on its feet roaring for one bird or the other, calling out bets of hundreds of dollars, until both cocks collapsed, exhausted, heads moving slowly, warily, and then the challenger cock made a sideways slice and killed the champion.

After the last fight, the crowd dispersed quickly, the vehicles inside the barn leaving through two side gated doors. A crew began tearing down the bleachers. Ouside, I wanted to follow the main videographer, but Ken just shook his head, knelt beside his Harley as though fixing a part.

Only a few vehicles left, the promoter finally walked out and headed toward a Porsche SUV. Ken motioned for me to get on the Harley, he kick-started it, we moved slowly across the parking lot toward the Porsche, and just as we came alongside the promoter, Ken threw out

an arm and knocked him to the ground. Ken quickly
stopped the Harley, killed the engine, and jumped off,
motioning for me to steady the bike while he sat astride
the promoter and punched him twice in the jaw.

"In the saddlebag," Ken said. "In the right saddlebag,
some duct tape."

I threw the roll to him, Ken duct-taping the promoter's mouth shut and then flopping him on his stomach and taping his hands together. Taking the Porsche's
keys, Ken toggled the alarm system off and swung the
promoter into the back seat.

"Get in," he shouted to me, and we drove away into
the desert.

25

The middle of nowhere, completely off-road in the desert. Promoter conscious in the back seat, lying still, eyes on us calmly. Ken motioned me to get outside, came around the front of the Porsche to talk.

"What you're going to see now," he said. Sheet metal hood *tinking* as it cooled, the night air intolerably humid and hot, sweat all over my body.

"Yes?"

"I've got to do something, with this guy, something I haven't done in years. I've got to make him afraid for his life, I've got to make him truly fear me, truly believe that I am the wrath of the Lord. But. Laura. Remember that what you'll see me do and say will *not* be me."

"All right."

"I used to be that kind of man," Ken said. "Let's just hope I remember what to do. But you, don't say or do anything, okay?"

"Sure, okay."

Around to his side of the Porsche SUV, yanking open the back door and pulling the man out, both Ken's hands on the man's belt buckle, dumping him crudely on the caliche. Ken took out a pocketknife, opened a blade, cut away the duct tape from the man's mouth, ripping out several chunks of blond hair caught in the tape. Rolling the man over, he flicked a wallet out of the man's back pocket, then cut the tape off his hands.

Ken knelt, pulling out a huge chrome-plated .357 revolver.

"Nice rodeo buckle you're wearing there," Ken said.

He bent over, hands on knees, focused on the silver buckle about the size of a salad plate.

"Broncs? Calgary? I can't quite read that, son. Take off your belt, I want to read what's on the buckle, I've got to take it in front of the headlights, so I can see what you rode to win that thing."

"Fuck you," the man said.

"Who is this jag-off?" Ken said. I'd opened his wallet, held a flashlight so Ken could read the name on the driver's license.

"Max Cady," Ken said. "Hello, Mr. Max Cady."

"He's not Max Cady," I said. Giggling, nervous, but it was still funny. "Oops." I'd already forgotten I wasn't supposed to say anything, but Ken didn't mind, eyebrows cocked into question marks, eyes cutting between me and Cady.

"You're not Robert Mitchum," I said.

The man's face immobile.

"You're not Robert De Niro, either."

A tiny smile on his lips, if the flashlight wasn't right on his face I wouldn't have seen it.

"So who's the real Max Cady?" Ken said.

"It's a part in a movie," I said. "*Cape Fear*. A sociopath is released from prison and terrifies the lawyer who sent him there."

"Let's have that belt, Max," Ken said.

"Not takin' my pants off," Cady said.

"Just the belt."

"Not lettin' my pants down, I don't do that except for ladies." He turned to me. " 'Less *you* want to see my bidness? I'll untuck it for you."

Ken swept the cowboy hat off Cady's head, stood back. "Just a moment," he said. Pulled me aside, back a few steps. "What I'm going to do next, Laura. It's just acting, remember, you've got to play your part."

"Acting, what do you mean, acting?"

"Don't you believe for a minute that what you're going to see me do is in any way the real me. Just a piece of acting, here." He turned back to Cady. "Now, bud, let's start the ball."

"Not takin' my pants down for you, homo."

Ken leisurely stretched out his hand with the .357, whacked Cady on the right elbow. "The belt first. That's for your attitude. Then we'll get to the questions. Now, this is the sticky part."

"Ask what you want. Let's get done with this, I've got two women to see."

"Gonna be like strip poker," Ken said. "You shuck off a question, you shuck off part of your clothes. You answer a question, you give me an answer I'd really put in the church poor box, you get to put something back on. Start with the belt. Get it off."

Cady removed his belt, held it out.

"Just drop it," Ken said. "Now. You got the rules? Only two answers possible to my questions. The right answer, or take off more clothes. First question. Who do you work for?"

"Nobody."

"You don't believe me, son. You're not really afraid of me, right?"

"I know who you are," Cady said. "You're that has-been cop. You used to work Vice, but you were a total fuckup. People saw you coming along, they didn't move away, they just laughed at your ass."

"Ezekiel," Ken said. "The Book of Ezekiel. Chapter twenty-five, verse seventeen. You can look it up, it's in the Bible."

"Ah," Cady said. "Now, that's real sweet. You're gonna preach on me, you're gonna save my soul."

"'The path of the righteous man,'" Ken said, "'is beset on all sides by the inequities of the selfish and the tyranny of evil men. Blessed is he, who in the name of charity and good will, shepherds the weak through the valley of darkness, for he is truly his brother's keeper and the finder of lost children. And I will strike down upon thee with great vengeance and furious anger those who would attempt to poison and destroy my brothers. And you will know my name is the Lord when I lay my vengeance upon thee.' "

"That's just from some stupid movie," Cady said. "And you aren't even a nigger, saying that dumb shit."

"Sit down," Ken said. Voice dropping at least four notes. "Pull off a boot."

Cady didn't protest, his face a mask. He leaned against the Porsche, slid down with his back against it, and tugged off his right boot.

"Twelve-inch alligator tops," Ken said. "From Paul Bond. Now, that's truly the finest boot made. Myself, I've just got some standard lizardskin boots. Hand-made, sure. But not so fancy as alligator. Too bad, looks like your feet are a couple sizes smaller than mine. Let's try that question again. Who do you work for?"

"Myself." Cady's face totally blank, as though he were concentrating on something entirely remote, like playing solitaire on a computer.

"The other boot."

Once it was off, Ken reached down, handed both boots to me with his pocketknife.

"Slash his boot tops."

I stabbed through the alligator skin, ripping long swaths through each boot.

"Now," Ken said. "I've just called some honest-to-God Jesus fire down on your boots. Next wrong answer, that Jesus fire lightning bolt comes right out of this .357, comes right down on your balls. So. There's no mistake here, you know what I'll do. Tell you what, though. We'll let that question slide awhile. Who do you work for, we'll come back to that. Who was the person who shot the video?"

For the first time, Cady looked surprised, his head bobbing from Ken to me and back to Ken.

"Deb," he said. "Deb. I don't know her last name."

"Deb No Last Name. Does she work for you?"

"No. I arrange the fights, she turns up with her crew. I never see pictures."

"So do you both work for the same person?"

"No. Yeah. I guess so."

"And that person's name?" Ken said.

"I don't know, honest to Christ, I don't know."

"Okay. Where do the fighting cocks come from?"

"All over, man, that's easy. The champion cocks come up from Sonora."

"Okay, third and last time. Somebody arranges all this, somebody further up the food chain from you. So, who is it?"

Cady didn't answer, Ken fired his .357 a foot away from and alongside Cady's head, black goo trickling out the left ear.

"God*damn*!" Cady said.

"You beginning to see a pattern in my questions?" Ken said.

"I'm just somebody in the food chain," Cady said. "I get cell phone instructions from somebody I've never met. He tells me where and when, I hire a crew and run the matches. But I can't give you no names, man."

Ken fired again, alongside the other ear. Blood trickled from the ear and the promoter wiped at it, groggy, wincing.

"Why are you so interested in cockfights anyway?" he said. "The real money is in the dogs."

"You stage dogfights?"

"No. Somebody else does that."

"Back to names," Ken said. "Is it the same person?"

"Do you work for the *maras*?" I said.

"Oh, man. Oh, Christ, man." Cady blanched in terror. "Come *on*, man! I'm not saying anything more."

"The videotapes," I said. "What happens with the videotapes?"

"I don't know, man. Please. That woman, Deb, she takes the tapes. That's all I know. I just run the cockfights. "Yeah, sure, okay? They own a lot of the birds, they dope the birds, they rig the fights, nothing is just fun for those people, not unless it makes money."

"How much do *you* make?" Ken said.

"I'm paid five thousand a fight."

"In cash?"

"Money transfer. It shows up in a bank account. Two thousand up front, the rest the morning after the fights."

"What bank?" I said.

"Bank of America."

"What branch?"

"Green Valley. The account's in the name of Dakota Barbie. Like the state, like the doll. Okay, that's all, that's all I know."

"Do we believe him?" Ken said to me. I nodded. "All right, Max. Whatever your real name is, I'll keep your wallet, we'll get your ID checked out real good. Hand me that duct tape."

After being wrapped in the tape, this time around both hands and ankles, Cady thought he'd go back into the Porsche, but Ken dragged him ten yards away. Cady tried shouting, but the desert swallowed his voice as we drove away.

He pulled up next to the warehouse, got out to slide open one of the doors, drove the Porsche inside. "These people who run the fights, they're worse than the animals that get slaughtered."

The barn was almost totally empty, the bleachers gone, nothing left but an ancient Ford pickup parked askew in one corner, the hood up, two fifty-gallon iron barrels on the ground near the tailgate.

"What will happen to this place?"

"I'll report it, cops might stake it out, probably not. These promoters move from place to place."

We looked in the barrels, both of them full of dead cocks. Ken went berserk. Finding a rusted tire iron in the pickup cab, he went to the Porsche, smashed all its windows, headlights, taillights, long scratches and dents in the body. Back at the pickup, he found two red cans of gasoline and dumped some of it in the barrels, then took some rags from the barn floor and soaked them with gasoline before cramming the rags into the Porsche's gas tank. The rest of the gasoline he sloshed over the wooden walls. Waving me outside, he stood in the doorway, touched a match to the trail of gasoline he'd laid down from the Porsche and lit it up.

We ran to the Harley and Ken popped a wheelie, he was so anxious to get away, fighting down the front of the bike as the warehouse burst into flame.

I flipped open my cell.

"What are you doing?" Ken shouted.

"Calling nine-one-one."

"Let it burn," Ken said. "Just let it burn."

26

Home.

I pushed through my bedroom door, going to the windows. The door hung slightly askew and swung shut behind me. When I turned, I saw myself in a full-length mirror on the back of the door.

Startled, I saw myself regard myself with surprise. Biker chick, that's not *me*, is it? Reddish spots on my bare legs, below the knee. More spots on my boots.

Still surprised, I bent toward the mirror to examine the spots, not even thinking to look at the real person. Speckles of blood all over my boots. I looked directly down at them. Sat on the floor, propped left boot on my right thigh. Boots flecked with rooster blood, like sprinkles on a mocha ice-cream cone. I'd not realized I'd splattered myself when dropping the dead rooster into the burn barrel.

I left my house at dawn. I drove west for a while, drove north, the sunrise low on the horizon and sometimes in my face, against my left cheek or my right and because I wanted its warmth, I turned south when I crossed I-10 for the fourth time.

Without noticing, I merged onto I-19, headed toward Nogales and the border, past the Desert Diamond Casino, with a dozen RVs parked on the edges of the

lots and fifty or sixty empty cars around the front and
side of the casino, early morning slot machine players.

At Esperanza, I exited into Green Valley, pulled up to
the empty parking lot near the Book Shop, where I'd
once parked window to window with Nathan. I read the
scrapes and oil markings on the pavement like they were
tea leaves, but found nothing there, so I eased out onto
La Canada and headed south again until by sheer coincidence I saw the Bank of America branch, its clock reading the wrong time, big hand pointed at six and the little
hand at eleven. I pulled into the parking lot, stopped, put
both hands in back of my neck, trying to stretch tension
out of my neck muscles. Using my fingertips, I tried a
shiatsu massage on my temples, but nothing stopped
my headache, so I turned onto Continental and saw I
needed gas.

A brand-new GMC pickup pulled to the pump across
from me. A tiny woman with pink hair jumped out to
pump gas, the driver eyeing me from underneath his
cheap straw hat, the straw crushed and folded until the
sides came up almost vertical with the brow pointing
down. As I pumped gas, I saw his eyes switch to the I-10
on-ramp, where three people stood in a huddle. A Mexican family, parents and a small boy.

"Damn Mexicans," the pickup driver said. "You hear
so many stories, you know, people down there on the
take, bribes, up the food chain the bribes get bigger. But
that's their country, I don't like 'em personally, I don't
want 'em in Arizona. Drive down here, look at that plastic everywhere, bottles, baggies, they're just litterbugs."

Wiggling his back against the beaded seat cushion,
scratching a spot somewhere below his shoulder blades,
then moving up and down, drawing his jeans tighter
against his crotch until he had to reach inside his belt
and rearrange his parts inside the white jockey shorts.
Jerking so much the pickup bounced until he got everything in place. He'd dropped his seatback almost to a

forty-five-degree angle, lying back like he was watching football on TV, his chin nearly on his neck, watching the road and his mirrors from the top of his eyes. I remembered a rodeo in Flagstaff, watching bronc riders stretched horizontal over the horse's back, legs extended to rowel the bronc.

"I mean," he said, "I got nothing against money, I got nothing against the smugglers and cartels and politicos and even the *policia* down there. What I got is this really pissed-off feeling that the money people are driving the poor people north, up here where they work illegally and take money out of *my* pocket. I could give a shit about what's legal, what's . . . how do you say it, what's right? Morals. Morally right. Money talks, it don't give no mind to morals."

Slim Pickens popped into my head, Pickens spurring the bomb, waving his crushed cowboy hat with a free hand, riding the hydrogen bomb in *Dr. Strangelove* and hollering, *YeeeeHaaaaa,* toward the end of the world.

Finished pumping my gas, I swung down Continental and onto the ramp, the man with his thumb out, but he pulled it back when he saw my face. I stopped just ahead of them, waved them to my car.

"Where you going?" I said.

"San Xavier," the man said. "The mission. Sunday mass."

"Let me give you a ride. Get in."

The woman and boy climbed in back, the woman smiling as she worked her way through a rosary. The man sat beside me, admiring the car's interior.

"*Mucho gracias, señora,*" he said shyly. "We light a candle. For you."

"No," I said. "I mean, thank you, but you don't have to light a candle."

"I will pray for you," the woman said, leaning forward from the back seat and pressing a card in my hand.

"No, no," I said. "Please, *por favor,* no prayers."

"But señora," the man said. "It is us who pray for you."

"Whatever," I said. I dropped them off near the front of Mission San Xavier and circled the parking lot to return to I-10, but stopped the car dead when I passed the W:AK minimall. Three stray dogs bounded over, tails wagging as I half stepped out of the car and immediately got back in and slammed the door shut, the dogs standing on their hind legs, all on my side of the car, my power window down and not going up fast enough, my thumb aching on the button to close the window faster. But the dogs only wanted to lick my hand, lick my face, get some food. They trotted off after the next car, ready to beg all over again.

Dogs. The W:AK minimall. This is the place of my worst nightmare. The night five years ago when Rey Villaneuva and I went looking for Miguel Zepeda, and Charley Not A Bear set a boy on fire.

We hurried through the doorway just as a large German shepherd lunged at my ankles. Rey slammed the door shut. Broken glass crunched under my feet. Rey flicked the flashlight down and around.

Plates, cups, saucers, bowls, everything breakable had been swept from two shelves above the sink and lay in pieces on the floor. Every drawer had been pulled out, emptied, smashed, and broken. One of three wooden chairs had been used to smash cabinets, the other chairs, and a card table. Two framed photographs lay in the sink amid shattered frames and glass.

The dog threw himself at the wooden bottom of the door. Rey played the flashlight around the doorway frame and down the hallway leading from the kitchen into the rest of the house.

A board squeaked in a front room as somebody put weight on it, and it squeaked again when the weight was released. At the far end of the cone of light I saw a shadow flicker from one room to the next.

I crossed both arms across my breasts and gripped my shoulders hard, blood pounding in the vein in my right temple.

I moved backward into the kitchen, glass crunching with every step. The noise really set off the dog and he tried to jump through the broken glass at the top part of the door. I hunkered on my ankles against the wall, hands over my ears, wanting to scream. My left calf muscles tightened in an excruciating cramp and I had to stand suddenly, banging against the wall and flinging one arm out to brace myself.

The dog leapt up through the window, knocking the remaining shards of glass into the kitchen just as three shadows exploded down the hallway. Somebody crashed into Rey, knocking them both to the floor. Rey's flashlight moved across a blue backpack and down onto a pair of lizardskin cowboy boots, one of them in motion, kicking Rey's hand.

The flashlight bounced and skittered on the floor and came to rest, illuminating Rey's head just as a second man burst into the kitchen, swinging a tire iron downward toward Rey. A third man got to the door and flung it wide open. Rey fired at him and missed, the man running toward the plaza as lights went on inside a house several doors away.

The dog snarled at the second man, sinking his teeth into the man's leg. The man screamed in pain as he smashed the tire iron into the dog's head so savagely it stuck there. He pushed Rey aside and ran out the doorway. Rey fell sideways, bumping against my leg.

I crashed to the floor, writhing among the broken dinner plates as he jumped out the doorway, turning to fire the Glock. My ears rang from the gunshots, the noise bouncing off the walls. Ejected shell casings clinked on the floor, and I drew in a deep breath filled with the acrid scent of sulfur and gunpowder.

Rey got up, unsteady, and staggered out the door and into the yard, streaked by the first rays of false dawn light. Charley stood there, his head angled sideways to keep his long black hair out of his eyes as he sighted along the barrel of his .30-30, tracking the man fifty yards away who was limping badly. He disappeared behind a house and we ran toward him as he entered the San Xavier Plaza parking lot.

Charley fired just as the man stumbled on a rock and lurched forward. The bullet caught him squarely in the center of his backpack. The man exploded into a fireball and dropped solidly to the ground, his arms and legs wiggling frantically as the fire consumed his entire body.

"Bad luck for him," Charley said. A siren sounded down San Xavier Road. "And bad luck for me if I stay out here and they find me with a gun."

"Give me the .30-30," Rey said. "I'll get it back to you later."

Without hesitation, Charley tossed the rifle to Rey and disappeared into the next house. The red-blue bubblegum police lights came across the parking lot, stopping abruptly when the car's headlights illuminated the burning man.

Two young Tribal Policemen crouched nearby, one with a nine-millimeter, the other with a riot gun. In the distance, a third man sprayed a fire extinguisher over the man's body.

Except it wasn't a man. Just a young boy.

"Geez, Rey," one of them said, coming up to us, his hands shaking on the riot gun. "What the hell is happening, anyway? Why'd you shoot that kid?"

And so I stared at the charred body, only partially covered with some EMT cotton blankets. Just for an instant, I tell you. I swear I couldn't have looked at the body for more than a few seconds, but that was enough for the image to get permanently locked into my head.

"Mary," I said.

A hesitation on the cell phone, Mary trying to register my voice.

"Who is this?"

"Mary. It's Laura Winslow."

"Laura. Have you, what, why are you calling?"

"Can you meet me somewhere? Right now?"

"What's wrong?"

Something in my voice alerting her, alarming her.

"It's nothing to do with you. It's just, um, I really need a friend. Right this time, this place, I really need a friend."

"Where are you?"

"The mission. San Xavier."

"I'll have to bring Ana Luisa. Is that all right?"

"Yes. I'll be up that small hill, to the right of the mission?"

"I know it. There's a resting place up there, wait for me there." I climbed the hill, alone at the shrine, the morning still early enough that those people arriving had come for early mass and not sightseeing. I'd taken the pink diary from my car, I'd hadn't yet read it, but I couldn't put that off any longer.

I read the only entry. Mary Emich finding two survivors of a terrible accident, the death of the boy, the discovery at the Arivaca Medical Clinic that both children were drug mules, each having swallowed somewhere around twenty balloons of heroin.

Diary clutched between my hands like a hymnal, like a prayer book, like a bad dream, I sat immobile for fifteen minutes, seeing only the contradictions of my life in front of me. The terrible chaos of the burned boy in the parking lot, the white towers of hope and serenity of the mission.

Shifting my body, a card fell out of my bag, the card that the Mexican woman had given me. A prayer card.

A beatific woman, head covered with a loose blue shawl, tears runneling down her cheeks, kneeling before a crown of thorns, hands clasped in prayer, looking hopefully upward.

Sorrowful Mother

*You who held Jesus in your arms, please intercede
with your Divine Son on our behalf. Ask Him to
help us to know one another more readily; to love
one another more deeply. Mother of all mankind,
inspire us to travel without falter along that road
at the end of which, under the Fatherhood of God,
there is true peace.*

Amen

Two shadows crossed my face.

"Laura," Mary said. "Meet Ana Luisa."

A shy brown face poked around from behind Mary's
waist, the head turned sideways as though to see me
from a different perspective.

"*Hola*, Ana Luisa," I said. She grinned, ducked behind Mary's back, and then held tightly to Mary's left
arm. The mission bells rang and rang. "It's a beautiful
morning," Mary said. "Please. Come with us to mass.
We'll add you in our prayers, and we'll all light candles."

I sat still and silent during the mass, barely following the
liturgy, not kneeling with Mary and Ana Luisa, but
gradually relaxing to the serenity of the service.

Afterward, we strolled the inner courtyard of the mission, the walls lined with tables of candles in glass jars.
Mary bought three candles and we each lit one, Mary
saying a prayer, Ana Luisa more attracted by the friendly
stray dogs that roamed everywhere in the courtyard. I lit
my candle and we walked back up the hill to the shrine.

"There are two or three hundred lit candles here," I
said. "What are they for?"

"To keep the flame of Jesus alive."

"Uhh, well," I said. "I thought they were lit to remember somebody."

"In keeping the flame of memory alive, sure. At different times, I light a candle for my husband, or Ana Luisa, or for her dead brother. For Mother Teresa. For Jesus. It's the everlasting flame of love and life and remembrance."

Dogs wandered around the courtyard, peering at us through closed wrought-iron gates. The courtyard itself peaceful and serene.

"And who was your candle for?" Mary said.

"I just did it. Because you did it."

She pinched out the flame on my candle, handed me a match.

"Light it again," she said. "But for a purpose of your own."

I thought of Nathan and lit the candle.

Inside the church, I sat in a wooden bench at the back and watched Mary dip her fingers in a stone basin hung along the right wall. While she touched her forehead and signed the cross, Ana Luisa stood on tiptoes and repeated the gestures. They walked together, hand in hand, down the center aisle to a wooden altar beneath paintings and frescos, they knelt at a railing for a moment and then came to sit with me during the ritual mass.

Outside, walking to our cars, Mary smiled, lifted her face to the sun.

"This beautiful old mission just radiates peace," Mary said. "It's like our park, places of serenity."

"I'm not feeling too serene," I said.

"But you've had peaceful times? In your life?"

"Sure."

"Tell me about one."

I remembered Nathan, naked, playing one of his wooden flutes. I remembered his face, lying sideways on the pillow, eyes shut, lips open and relaxed as he breathed. It was the first time I'd seen him so relaxed. No vertical furrows on his forehead between the eyes, sleep even softening the lines which runneled down from the sides of his nose to the corners of his lips. I realized he was the kind of person who had to compose a business face, probably a

Law face, tighten things down, form a skin barrier against
showing emotions, eyes narrowed with a private, encoded
life force and lips that would never reveal it.

A face so guarded it reminded me of mine.

"What?" Mary said. "Was it a good time?"

"Yes," I said finally.

"So why are you crying?"

"It ended badly."

Mary sat awhile, nodding to herself, humming a tune
I didn't know.

"I remember a time," she said. "My husband, Jim, he
was stationed for a time in Kentucky. I used to drive the
back roads, up into the hollows where strangers didn't
much roam. One day, I pulled off the road to read a map
and saw a waterfall beside me. I got out of the car, went
down close to the creek so my eyes were level with the
lip of the waterfall, just before everything dropped about
twenty feet. It was October, the leaves were changing,
leaves were falling, floating down the creek and rushing
over the lip of the waterfall. Everything was blurred, the
water moved so fast, and I was looking upstream, fixing
my eyes on a leaf, and I followed that leaf with my eyes
right to the edge of the waterfall and in that moment
everything slowed down a hundred times, it seemed, I
could see every splashed drop, every twig and leaf, see
them crystal clear. Jim told me later that's what athletes
feel when they're in the zone. Like a baseball hitter, who
sees the ball coming toward him at ninety-five miles an
hour, but because the hitter's in the zone, the ball just
floats in slow motion and he can see every seam on the
ball and know if it's a fastball or a curve and he knows
exactly where to swing his bat to meet the ball."

"I know that feeling," I said. "Sometimes when I'm
swimming, I get beyond everything, I don't think of fatigue or control or what's troubling me. I stroke and
stroke, my hands reach out, I almost see my hands part-
ing drops of water."

"That is so," she said.

"But my past . . . some of what I remember from those times isn't something I really *want* to remember. Can I ask you a personal question?"

"Sure."

"How much did you love your husband?"

"My, my," she said. "My, my my, talk about love. Well, for nine years, no love could ever be better. But he had this, I never understood it well, he had this sense of a calling. During the first Iraq war, we were so young, we'd set aside having a child until the war was over. But in the next ten years, he was gone most of the time. Afghanistan, all the 'stans, all kinds of countries. It's very hard to hold love in your heart when the person is alive but not in your house, when your man is not in your kitchen, in your bed, inside your very body and soul."

She stood up, brushing sand and small twigs from her dress.

"Come to my house," she said. "We'll make blueberry pancakes."

27

Pomelo Road lies just north of Orange Grove, between Oracle and La Canada, the whole area the site of many old ranch estates built in the twenties. At that time, Pomelo lay far north of Tucson's boundaries, and the ranches were owned by a single families and covered twenty acres or more.

Now most of these estate owners had succumbed to the exploding real estate market in northeast Tucson, the estates parceled into one-acre properties with very new houses that sold for half or three quarters of a million dollars.

No streetlights in this older section of Tucson. The other houses barely five years old, but Mary's place had a peaked roof to accommodate the swamp coolers in the attic crawl space. None of the yards fenced, although most houses were secluded by heavy shrubs and saguaro-ribbed borders. Shadows not so stark, the moon barely half full, but shadows, yes. Stepping out of my car, I twisted my left foot slightly, my sandal fell off, and as I rested the foot momentarily to locate the sandal the day's heat came up from the rough paving. Mesquite seedpods everywhere, an inch long, black and bumped from the seeds bulging against the hard skin.

Two young men came down the other side of the street. Hand in hand, the shorter man leaning his dread-locks on the heavyset man's shoulder. Talking and laughing, but soft and quiet. They saw me fumbling my sandal on. They nodded, went on, I could hear one of them jingling keys in his pocket. Four houses down a woman shouted, *Harry! Rosie! Get in here!* and a border mongrel lunged across the street, followed by a larger dog with a thick coat, the mongrel saw me and looped around me, tail wagging. No threat, just a romp.

Mary's rented house sat in the middle of one of these estates. Still the original property, but on a smaller lot, with most of the acreage long since sold off, so that the original hacienda sat in the middle of three acres, separated from the modern homes by thick hedges of mesquite bushes and trees and rows of eight-foot-tall saguaro ribs linked vertically in fencing that kept the coyotes out. The original hacienda gate-arch remained, although the late nineteenth-century wrought-iron gates, imported from Chihuahua, had long been discarded or stolen.

While Mary made pancakes, I wandered through the old house. The kitchen was placed between two wings, one with a large bedroom and two bathrooms, the other with two more bedrooms and a living room. All of this surrounded a partially tiled garden and courtyard, separated from the road by a six-foot-high brick wall.

In the back bedroom, I found a photograph out of my past.

"This is the rez at Pine Ridge," I said.

"Yeah. Mom gave that to me. I was about six or seven. We were there."

"During the firefight?"

"Yes. I just hid, my mom helped load rifles."

"So did I."

"You were at Pine Ridge?"

"In 1975. Yes."

"I don't remember you," she said. "But I mostly just remember being terrified, and all the guns banging, and once in a while a bullet would come through the walls of the bedroom where I was hiding."

"How about that," I said. "We were in the same place, at the same time."

"How old were you?"

"Fifteen. I think. But I don't know when I was born."

"You don't . . . what? You don't know your birth year? Your birthday?"

"No."

"Are your parents alive?"

"No. My mother, I never knew her. All my dad said to me was that Mother was a bar girl, on the rodeo circuit. Dad, his name was George Loma, he was Hopi, my mother was white. I guess. Dad rode broncs, bulls, all rough stock on the circuit. I ran away from home, he died some time after."

"And you went to Pine Ridge."

"My husband at that time, he was a member of AIM. I was pregnant, I think, at Pine Ridge."

"You think? You don't know, Laura, are you saying you're not sure when your daughter was born? When *you* were born?"

"It happens that way," I said finally.

"Does that bother you?"

"Never used to," I said. "Lately, it's really a puzzle."

"But you know how to solve puzzles."

"I find people," I said. "Given a client with unlimited money to spend, unlimited time, I almost always find whoever I'm looking for. But with all my expertise in looking through databases, no way can I find myself."

Mary left for a moment, brought back the Pine Ridge photo.

"I wonder," she said finally. "I know other people who were there. Maybe they've got pictures. Would that help, if we found you in a picture?"

"It'd be a novelty," I said. "I have only one picture from when I was young."

"Pine Ridge," Mary said. "That was a long way from Kansas, but my father and mother said we had to go. Our pickup would never make it, I think it was a '59

Chevy vee-eight stepside, great for migrant picking work, but we'd never make it all the way to Pine Ridge. One of my uncles, a Chippewa from Michigan, Ralph Pinto Three Mares, he came through Kansas with this borrowed Land Cruiser, a totally new aluminum-cocoon RV, I think it must have been over thirty feet long, it was huge. Had four beds, one was a king, two queens, a regular double bed, then the dinette cushions came out to be single beds on the floor, so the whole RV could sleep four families with room left over for the three dogs, I think there were two cats in there somewhere. He said it was borrowed, he might have stolen it, or traded all his fishing gear and special Wisconsin fishing holes for it."

"I can't follow this," I said. "My whole memory of Pine Ridge was guns, gunpowder, my ears shattered one night by this idiot who brought in a ten-gauge shotgun and fired that goddamn thing for half an hour straight, I couldn't hear anything for hours."

"I guess some people saw it like a happening?" Mary said. "But I don't understand how they could. People died."

She reached out to hug me. I didn't know what to do, I turned a bit sideways, leaned into her, hugged her like that.

"Hugs," Mary said. "You don't seem too, uh, well, you don't hug too many people, right?"

"No," I said. Shrugged, with a smile.

"There's all kinds of hugs," she said. "You ever watch people, say, at an airport? People saying goodbye? Hello? Canoodling while they wait for their flight?"

"No," I said. "I don't watch things like that."

"Huh. But, you've said this to me more than once, you *do* watch people. Right? You look for, what do you call it?"

"Tells," I said.

"Tells. Right. You could say, nonverbal things, but no matter how subtle, they tell you something basic about the person."

"Not basic," I said. "It's more, I don't know, I guess I'd say there are a lot of things people do that really don't mean anything. Like, say, somebody who just scratches the top of his head because it's a habit. Okay, maybe that person is nervous, maybe his mother scratched his head, his mother's died, he likes the feeling, and he doesn't have a wife. But a real tell . . . here's what it means to me. A person does something unconsciously that reveals a weakness."

"Why couldn't it reveal a strength?"

"Then you know you're up against a wall, and to go down some other road of communication. But weakness, when you spot that kind of tell, you can use it. You can leverage what you've seen against that person."

"Sounds kinda . . . negative," Mary said.

"Exactly."

"Why would you mainly be interested in somebody's weakness?"

"That's life," I said. Not too happy anymore with this discussion. "That's survival. You use it to survive."

"So," Mary said. "So . . ." I could see this was a shock to her, as though she'd not ever considered life as more of a struggle than a celebration. "Your voice just dropped a few notes, when you said that word. *Survive.* Your mouth . . . changed, I guess your lips tightened. And so, if I live by your 'tells' and your 'rules,' I'd now have an advantage?"

"Yes." Really angry that she'd picked up on my irritation, trying to mask that I'd moved from irritation to anger, but her eyes widened and I knew, I *knew* she'd sensed my anger.

"Okay," she said shortly. "Okay. So let's just rewind here, okay? Let me go back to hugs. If you were going to hug me right now, you'd do it how?"

"I wouldn't."

"Ah."

Mary's face flickered with every emotion in her body, nothing held in reserve, she felt something, her face displayed it. Right now I expected her to take a step back from me, to distance herself from my anger. But she astonished me, *Jesus,* this woman astonishes me. She stepped right up and wrapped her arms around me. I didn't know what to do, I held my arms to my side, I couldn't move them anyway even if I wanted to, she pinned my arms to my body, she molded herself against me, and I thought immediately of Nathan and how he'd hold me like that. Unconditional love. I relaxed without even thinking about it and laid my head on Mary's shoulder and sobbed and sobbed, people walking near us made detours to keep their personal zones clear of my loud, fierce release of anger.

Mary held me and held me. Gradually, she rocked from side to side, I knew, I just *knew* from a long time ago that's what mothers did with their children and I laughed, my face drenched with tears, Mary's white blouse soaking where I'd laid my head on the shoulder.

"Hey, girl," she said.

"Hey, girl," I said.

We stood apart, just a foot or so, arms still touching each other.

"Whoa," I said. "What kind of hug was that?"

"Full-body hug. If you were my husband, I'd call it a full-genital hug. It doesn't mean what it sounds like. I don't want to have sex with you, but I want to touch as much of your body as I can, so you feel my love for you."

"That is so clichéd," I said.

"So get googoo. Sometimes I love getting googoo. So what do you want?'

"More coffee."

We sat at her breakfast table, sipped the hot coffee.

"Thanks," I said. "I guess, okay, I really learned something there."

"Me, too. I never thought of different kinds of hugs as, what do you call it? A tell? Okay. You want my full tell-all catalogue of hugs?

"Snotty women. Bitches. They don't want to hug you, you sure as hell don't want to hug them, but say it's a party, it's a formal affair, women hug at those things. So a bitch hug is like this. They turn sideways, they lean forward from the waist, so if they touch you at all it's from their side. They touch your back and immediately pull away from you."

"Hey," I said. "I've got a variation of that. Let's call it, uh, shy guy, no, don't-really-know-how-to-hug guy. Turns his whole body sideways, not all the way, forty-five degrees, and steps into you. Pats you on the back. Three, four pats at most."

"Not a genital hug at all, that's for sure."

We finished the coffee and poured two more cups, but in the process we lost track of any need to talk about hugs. I've never, *ever* felt so close to another woman.

"God, you're something," I said.

"Well, God has a lot to do with it." We clinked coffee mugs, and simultaneously said the exact same thing. "Hey, I just got a new girlfriend."

She giggled, held a finger to her mouth, lips pressed together, held out her right hand, extended the pinkie, waved the hand at me to do the same until I linked my pinkie with hers. "What did you wish?" she said.

But my wishes were far too complex to even describe.

She walked me out to my car. We fiddled with the sense of not wanting to say goodbye, but having to do it any-way. Leaning on the mailbox, we both heard a rustling inside and without thinking she grabbed and pulled down the lid and jumped back in fright as a huge dia-mondback rattlesnake uncoiled and dropped to the ground to slither away.

"My God," Mary said. "My God, my God, my God."

"Let it go," I said. Reaching inside the mailbox, a postcard inside. I handed it to her and she blanched and dropped the card. I picked it up, recognized the card

from the online casino website. The movie promo postcard for *La Bruja*.

Bold, red handwritten words across the card.

No me jodas.

The death card.

I called Alex for help.

"Alex!" I shouted. "Alex, whoever we use for personal security. Get a team out to my house. Right now.
I'll explain. Just do it.

"You've got to come with me," I said to Mary.

"Where, what do you mean, I can't leave."

"Get Ana Luisa." Pulling the Beretta from my back,
waving Mary back to her house. "Just get her, now."

"What should I, I can't just leave."

"Don't bring anything. Get Ana Luisa, come back to
the car."

I racked the Beretta's slide, the *clickclack* reverberat-
ing. She ran into the house and returned immediately
with Ana Luisa and I drove like a drunk, weaving in and
out of lanes, up to River and down to Campbell, south
of Campbell, eyes always on my mirrors, until I cut in
front of a silver Hummer and dropped over the hill
down to my driveway, where two cars sat, doors open,
and five men with weapons pointed at us.

28

VIDEOCONFERENCING ON A SECURE HIGH-SPEED
CONNECTION.

ALEX: We're good to go.
LAURA: Who's in the shop?
KELLE: Me.
ALEX: Guy in the background is Kelle's boyfriend.
NORMAN: Norman Don. Hi.
LAURA: First, anything on the cockfight video I shot?
ALEX: Wait, Laura, wait. How you doing over there?
LAURA: Sniper on the roof. Four men on the grounds.
How would you feel about being in a small castle
with the drawbridge up?
ALEX: Scared as hell. What do you want first?
LAURA: The video I shot at the cockfights. Anything us-
able?
KELLE: I isolated the videographer's face. Clearly a
woman. Here's a frame from the video. Her face en-
hanced. Sending you a graphic file.

> [face appears on-screen, white woman, mid-
> to upper thirties in age, short-cropped white
> hair, obviously dyed, nose slightly broken,
> full lips, what look like huge green eyes,
> wearing headset with mike stalk.]

KELLE: We're calling her UNSUB two. From the way she handles her gear, she's a pro. We're hoping she's not from out of town. I've sent her image to contacts all over Tucson and Phoenix. Nothing yet. The other videographer, diagonally across the fight pit, probably a young male, but I can't enhance his face at all.

LAURA: Okay. Sticking with the cockfights. Can you make any digital connection between the actual videotaped fights and the animated version that shows up on the casino website?

ALEX: Got three different answers to that. [*drinks from liter plastic bottle of Mountain Dew*] First. The casino website is gone.

LAURA: Just the cockfight part?

ALEX: All of it. But somebody is really savvy. The website is up and running at a different web address. So they know what they're doing, they have capability to switch IP, Internet Protocol, numbers, get the site switched. Took us only an hour to find the new site because part of the IP is identical.

LAURA: So they must have some way of notifying people where to go.

ALEX: Right. Maybe an email list. More probably instant-messaging, something that's dynamic and is very difficult to hack in to.

KELLE: [*winding and unwinding a ringlet of hair over her forehead*] I've compared camera angles that UNSUB two shot, you can see, in your pinhole video, where'd you have that hidden, anyway?

LAURA: In my leather bra.

KELLE: Must've tickled. Anyway, you bracketed UNSUB two really really well, so I worked up pretty much what she shot versus the camera angles on the video game. We saved that just in time, before the website moved somewhere else.

LAURA: Could the videographer also be the animator?

NORMAN: [*comes to videocam, face momentarily distorted, a fish-eye effect as he gets too close and backs*]

off a few inches] That's what I'm working on. Same
person? Very hard to tell. Animation is both labor- and
computer-intensive. That tells us something right away.
In addition to being able to switch websites to another
address, this operation probably includes a separate
animator. We're calling that person UNSUB three.

LAURA: What happened to one?

ALEX: Somebody's running this operation. UNSUB one.
Don't know anything yet. Could be one person, could
be a dozen, could be more people rotating in and out.
UNSUB. Totally unknown suspect.

KELLE: I've got feelers out for any information on local
graphics whizzes. Nothing so far.

NORMAN: We've not yet found any animated gambling
sites with dogfights. But cocks, dogs, my guess is we'll
find just about anything.

LAURA: Okay. It's the people behind this, anyway. Dead
animals is bad enough, but we have to focus on who's
running things. The bank account?

ALEX: Not a gold mine, but we got some product.
Dakota Barbie, we're assuming that's a fake name. At
the end of the trail, after all the intermediary transactions in Europe, Japan, and the Caribbean, it ends in
one Tucson bank account with all kinds of deposits
and withdrawals, all by wire transfer. That took real
finesse, getting into the local bank. These people are
getting better at protecting their digital data. We're
still trying to work out where the money comes from
and where it goes.

LAURA: That's it?

ALEX: That's it. What next, Laura?

*[faces of Alex, Kelle, and Norman side by
side, nobody smiling, three young faces
showing fatigue but dedication]*

LAURA: Any useful data on the *maras* cartel?

ALEX: Lots of data, nothing useful. They're not really

cartels, like the traditional Central and South American drug cartels. The *maras* are more like gangs, some of them formed in prison. But depending on the city, or even the territory within a city, the gangs operate in a very loose confederation, if they're not killing off the competition.

LAURA: Let me handle that end. Last thing I want is for you to get nabbed hacking into NCIC or INTERPOL or any law enforcement source. Anything on the name La Bruja?

ALEX: Nothing.

LAURA: All right. Keep whacking away, kids. Thanks. Let's conference again in, say, two hours.

ALEX: Cell phones?

LAURA: I've got five totally clean phones here. You know the numbers. Don't call unless you've got something important

ALEX: We never close.

[connection terminated]

VOICE MAIL, CELL THIRTEEN, SEVENTEEN MESSAGES.

JORDAN KLIGERMAN: Laura. Laura Winslow. Please contact me, contact anybody in my office. You have the numbers. Urgent we talk.

[remaining sixteen messages all from Kligerman]
[all voice mail messages deleted without response]

INCOMING CALL ON CELL THREE

KEN: Laura?

LAURA: Hi, Ken.

KEN: You disappeared on me.

LAURA: Are you on your cell phone?

KEN: No. Landline. Pay phone. Are you all right?

LAURA: Yes. We're doing, we're okay.

KEN: Mary's not home, either.

LAURA: She's with me. And Ana Luisa, they're both with me.

KEN: At your house?

LAURA: Yes.

KEN: I'm coming right over.

LAURA: No! Don't do that.

KEN: Don't, what, why not?

LAURA: It's not safe.

KEN: It's not safe?

LAURA: Not for a while, no.

KEN: It's not safe? What do you mean? You're not safe?

LAURA: Ken, please. We're here, but it's not safe. And I don't have time to tell you everything.

KEN: I'm coming over.

LAURA: You've got to trust me. Work your contacts at TPD.

KEN: I want to see you.

LAURA: We're all right.

KEN: I want to see *you*.

[long pause, traffic noise from Ken's phone]

LAURA: Do this. Go somewhere and buy three new cell phones. Don't transfer over any existing numbers. All new phones, new numbers. When you've got them, call me from another landline, give me the numbers of all three phones.

KEN: This isn't making sense.

LAURA: Trust me.

KEN: Give me an hour. Why all the phones?

LAURA: We don't know who we're up against. But we do know that they're extremely technologically sharp. So maybe somebody monitors wireless cell calls. It's not hard to do, once you find who you're looking for, then you can easily triangulate the call and get a location.

KEN: You're telling me to watch my back.

LAURA: Call when you get the new phones.

KEN: I'm on it. I really want to see you.

LAURA: Not a good time for that, for . . . not a good time for me and you.

[connection terminated]

OUTGOING CALL ON CELL FIVE

KYLE: Homicide. Kyle.

LAURA: It's Laura Winslow.

KYLE: Where you been, girl?

LAURA: Busy.

KYLE: So what's up?

LAURA: Max Cady has a real name. Tuglivik. Tuglivik Taerbaum.

KYLE: Not on VICAP or NCIC.

LAURA: We got this through a U.S. Customs database. Taerbaum. An Alaskan Indian. An Inuit. His Customs jacket's half an inch thick. Armed robbery, armed robbery, manslaughter, that's how he went down to Florence seven to twelve, paroled in the eighth year. Also suspected in thirteen murders, all cartel assassinations. A muscle man, an enforcer. The cockfight thing, probably a sideline. Or he's moved up with added territory of his own.

KYLE: A total mystery to us down here.

LAURA: Anything more on the gardener? Carlos Canas?

KYLE: Still trying to decipher the meaning of that tattoo. E210.

LAURA: Yeah. Could be anything. E210 . . . E210 . . . useless, without something else. You'll keep me posted?

KYLE: Sure. Hey, listen, word's out everywhere in TPD, if you contact anybody here, you're to know that Jordan Kligerman wants you to call.

LAURA: So tell him you called me?

KYLE: All right George. [Obviously being overheard on his phone.] Sunday night, my place. See ya.

[connection terminated]

OUTGOING CALL ON CELL FIVE

[five calls to Nathan, all unanswered]

INCOMING CALL ON CELL THREE
KEN: Got the new phones. Laura, I want to know what's going on.
LAURA: Have you got half an hour?

29

And we waited. And we all waited. One day, two, three days, four.

Not much happened, except routines, swimming, eating, staying away from windows at night. I thought Spider would complain, but she did most of her business by phone or computer.

And then one day the crocodile arrived.

Among Spider's many clients, she did public relations for a local gallery, which just opened a show titled Concert Party. Curated by Michelle Gilbert, an art historian at Sarah Lawrence College, the entire exhibit consisted of huge hand-painted signs on sheets of plywood.

After half an hour's bickering with our private security, a U-Haul van came up the driveway and three men unloaded a painting on two joined four-by-eight sheets of plywood. A lady sat on a crocodile in the middle of a river, her face serene as she gripped the crocodile, a large wooden box inside its gaping mouth as it moved downstream.

The men installed the artwork on an inside wall of our three-car garage.

"That is totally weird," I said. Our cars moved out of the garage for the viewing.

"It's an advertisement," Spider said. "In Ghana, local

pop artists work with singers and bands to prepare advertisements for what they call concert parties. Singing, storytelling, dancing, a band, the working out of legends. This is A. B. Crentsil's band. Not that I'd know the difference. They play a local style of music called highlife. Michelle collected the advertisements during several visits to Ghana. This artist is Mark Anthony."

"This is for a play?" I said.

Spider consulted her catalogue.

"It's a proverb about selfishness. Literally, it says,

> *'If you don't let your friend harvest nine,*
> *you will not harvest ten.'*

"Or, more or less, 'If you do not allow your brother to climb, you also will not climb.' I got this one for you, I was thinking you miss Nathan."

"I miss him awful," I said. "But a crocodile?"

"It's a Ghanaian reworking of the legend of Snow White. It's about the jealousy and envy of an older powerful woman towards her junior. You know how it goes, that children's story. A treacherous and destructive Queen Mother has the power of life and death over the good, obedient, religious, and beautiful daughter Snow White. In this play, Snow White survives each trial placed before her by the Queen Mother and ultimately is rewarded and in the end the Queen Mother dies."

"All I remember is the poisoned apple," I said. "Why is this woman on a crocodile? And what's that in the crocodile's mouth?"

"The Queen Mother has given the girl a box and told her to collect something from a distant Queen Mother, who lives in the land of the dead. On the way, an angel tells her how to proceed on her journey and gives her some gold to throw into the river which she must cross. The angel tells her not to open the box which the Queen Mother will give her, and on her return, she must throw a gold piece into a river and a crocodile will come to carry her across. The girl returns and gives the Queen Mother the box and the Queen Mother thinks the girl has opened it, and so she herself opens it, discovers it is full of gold coins, and goes mad. She then tells everyone how she wronged the girl. She dies and the girl becomes Queen Mother. End of story."

"What's the moral?" I said.

"I don't know. A morality tale about envy, pride, step-mothers, and royalty? In the end, the intended victim survives and the evil perpetrator dies."

"I meant, what's the moral for me?"

"I love you, Mom."

"I'm not an evil mother?"

"No," she said. "You just miss Nathan. I thought this might cheer you up."

"Thanks, sweetie. Thanks a lot. But it is totally weird."

"Also," she said, "I guess . . . I really don't want to know why there are men with guns all over this house. Last night, when I went into the kitchen to feed Sarah Katherine, one of those guys was sitting there drinking coffee. I'm not sure which of us was more freaked out, me seeing a gun, or him seeing me breast-feed."

"I'll tell you why he's there—" I said.

"No. I don't want to know. I trust you, I love you. If it's something you really believe is necessary, that's enough for me."

And for me, the real moral of the crocodile is trust.

30

On the fifth day, a commotion in the driveway, two security guards escorting Ken up the back stairway to where all of us sat around the outdoor swimming pool.

"Do you know this man?" One of the security guards, hand on his weapon, the other hand bunching up Ken's shirt at the back to restrain his movement.

"Ken," Mary said. Rising from beside the pool.

"Yes," I said. "He's a friend."

Without apology the security guards let Ken go and disappeared. Above us, Jeff Miller, the sniper, stood at the edge, finger on his rifle. I waved and nodded to him, Ken staring until Jeff backed out of sight.

"That's an M-40," Ken said. "Ten-power scope. What the hell is this?"

"It's a fortress," Spider said. "And we don't much like being in it."

"Hey, honey bunny. I haven't seen you in days," Ken said. He wanted to hug me, wanted some physical contact, I couldn't tell what he wanted, so I gave him a quick hug and when he nuzzled his nose into my ear I pulled away.

"Wow," Spider said. "That must've been some bike ride the other night."

"Wanna cool off?"

The only thing I could think to say.

"Wanna jump in the pool?"

*   *   *

An hour later, a security brought us a sausage-and-extra-cheese pizza.

Beside the pool, afternoon sun on our bodies. Mary turned off the hydrojets for the small spa at one end of the pool, the surface of the spa slowly flattening, no breeze, sun angled just enough to the southwest so that it reflected off the pool. Drying Ana Luisa's hair.

I put on my sunglasses. Mary bent over Ana Luisa's head, Mary's bikini top hanging loose, her left breast mostly outside the bikini, the nipple still hard from lying against the hydrojets. I looked over at Ken, but he'd turned away to the west, I admired that in him, I liked that in him.

Not a looker, an ogler, a secret watcher, not one of those men, especially married men, even with their wives and children around, those men who can't resist scanning any good-looking woman of almost any age that passes near them, like that glowing tube inside a copier if you hold the lid up, those men's eyes traveling down and up the woman's body, scanning as though she were naked.

Gave Ken a kiss on his shoulder, rubbed his nose.

"What?" he said, still not looking at Mary.

"I think I kinda . . . I'm kinda going with the flow here."

"The pool? Don't you get half topless on me."

"Phhht," I said. "You can look at her now."

Looking behind the house, staring up at the Santa Catalinas, Ken shielded his eyes.

"Do you hike?" he said.

"Hike?"

"You know, walk with a little extra momentum."

"Sure," I said. "I've hiked all over the Santa Catalinas."

"Cool," he said. "I've got boots in my car. Let's ditch these guards, spend a few hours up in the canyon."

"Not a good idea," I said.

"You've been laid up here five days. You've got a gun,

I've got a gun, up in the canyon we'd not be exposed, anybody got near enough to shoot us we'd shoot them first. Ah, come *on*."

Pushing up the canyon took so little energy that Ken and I decided to hike toward Kristen Peak. There was no marked trail, so we started bushwhacking up from the west side. The only real adventure on the way up was a brief encounter with a banded rock rattlesnake. Storm cells were developing toward the south, but they all looked pretty mild.

Once we reached a plateau about four thousand feet high, and could see clearly to the south and east, it was a completely different story. Two storms looked potentially tornadic, especially since they were both drifting slowly our way. The one immediately to the east of us did drop a mini-tornado into the valley, but the major storm motion was to the northeast, and that one missed us.

I initially thought the one southeast of us might pass us on the east, but I quickly became concerned. Ken later said he should have known by the fact that I never sat down. I pointed out to Ken that clouds were forming under the cloud base so quickly that you could watch them spring into existence. But Ken's basic attitude was that he'd hiked many ten-thousand-foot peaks all over Arizona, Utah, and Colorado, and there was nothing here that could scare him. I pointed out that the entire storm appeared to be rotating.

"That looks something from Ghostbusters," he said.

"One or two?"

Actually, I was thinking, if it looks like special effects, it's time to hike down to safety.

"I think we should go," I said.

"Go?" he said. Stretching his arms out like Moses, daring the storm. "Go?" he said, ripping off his shirt and beating his breast, then turning to look at me just as a few raindrops fell, his face to the rain, and mine also. I rubbed rain into my hair, and the next I thing I remem-

ber is rubbing rain into *Ken's* hair and rubbing his body,
both of us carefully removing the other's clothes until he
couldn't unhook my bra and grabbed the back of it in
both hands, my breasts falling free, and we couldn't
arrange our clothes quick enough on the ground, we fell
naked together, Ken underneath me and then inside me
and as the storm let loose two minutes later we'd both
gasped and finished and lay side by side, soaked with
rain and caressing each other's bodies until I looked up
and saw everything black above us.

"We've got to get out of here," I said.

The storm base had dropped down completely out of
sight, doing violent gyrations on the other side of a rise.

"I think we should run!" I said.

"No, no." Ken fumbled in his wet jeans pocket, took
out a small digital camera. "Here, just take my picture
first. No, wait a minute, take another from farther, behind those little rocks. Oh, I've got an idea, I should be
holding out the Blair's Death Rain habañero potato chip
bag!"

"Ken!" I shouted. "We've *got* to go."

But first he dug the chips out of a small pack, made me
take his picture. Finally dressed, we started to move
downslope. About one-third of a mile away and one
hundred feet lower, French Joe Peak suddenly disappeared behind a solid wall of water.

"Have you ever seen anything like this before?" Ken
said.

"No," I said. "No. I've never seen anything like that
in my entire life, but if you don't stop looking at the special effects, we could die up here!"

Clouds blew from below the peak, flickering in layers
above us like ribbons at a birthday party, like streamers
attached to a fan. Ken suddenly comprehended the grav-
ity of our position, and was in such a state of panic that
we started running in the wrong direction, running right
toward the storm. We changed direction, found a spot
about one hundred yards from the top of the peak and

opposite the storm strike side. We huddled against the
base of a limestone cliff as the storm struck, clouds flying around like trash in a dust devil, the storm a direct
hit on top of us.

In a matter of seconds, it became almost dark. The
driving rain suddenly freezing cold, both of us shivering
until we decided to run down the hill. We charged
blindly, Ken leading, totally drenched and half blinded,
the starkness of our peril totally clear as a lightning bolt
struck ahead of us and thunder crashed immediately and
I knew we were dead perfect in the heart of the electrical
part of the storm, lightning striking viciously all around.

When the storm finally relented, we realized there was
very little chance we could get out the way we came, but
Ken unerringly sensed where we were, extended his arm
forward like a karate chop, *go this way*.

An hour later, we were home.

31

"I need to tell you something," I said.

Ken and I nibbling on cold pizza crusts, the last of the monsoon rain splattering the skylights.

"Right now things are kind of uncertain for me," I said. "Spider calls it Jumping The Shark. When you lose your bearings, you want to know the quality of support you can trust from your friends. Are they with you, down the next block, into that house, across that street? Some people, you can't trust yourself to guess their motives, you've got to just give complete trust. Or no trust."

"You can trust me," Ken said.

"I don't really know that."

"No," he said finally. "You don't. I like you a lot, but I don't know you very well, and you know me even less."

"It's not the sex," I said.

"I liked that, too."

"Trust, that's what's on my mind. How much do I trust you?"

"You've got to decide that," Ken said. "To me, my life seems so, hey, I'm eight to one at the park. Weekends are mine, but it's a steady thing, working at the park. It's a routine, it's steady, I love doing it, right now it's my life. You, you're no way ordinary. But you're asking me the wrong question."

"What?" I said. Thinking, *I don't have time for this.*

"Why do you need to trust me?"

Blinked twice, tried to focus on the question.

"See," Ken said, "I want to help you because it's instinctual. I'd do anything to protect you, protect your family, even to protect Mary and Ana Luisa. It's from my heart, my gut, I've told you that, it's completely a gut response."

"And?"

"You're always working things over in your head."

"Say again?"

"Laura, what are you thinking right now?"

"Uh," I said, "uh, I don't understand what you're telling me. I don't have time to try and figure those things out."

"You're in your head," Ken said. "Not your heart. You toss everything around, backwards and forwards, flip it side to side, you've got to look at a question from a dozen different ways until you decide how to answer it."

You're a Libra and a Gemini rising. Sandy. My astrology chart. *You've got four different people in there all competing against each other. Like a split personality.*

"Is there another guy?" he said. "Somebody else? In your life?"

"There was, there . . ."

"Was? Or is?"

There's the moment. Which side of the border are you on? Do you look at a glass of water being half full or half empty? Or do you see whatever water's in the glass as what *was,* and the empty space as what will be? Or is it just water and you're working your head too much instead of your spirit?

"I can't say."

He let the moment pass.

"Okay," I said finally. "The Tucson Police Department has a bad cop."

That blindsided him, not the fact itself, but that I'd said it.

"For the record, for the somewhat public record, TPD

hired me to look at all kinds of financial records relating to drugs. But what they *really* hired me for is to look at the financial records of several hundred cops, looking for a pattern of unexpected income or purchases."

"A dirty cop," Ken said.

"Except, I haven't done anything about it."

"You know the cop's name?"

"No."

"Does TPD have somebody in mind?"

"They're not telling me."

"So let me get this right," Ken said. "You're looking for a bad cop who's probably taking money from drug cartels? From the *maras*?"

"Yes."

Anger flashed in his eyes, crinkled his face muscles.

"Just tell me one thing, Laura."

"I'll tell you *anything*."

"You're not using me?"

"Using you?"

"Using my connections with the police department?"

"How could you think that?" I said.

"Trust cuts both ways."

"No," I said. "Does that help? No, it never occurred to me."

"Whew," he said. "I just had to be sure about that."

"Be sure about that."

"So tell me, Laura. What the hell are we doing with each other?"

"You're a good friend," I said.

"Nothing more?"

"I don't know you enough. Not yet."

"There's something going on between us."

"I've more to tell you," I said. "About my life. But I'm not sure yet I'd want to trust myself, trust my reason for telling you."

"Fair enough."

"You're not disappointed?"

"Disappointed?"

"In me, in us. That there's nothing more than friend-ship?"

"I don't live for the future," he said. "But . . . uh . . ." He turned his head slowly away, eyes unfocusing.

"You *are* disappointed."

"No no no no no," he said. "Forget talking about us. Laura. About this bad cop. I think . . . I think I might know who it is."

Mary and Spider burst into the kitchen.

"Come on," Spider said. "Let's all go out to eat."

"You know who it is?" I said.

"No."

"What are you guys talking about?" Spider said.

"But you *think* you know?"

"Come *on*!" Mary said. "We want to go out to eat."

"No," I said. "You're not going anywhere."

"Whatever's threatening you, Mom," Spider said, "they're gone. Let's celebrate, let's go eat."

"No."

"Come on," Ken said. "Just a quick meal."

"You're not helping, Ken. My daughter's not going anywhere."

"All right. You and Mary and I. We'll go out."

"Yes," Mary said, turning to Spider. "You watch the kids. Tomorrow, I'll watch the kids and you go out."

"Mom," Spider said. "You're treating me like another kid. I'll do what I want, I'll go out if I want."

"No," Mary said. "You go tonight, and I'll stay."

Spider looked us over.

"All right," she said. "You three guys go tonight."

In the car, Ken tapped on the dashboard, nodding to himself or shaking his head. I didn't ask him anything, didn't want to talk about it in front of Mary.

Ric's place stayed open until ten, we piled in the front door just before closing and begged for three meals and a bottle of zinfandel. We sat out on the patio, the sky darkened, the moon bright, occasional traffic noise humming from Sunset Road just to the south of the restaurant.

At ten-thirty, the restaurant staff locked up and left us alone, drawing a large chain around the entire plaza but leaving a space for us to walk out. Once the staff had all driven away, Ken went to his car, brought back a yellow plastic bucket, like a kid's sand pail for the beach. Popped the lid off the bucket and spooned icy slush into our three empty wine glasses.

"Margarita mix," he said. "You buy the bucket at Costco, you fill it with tequila, you got instant cold margaritas. Hand me that saltshaker."

Somewhere around midnight, we'd run out of stories and Mary asked Ken to tell about any other incident happening when he was a detective. He ran a finger inside the yellow bucket, licked his finger. The mix had long since melted, still drinkable but not cold.

"I ever tell you about the Iceman?" Ken said.

"Nope."

"Iceman loved NASCAR races. He'd drive all over the circuit, every year he'd follow the circuit. Never had a job, but he did have steady income. Had this three-quarter-ton pickup, rigged with those mechanics' boxes? You know, those ribbed, galvanized boxes along each side of the pickup bed, you stored your tools in there, whatever. Well. Iceman, at some time he'd learned how to repair refrigeration equipment. Residential, commercial, he could fix anything."

"So he'd take jobs in towns?" I said. "To pay his way? Around the circuit?"

"You know, when you stay in a motel, they've got these ice machines. You got your room, you got your empty bucket, you go outside to the ice machine and fill up on ice cubes. Well, Iceman, he'd steal the machines."

"For the ice?" I said, poking him in the chin.

"He'd empty out the ice. In one of those mechanics' boxes, on his pickup, he had a heavy-rigged dolly. He'd disconnect the ice machine after he emptied it, he'd haul that machine to the power tailgate on his pickup and load it aboard. Next town, he'd sell the machine. He got these official stickers he'd paste on the machines, look like they'd been inspected and approved. Sometimes he'd clean up the machine, spray-paint the rusted or dinged spots, and go back to sell it to the motel owner at the very same place he stole it from. Must've stolen . . . I don't know, hundreds of 'em."

"How'd you ever catch him?"

"Didn't. Some deputy sheriff in some back-country Texas town decided to look into ice machine thefts in his county. Got license plate numbers, starting coordinating with other sheriff's offices, they noticed the pattern. Same deputy that started the search, he got so addicted to finding this guy, he quit his job and drove across thirteen states until he realized that he'd been following the NASCAR circuit. Being a race fan himself, he'd go the races, probably same day as the Iceman. And that's a true story. Want to hear another one?"

A car backfired on Sunset Road and Ken whipped out his .357, my hand behind me, reaching for the Beretta.

"Wow," Mary said. Loopy, but not drunk, none of us really drunk but high. "I want a gun."

"No, you don't," Ken said.

She picked up his .357, broke open the cylinder, checked the loads. "Grew up on farms," she said. "I don't have a gun, but I know what to do with them. You've got the hammer on a loaded cylinder." She put the .357 down, touched my Beretta. "Laura, why do you have this?"

Three margaritas loosened my self-control. Mary and Ken waited, my mouth opening and closing like a guppy grazing for surface food. I had no answer for them, none for myself, and in that moment a car backfired on Sunset Road and I said the first thing that popped into my head.

"Target practice."

"What?"

"Let's shoot some rounds. See who's better."

"Not a good idea," Mary said.

I looked at Ken, gestured. "We're at Sunset and Cray-croft. Right? A little east of here, we turn north into the canyons, go all the way to the end, there's an outdoor shooting range."

Mary watched, hands over her ears, as I matched shot for shot with Ken, his .357 incredibly loud, the Beretta sounding only like popping corn.

"I've had four margaritas," Ken said. "But I hardly feel them. At thirty yards, you're just plinking, I'm blast-ing. Mary, you want to shoot?"

"Yeah," I said. "You've talked about it. Show us."

Ken palmed his .357, offered the handle to Mary.

"I've mainly fired rifles and shotguns," Mary said. "I've been watching the recoil when you fire that can-non, what would it take to learn?"

"Could you do it?" Ken said.

"Why would I want to?"

"Is this more of your pacifism?" Ken said, and every-thing got quiet because his good humor was entirely gone, replaced with a cold, serious tone.

"No."

"Then why not?"

"If I had to," Mary said, "I'd shoot it. But I don't have to."

"And what would it take?"

"I don't know."

"Protecting Ana Luisa?"

She ducked her head, held both palms up, no.

"If you had to protect Ana Luisa," Ken said. "To the max?"

"Then? Yes," Mary said. "If pushed into that corner, no matter what the consequences, I would shoot a gun."

"Would you kill somebody?"

"Why are you doing this?" Mary said.

Ken stood against her, pushing her body so they both faced downrange.

"It's heavy," he said.

Heavy pressure. That's what I felt, sweat running freely in defiance of the cool evening air. Took a small pack of tissues from my bag, wadded them together, and wiped my forehead and across the back of my neck, the tissues quickly sodden and crumpling in my fingers while the sweat kept running.

Panic sweat, flop sweat, the moisture cooled just enough by the air to work like an evaporative cooler. Sort of. I'd rarely known this kind of sweat, rarely felt this degree of tension. A diver friend told me about undersea pressure, she regularly descended to six, nine, even twelve fathoms below the surface. Each fathom approximately six feet down. At six fathoms, the pressure per square inch was double that at the surface. Twelve fathoms, triple the pressure, and so on and so on to the limits of a survivable dive.

I figured I must be somewhere down around one hundred feet, watching Ken level his .357 and fire a round.

"About six, eight inches of recoil. So. Ana Luisa is at your back, you and this gun are all that's between her and whoever stuck that rattler in your mailbox."

He fired again.

"You and this gun are all that's between Ana Luisa and the *maras*."

He fired again.

"You see how to do it?" He put the .357 in her hand, started backing away. "You're all that's between Ana Luisa, between all your love and something evil." Fifteen yards away, shouting. "Aim the gun." Twenty yards away. "Aim it at me, Mary. Lift it up, aim it at me." Thirty yards away. "Shoot me, Mary." He stopped. "You've got one round left. Shoot me."

Mary stared at Ken, muscles working all over her face. "*Shoot me!*"

She aimed the gun, Ken threw his arms out wide, waving his palms at her. She pulled the trigger just before I could deflect the pistol, but it clicked on an empty chamber. Astonishment all over our faces, she pulled the trigger twice more.

Click. Click.

"You knew it was empty!" I shouted into Ken's face when he came back to us. "You knew, you made her try anyway."

"I knew," Ken said. Palming the .357. "But she didn't. Come on. We've had a party. Let's go back to your house, you two get some sleep."

But at home, nobody guarded the driveway entrance. Winding clockwise up the drive, apprehensive, we came into the parking lot and saw two TPD cruisers.

"Miss Winslow?" an officer said, Maglite in my face.

"Yes."

"Miss Winslow, I've been ordered to take you to headquarters."

"It's two in the morning," I said. "Can't this wait?"

"Lieutenant Kligerman said to bring you in. Now."

"Is there a charge?" Ken said.

"The lieutenant will discuss that, ma'am. But we have orders to cuff you if necessary. So please get out of your vehicle and in back of the cruiser."

"Call Christopher Kyle," I said to Ken.

"Detective Kyle will meet you at headquarters," the officer said, one hand holding out handcuffs, the other hand on his duty weapon.

32

The four of them huddled around one end of a huge oak table, elliptical in shape, with a rounded notch cut into the far end. TPD Chief of Police Rich Wallach, Assistant Chief Django Manouche, Bob Gates, and Jordan Kligerman.

At fifty-seven, Wallach's hair still more blond than gray, cut in military style, shaved at the sides and sparse bristles on top, no more than an inch high and dead flat across the crown of his narrow head. Jarhead, I thought. But just the hair, his voice not that of a Marine, but very soft, a faint burr, Scotch or Irish, long since smoothed by Arizona's slower pace.

Wallach wore a short-sleeved Brooks Brothers shirt, a button-down collar with the buttons cleverly tailored underneath the collars. A very light orange shirt, tucked into carefully creased seersucker pants, held up with braces, the pants in turn tucked into sixteen-inch-high cowboy boots with a two-inch roping heel.

"Bob?" I said. Gates didn't even smile. "Bob, what is this?"

"You know who I am," Wallach said.

"Chief of police."

"And you know these other men?"

"Yes."

A fifth man entered the room, left the door open, pulled out a chair next to Gates but didn't sit down. Lids

falling slightly over light blue eyes, no crinkles at the
sides as he smiled, lips wide and curved, the smile broad-
ening to show impossibly white teeth, capped or a dental
plate, the smile as fake as the teeth.

I'd met him three years ago.

I couldn't remember his name, couldn't remember if
I'd ever known his name, and he wasn't introduced.

An assistant United States attorney who'd threatened
me with old FBI arrest warrants if I didn't work with
him. This guy, he'd been at two or three meetings back
then. Sat away from the conference table, took no notes,
never said a word. Another U.S. attorney. From the
Phoenix office. My hair was different, shorter, redder, I
was three and a half years older.

Maybe he didn't recognize me, but I knew him.

Taut body stretched out for my file, muscles rippling
inside the starched blue shirt, and he twisted sideways.
He looked down at the file, turned his head slightly, sunlight across his reading glasses, I couldn't tell if he was
looking at my file or me. Idly licked an index finger,
pushed up one page after another, he *was* looking at me,
he already knew everything in the file. Finger pushed out
a photograph, he nudged it free of the folder and across
the desktop.

"This *is* you," he said. Not a question. He was pleased.

A Washington State driver's license. My face, no doubt
about it, the long wig I'd worn, fake eyelashes, huge earrings, smeared lipstick, it looked so fake I wondered
what I'd ever thought I could get away with back then,
fifteen years ago in Yakima, when I had half a dozen
grifts working at the same time. I don't even remember
what name I'd used, what name was on the license.

Oh, yes, he was pleased. He gestured at the doorway
and a woman came tentatively into the room, two steps
at a time, like a dance movement.

"Is this her?"

The woman came halfway down the room, placed her
hands flat on the desktop, nails trimmed but not painted.

"Yah."

"And what's her name?"

"Katrina Mangin. When I knew her, she called herself that."

"I'll show you a Washington State driver's license. What is the name?"

She held the license about six inches from her eyes.

"Katrina Mangin."

"Who are you?" I said.

The woman wouldn't answer, wouldn't even look at me.

White spots at the ends of each nail, her way of control and misdirection so she wouldn't have to answer my question quickly, hands straight out, fingers slightly separated and pointed at me.

"I don't have to say, do I?" she said. "I don't give my name, right?"

Those fingertip white spots, she was pressing very *very* hard to keep control. A bit of a smile, perfect teeth, just a wee tilt of the head, used to flirting, and she *laughed* just a bit, inhaled and just as quickly exhaled.

I stared at her, walked over to her, she recoiled as I looked into her face, but I didn't recognize her from anywhere. Her eyes cut from me to a credenza along the wall. Restless, not given any direction, she picked up a silver frame, photo of a young girl on a merry-go-round horse, photo of some young woman and an older man, swimsuits, from the pilot deck of a thirty-foot powerboat rigged for deep-sea fishing. She set the frame down, looked all around the office, at every square inch of floor and walls and furniture and finally the ceiling.

"Jesus," she said. "What do, what *else* do you want me to do?"

Her arms locked in front, hands on elbows. I shifted my eyes to her open-toed hump-me pumps, her toenails a bright, deep orange, but chipping.

"That's all," Kligerman said. "Send in Heather."

Heather. Heather. Celli, I remembered her vaguely

from my visit to Kligerman's squad room. Not nervous, not showing any kind of emotion, she laid a laptop on the table.

"Miss Celli," the U.S. attorney said.

"Excuse me," I said. "I didn't get your name."

"I didn't give it," the attorney said. We locked eyes for a while, then he turned slowly back to the papers in front of him. "Miss Celli. Just summarize. Right now we don't need anything but a summary."

"Four times a day, I check a lot of files, a lot of computer logs. I look for any trace of somebody hacking into our system."

"And, in summary, what did you find yesterday morning at three oh two?"

"Five illegal entries."

"To the TPD databases?"

"No. To our entire system. All files. Personnel, financial, long-range planning, criminal investigations. Everything."

"And, again, just summarize, what happened?"

"Several files were altered. One deleted. One new file added."

"All at once, Miss Celli. Tell us everything, all at once. I don't want to drag this out with a thousand questions."

"Seven files on our latest investigations of the *maras* gangs. They'd been altered to show negative results of searches, identity checks, mostly financial transactions. A master file of financial data was deleted."

"But you were able to reinstall those files? In original formats?"

"Yes. And we immediately began backtracking, trying to work out where the hacker came from. The IP numbers."

"Don't get techie on me. Just summarize."

"We traced all the illegal entries to computers at the offices of private investigator Laura Winslow."

"That's a lie," I said.

Heather held out some papers, shook her head. Nobody objected when I took the papers, flicked through them. It was my office.

"And the file that was added? You said one new file?"

Heather flipped the laptop open, pressed a few keys, swiveled it so the men could see something hidden from me.

"Again. Show her this time."

Approximately ninety seconds of video. Me, in my biker outfit, standing on the top bleacher of the cock-fight, shouting, laughing. I was stunned.

"Where did you get that?" I said.

"That's all for now, Miss Celli." She left the room.

"Laura," Gates said. "For God's sake, Laura. Why?"

"I didn't do this."

"That's you, Laura. That's you at an illegal cockfight."

"Yes, that part, yes, that's me. I was there undercover."

"Part of an investigation?" the attorney said.

"Yes."

"And who is your client?"

"I don't have to tell you that."

"And all this other stuff?" Gates said.

"It's fake. I didn't personally do any of it."

"Then one of your employees?"

"Never."

"The evidence," Gates said. "It's all there."

"It's fake."

"You're despicable," the U.S. attorney said. "The last time we met, that whole business about smuggling women across the border, I didn't have enough power to charge you with complicity. Now I've got the power, and trust me, if there's any truth in these charges, I will take you down for good."

Chief Wallach raised a finger. "I don't understand any of this," he said. "Laura, you're saying, you're an expert in identity theft, and somebody has apparently stolen your own identity?"

"Yes. I could fake this myself. It's not hard."

"I have all your files," the U.S. attorney said. "Your

old arrest warrants, as much of your background as anybody knows. A lot of different names. What is your *real*
name?"

They all froze, they all waited for me to talk.

"Kauwanyauma," I said finally.

"What exactly is that?"

"My Hopi birth name. Am I under arrest?"

"Laura," Gates said. "I, personally, I can't protect
you."

"You're a flight risk," the attorney said. "No use asking you to surrender your passport or any documents.
You'd just create a new identity."

"Bob," I said. "You came to me. You knew I didn't
want this, you talked me into it, you *led* me into this. I
trusted you."

"I can't help you."

"You people," I said. "You came to *me,* you asked for
my help, and now you can't even imagine that somebody
has set me up."

"Set you up?" Wallach said.

"You people. You're all so totally *i*gnorant about computers, you have absolutely *no* idea what can be done
with them. I'm being *framed,* this is so totally a setup.
You assholes. You're being set up yourselves, the entire
Tucson PD is being set up, and you're letting it happen.
You don't even trust the one person you brought in from
the outside to find one of your dirty cops."

"What is she talking about?" Manouche said.

"Later," Wallach said.

"What the *hell* is she talking about? A dirty cop?"

"*Later,*" Wallach said.

"So," I said. "You arresting me? Or what?"

"Chief?" Gates said.

Wallach twiddled his fingers. "Is there a federal
charge?" he said.

"Not at this time," the U.S. attorney said.

"It's my jurisdiction?"

"Yes. But I'd advise you. Don't let her go."

"Bob," Wallach said. "Miss Winslow. I'll give you twenty-four hours. Show me *any*thing, disprove *any*-thing. But just twenty-four hours."

"Chief," Kligerman said. "That's the wrong thing to do."

"And if I'm wrong, it'll cost me my job. You have your twenty-four hours, Miss Winslow. If you're guilty of this, God help you."

"What happened in there?" Ken said. He'd followed me to police headquarters, waited for me to come out, expected the worst, that I'd been arrested and speed-booked without remand.

"Something really weird," I said. "Something . . . I don't know what happened in there, but I was being set up."

"For what?"

"That's what's so weird."

"What did they say?"

"It's what they *didn't* say. I can't explain, it's not logical yet, I can't figure out what they didn't say. Take me to my office."

But before Ken could turn on the engine, Bob Gates banged on the top of the car and slid into the back seat.

"Around the block," he said.

"Bob, Bob," I said. "Why am I being set up?"

"It's not real."

"Not real?"

"We know you didn't hack into the TPD computer network."

"You know?"

"You knew?" Ken said.

"Only two of us. Wallach and myself. We trusted nobody, Laura. Having Django Manouche in that meeting means half the department will know about it in an hour. Manouche can't keep secrets, he needs to tell secrets to get people to believe he's got the power. When I first talked to you about this, Laura, I figured you'd get your company on it full-time. I didn't think you'd wait."

"I wasn't sure what to do."

"When you did nothing, I set up this meeting. We're just hoping we force somebody's hand, it's a long shot."

"It's so long it's invisible," Ken said. "Just one thing. Who do you like for the bad cop?"

"We don't know."

"He's in either Narcotics or Homicide."

"We agree."

"I think . . . Homicide."

"Yes. We agree on that, too."

"How many people in Homicide?" I said.

"Way too many. Drop me off here. I'll walk back to headquarters. Twenty-four hours, Laura. Get out there, do your magic."

33

I flipped open a brand-new cell phone, called Alex.

"Listen," I said. "Get everybody there you can."

"What up?" Alex said.

"First, I don't care how you do this. There's a bank account in the Green Valley branch of Bank of America. Under the name Dakota Barbie. I want a complete record of all transactions in that account. Focus mainly on where the deposits come from. Track them back as far as you can."

"Okay."

"Next. That online gambling casino. A lot of different kinds of games listed in the menus. Did you look at anything other than the one about cockfights?"

"Not had time. Didn't know it was a priority."

"You're looking for the same kind of animated thing. Except with dogs."

"Eeeeeuuuu," Alex said. "Okay."

"That's it. You got anything for me?"

"Not yet."

"Oh. One thing more. Run the name Max Cady through every police database. It's an alias, you'll find he probably uses a lot of names, including Taerbaum. Find anything that connects him with Barbie."

"Max and the doll, okay. You coming here?"

"Sometime tomorrow."

"Check. We'll pull an all-nighter, Laura. I hope we're getting paid well."

"You can do that?" Ken said when I disconnected. "Get bank information? Things like that are supposed to be confidential."

"With all the fake names as cutouts, I'm not sure we'll learn anything. But yes, we can do that. We can do anything, looking for information."

"It just kinda . . . floats through the air?"

"Air, telephone lines, TV cables, satellites. I said.

"Don't know yet. Dogs. Doesn't surprise me. Pet dogs in Tucson have disappeared for years, there's now a state law with penalties for dog-napping in Pima County."

"What happens to the pets? To the dogs?"

"Training bait. You don't want to know any more."

At three o'clock in the morning, I sat at my workstation computer, Cady's wallet in my trash basket and everything inside the wallet spread under a desk lamp:

driver's license
VISA card
Master Charge card
membership card for Sam's Club
photo of three naked women
a dozen business cards

I'd phoned Alex with the credit card numbers. She'd sent most of the workers home, put our A team on the Bank of America bank account.

The A Team. The two Sarahs.

Sarah B worked with her head, Sarah C . . . well, she'd get locked into some endless search routine, no sense of how long it would take to run, Sarah C dreamed herself across the world to places she'd been or not. *Not daydreams*, she'd say, *I am so not daydreaming, this is just astral traveling. You're running a computer program*, Sarah B would snap at her. *All right,* Sarah C would always come right back, *so let's say I'm an astral data traveler.* Of the two sisters, Sarah C usually did the best, most intuitive work, so we let her travel, and if somebody'd notice that her program routines were completed but she'd still be locked off in Asia or Machu Picchu, we'd just rap her gently on top of her head and without complaint she'd come back to us.

With nobody in the office with time to run the credit cards right away, I said I'd do it. I rifled through the business cards, most of them for bars or strip joints. Only one looked promising. A totally blank card except for a handwritten telephone number.

"Laura?" Alex, on my cell. "Bank of America is just a drop box. Money comes in, it's wired out within twenty-four hours. So far, we've chased the transactions over three continents."

"Keep at it," I said.

I could see long keyboard hours ahead. You have to treat these random searches with infinite patience, my friend. You shove time off to the side, you remove any clocks from the screens or the desks or the walls. You set a finish point, somewhere out there, you *know* it's out there and you'll finish. What you *don't* really know is whether the finish will produce useful data.

And that's why you learn to master patience. One friend of mine used to whistle toneless tunes, he never even knew he whistled. Another hacker conjugated German verb tenses, this guy's phenomenal memory led back to high school German. He never spoke it, but he could conjugate all tenses of nearly three hundred verbs, and when he got to the end he'd start the process backward.

But tonight, *im*patience was my master, not the other way around. I laid my head on the table at one point, closed my eyes, and leapt up a silent dream of fighting, bloodied cocks.

* * *

I must have fallen asleep again, without dreaming. My cell went off right next to my ear, but I barely flipped it open before the call switched to voice mail.

"Laura. It's Christopher Kyle."

Oh, God, I thought. *Not more bodies.* But that's what it was. A TPD sector car found a body burning in a vacant lot.

"Who?" I mumbled.

"Laura. I heard . . . everybody's talking down here."

"About computer hacking?"

"Yes."

"They've got solid evidence," I said.

"But you didn't do it."

"No. But I can't prove that."

"I'm sorry," Kyle said. "I'm . . . I guess I don't know you after all."

"Christopher," I said. "Please. Don't give up on me. Trust me, I didn't do this. I need you to believe in me."

"Why should I?" he said finally.

34

Late morning. Late morning. Beside the pool, Ana Luisa playing with Spider's baby. Sarah Katherine couldn't talk, Ana Luisa only understood Spanish, but they made sounds to each other, that rarity of human communication that extends beyond the normal senses.

Once they returned to the house, feeding time for the baby, lunch for everybody else, I sat on the edge of the pool, legs in the water, arms back and bracing myself, head to the sun. Another blue, high sky over Tucson. More cloud formations south, building toward another monsoon.

What *is* this case about?

Who faked the computer hacking at TPD? Why involve me?

Should I stop being involved?

I suspected everybody, I suspected no one.

Spider came out with a cup of coffee for me, saw I wanted to be alone.

I felt guilt about sex with Ken.

One more guilty phone call to Nathan, but getting only the familiar message that his cell phone was out of service. I called Ken and found his voice mail greeting had changed. An oblique mention of hiking in the Santa Catalina Mountains, getting away with a friend, would his friend please leave a message.

I am *that friend*, I thought. But I didn't leave a message.

What *is* a friend? How do you tell the difference between a man who's just a friend and a male friend who's
maybe something more?

David Schultz came at noon. Despite a temperature over
one hundred degrees, still dressed in a seersucker suit,
white dress shirt buttoned tight, tie a solid pale blue,
shoes polished to a glimmer.

I offered coffee or lunch, but he didn't have time.

"I don't know much about *La Bruja*," Schultz said.

"It's probably not going to help me anyway," I said.

"Still. You asked. I was curious. At my age, curiosity
is a good thing on a sunny day. Especially with the fem-
inine instead of the masculine. *La Bruja*. Not *El Brujo*. I
guess, I just assumed it's a woman. Really, I don't know
much. But there is such a woman."

"Here? In Tucson?"

"Oh, no. Somewhere in Mexico. My sources say that
people speak of her with respect, but nobody spoke out
loud, they'd whisper of her. Lives in a castle, they said.
Somewhere way south in Sonora, or maybe Chihuahua.
A castle on the side of a mountain, you know, what we
call a sky island, just the single mountain rising out of
the desert. A valley and lots of water below, a good-size
village. Not a town, certainly not a city, but protected,
that's what people said of La Bruja. She protected the
people."

"Drug lords in Colombia," I said. "They protected, so
the people would serve."

"Not the same, Laura."

"It's drugs and smuggling," I said.

"And you know this how?"

"A client."

"Ah," Schultz said. "A secret client."

"The woman makes a fortune through drugs, spends
money around her own village, keeps the drugs out of
those people's hands."

"There was a movie. Nineteen fifty-three. *La Bruja*.

Here's a color reproduction of the poster." Handing me
an exact duplicate of the card left in Mary's mailbox.
"The leading role played by an actress named Marilena.
My source in Mexico City says she only used the one
word because she was half Austrian. Full name was
Marilena Stimpfl."

"Is she still alive?"

"Nobody knows."

"And this town, this castle, where is it?"

"Nobody knows. And I've got to run."

"Thanks, David. Thanks a lot."

"I don't think I've been of much help."

"At this point, any information helps."

Staring at the pool, the surface absolutely calm. No ripples, no insects skimming along, no leaves or debris, just
a large oval of water, bluer than the sky.

Look into the water.

The thought so random and unsuspected, like Obi
Wan guiding Luke Skywalker near the end of *Star Wars*.

Delilah. The woman I'd met a year ago, on the road
near Ruby. A flash flood blocking the road, she pulled
my car across with a winch, she took me to Monica's
birthday party in Arivaca.

Arivaca Road. Where Mary found Ana Luisa.

Look into the water.

I remembered why Delilah said that.

*You've got to do the work, girl. You've got to see a
mirror image of yourself, you've got to mirror yourself
and illuminate the anger you see in yourself instead of
just figuring what your emotions are toward other people. Flip those emotions so you see them in yourself, then
you work on what that's doing to you.*

But instead of working on my anger, I flipped everything I knew about the events of the past days. Starting
with the visit from Bob Gates, I turned over all conversations and phone calls and computer data search results, I
questioned everything about these events.

What if. That's the process. What's on the flip side of this coin?

After an hour, there were only two pieces of data that might have other explanations. E210. The answer to most everything had to be in E210.

I ran into the house, dressed quickly, packed my shoulder bag, stuck the Beretta underneath a pale yellow jacket I wore with sleeves rolled partway up over a tank top, nothing coordinate, just dressing quickly.

I went looking for Christopher Kyle.

35

But Kyle had been suspended from active duty, pending . . . pending something the desk sergeant wouldn't tell me. One of his partners in Homicide finally told me that Kyle just couldn't put in the long hours, his hips burned with pain. I finally found Kyle at a baseball practice batting range, working out his frustration at his failing hips by using the muscular top half of his body.

Stood in the batting cage, punched the button to start feeding him balls. Metal canes at his feet, propping himself with determination to stand unaided. First ball came at him right in the sweet spot, but he swung under it. Adjusted his stance, smacked the next ball just above his hands. *Tink*. From the aluminum bat.

"It was me," I said. "I caused this."

Tink. Solid hit with the barrel of the bat, the ball rising continually until it caught the steel mesh wiring thirty feet away. Two other men started up in the cages beyond Gates, all three ball-feed machines operating at different time intervals.

"Computers don't lie."

"That *wasn't* me."

"You're guilty," he said.

Tink. Gates swung off-stride, slicing his next ball so it whacked the steel mesh near my face.

"Don't hook your fingers through the wire," Kyle

said. "I hit any more as bad as the last one, I'll bust a few of your fingers."

"Is that a threat?" I said. *Tink*. Getting damn tired of these men, swinging a bat like they were just a signed contract away from the bigs.

"Negative." Not flinching when he stepped too close into the next ball, drove in down off his instep.

"Sure sounded like a threat," I said. Regripped the mesh, lacing my fingers through the diamond-shaped holes.

"Suit yourself. Busted fingers, can't work a keyboard."

"What's happened, Christopher?"

"You're poison, Winslow. Worst thing of all, you've poisoned yourself."

He stepped into another pitch, I saw him turn sideways, deflecting the ball toward me, but too low, it struck the fence around my knees.

"That's definitely a threat," I said.

Gates stepped away from the next ball, rested the bat on his shoulders. "Negative, Winslow."

A ball floated past, right in the zone, a home run ball, but he didn't swing.

"Listen to me, listen to me. I believed in you, I trusted you. But no more. You're guilty. And because I spoke up for you, I'm now under suspicion of . . . they don't even tell me. So. Just leave me alone. We're done here."

Kyle went to the ball-feed control panel, slid the single switch fully open. Balls streaked at him every fifteen seconds, he swung and connected with almost every pitch, spraying balls everywhere inside the cage until the feed bin emptied.

I called Mary's cell. No answer, but my phone rang just after I'd disconnected.

"Laura," Mary said. "Something really bad's happened to Ken."

"What?" I said. "What, where is he?"

"St. Mary's Hospital. Intensive care."
"I'll be right there."

Any ICU is brightly lit, rooms arranged around a central nursing station, patients in most every bed, either recovering or dying, all kinds of continual monitoring of vital signs, breathing, heart machines that beeped steadily, the atmosphere charged with the starkness of these choices. You went to another bed, you got better, you went home. Or you went to the morgue.

Mary sat beside Ken's bed, Ana Luisa asleep in a hard plastic chair, a rosary in Mary's hands, her fingers quiet on the beads. She'd been crying, her face now grim but dry.

"I've kinda forgotten how to say a rosary," she said. A quick smile, but her face lined with frowns and sadness.

"What happened to him?"

"Getting in his car, right in front of police headquarters. He started to pull out of the parking spot, a garbage truck rammed him sideways, crushed him into his car. Somebody jumped from the garbage truck and ran."

"Just tell me he'll live."

"Mostly broken bones. Left ankle, right thigh. Two ribs broken, four more cracked. He's on morphine, he's had surgery, their biggest concern is whether he had a concussion." Fiddled with her rosary. "I know the sense of what I'm supposed to say, I don't remember the rituals. Hail Mary. Our Father. Dark beads. Red beads. Mostly, I've been praying to Mother Teresa. Praying she'll intercede for me, help Ken's recovery, help keep him alive."

"It's not your fault," I said.

"It *is* my fault. I saw that first image on Ken's computer, I got him to contact you, I pulled you and your family into this. I'm guilty of all that."

"You'll be forgiven," I said. Unsure what that meant to her.

"But will I forgive myself?"

"I've got to tell you this," I said finally. "You realize, if this wasn't an accident, if somebody tried to kill him, then you're in danger."

"Yes. I know that. I still feel guilty I pulled all of you into this."

My cell rang. Tempted to ignore the call, I glanced at caller ID and saw it was Alex. Held up a finger while I flipped open the cell.

"Laura!" Alex was triumphant. "We've found the woman."

Finally. A break.

"Her name's Deb Carlin," Alex said. "Norman Don is parked a block away from her house. She's inside, Norman thinks she's alone."

"Call our security people."

"Shouldn't we really call the police?"

"No. Get security to St. Mary's Hospital. Mary's also here."

"Is she all right?"

"Yes. It's Ken. Somebody tried to kill him, but he's alive. Get security people here, outside the room. Protect Ken, Mary, and Ana Luisa. I'm going to meet Norman. We'll then brace Deb Carlin. This has to end."

"I'm going with you," Mary said.

"No."

"I'm going."

"No way. This is *my* responsibility."

Mary opened her purse, showed me what was inside. Ken's .357.

"I started all this," Mary said. "I want to help finish it."

36

A huge, sprawling million-dollar home in Ventana Canyon, sitting on two acres of foothill property. We pulled up behind Norman Don's car, parked on a road about a hundred feet higher and overlooking Carlin's backyard. A woman lay flat in a lounger, topless, face up to the sun.

"I don't have binoculars," Norman said. "But I wouldn't want any reflected glare from them anyway. I've moved my car every twenty minutes or so, but there aren't many places nearby to park. Alex wants you to wait for backup."

"Give me that," I said. Reaching through his open window for some Watchtower pamphlets. "I'm going to witness for Jehovah."

"What do we do?" Mary said.

"You're staying here."

"Don't argue with me." Reaching in her purse, she grabbed Ken's pistol, pulled it out.

"Whoa!" Norman said. "Easy, easy."

"I'm going with you," Mary said.

"All right," I said finally. "All right, all right."

"What do you want me to do?" Norman said.

"We're going up to her front door. We're Witnesses, working her neighborhood. Chances are, she won't even see us coming. We can take her at the swimming pool. Where's your cell?" He handed it to me, I called my own phone, and when it rang I left the connection open. "We'll be at her door in ten minutes. If she gets up from that lounger, if she goes into the house, it'll be us at the front door. You tell me exactly what she does. Okay?"

"Okay."

"Put on your sunglasses," I said to Mary. "Take these two pamphlets, make sure you walk tall, work your smile. Here." I pulled a straw hat from the back seat, put it on her head, but she had too much hair so I wore it. Ready?"

"She just sat up," Norman said. "She's looking around, waiting."

"Ring the doorbell again," I said. Mary pushed the ivory button, chimes rebounded somewhere far away from the front door.

"She stood up. She's chewing a fingernail, she's picked up a big towel, she's holding the towel like there's something underneath. She's going inside."

"Ring it again. Smile."

"God is with us," Mary said.

A slot opened in the thick oak front door.

"Go away." A woman's voice, husky, without much emphasis. "I don't want your kind around here."

"Oh," I said. "I'm sorry, I know you think we're Jehovah's Witnesses. But actually, we both live two blocks away. We're circulating a petition against one of the homeowners. He's, well, he's decided to plant grass, I mean, *grass*. Here, in this development. When it's been perfectly landscaped. A riparian habitat."

"Grass?" the voice said.

"Yes. Actually, some of it won't even be real grass."

"Plastic," Mary said. "Like, say, on a football field. Plastic grass."

"For Christ's sake," the voice said. "Fake grass."

"Exactly," Mary said. "I've got a petition to the zoning commission, complaining about the grass. Most everybody on our blocks have signed, today we're trying to get other signatures. It'll just take a minute, just print and sign your name, we'll fill in the address."

"Shit. Sure, okay, sure."

Two deadbolts released, the door opening about a foot, and I rammed against the door, knocking the woman backward, her towel flying up and out of her hand and dropping a small automatic pistol that gouged a chip in the entryway tiles.

"Down, down," I shouted.

Kicked the automatic to one side as the woman lunged for it and I drew back my foot and kicked her on the right breast and that hurt, she grabbed the breast, rubbing it with one hand, sitting quietly now and looking for an edge. She cut her eyes between my face and Mary's and then she smiled.

"I know you," she said. "I know you both."

"And now we know you. At last."

"We've seen each other before."

"Yeah. You videotaped me and I videotaped you."

"In your leather bra," she said finally. "Should have thought of that." She turned her face to Mary. "And how's that little girl?" she said.

"She's safe," Mary said. "She's in God's hands."

"Where we want to send all of you. Straight up to God."

She made no effort to cover her naked breasts, she sat with both hands braced behind her, firm, large breasts hardly moving, but I saw muscles rippling in both arms and knew she'd launch herself at us if she saw any edge.

"Mary," I said. "Move over near that chair. Put that .357 on her."

"Wow," the woman said. "Tall lady. Big gun. Wow."

"I only want one thing," I said.

"Cockfighting is a misdemeanor. Small fine, no jail time."

"This has nothing to do with cockfights."

"I've nothing really to say. Really. Nothing."

"Is Deb Carlin a real name?"

"It's a name."

"But you've had other names."

"So have you," she said. "Really. This is a waste of time. I'm getting up."

"Have you heard about Carlos?" I said. She blinked, lips twitched slightly, hardly noticeable if I weren't two feet from her face.

"Who's that?"

"Carlos Cañas."

"Don't know him."

"He's dead. Burned to death two days ago."

"Is he with God?"

I backed off two feet, sighted my Beretta, calculated the angles, and fired, the bullet runneling a deep crack in three of the tiles. She flinched, regained her composure.

"Shoot up the house," she said. "But you won't shoot me. I'm getting up."

"Five days," I said. She stopped, halfway from a hallway to the back of the house. "For five days, I've been wondering if I should stop carrying this Beretta."

"Oh fuck that," she said. "You're gonna shoot me, for Christ's sakes, shoot me. But I'm going to get dressed."

"Please," I said. "Don't move."

"Oh, by all means," Mary said. "Move."

"That goddam girl of yours," Carlin said. "The people I worked with, they've got these lists. When something goes wrong, they've got to take care of *every*body on those lists. And that girl saw too many people. A pity she didn't die in that crash. You're Catholic, aren't you?"

Mary nodded, the heavy .357 wobbling a bit in her hand.

"So let me ask you," Carlin said. "Is the hand of Jesus on that gun?"

"No," Mary said. "This is all on my own. Your future is between God and yourself. I'm just here to help arrange the meeting."

"Wow," Carlin said. Laughing. "Right out of a movie.

Listen, you two. I'm not somebody who stays in the shallow end of the pool. I'm gonna get dressed now."

"Don't move," I said.

She shrugged, started to turn her back.

I shot her in the left knee, blood spurting on the cream-colored tiles, and she writhed in agony. I stuck my shoe under her bathing towel, flicked it on her.

"Find the bathroom," I said. Mary in shock, her pistol drooping. "Mary. Find a bathroom. Get more towels. Do it."

"You shot her," Mary said.

"And I might shoot the other knee. Get some more towels."

Mary ran down a hallway and returned quickly with two huge terrycloth towels. She started to kneel at the woman's side, but I motioned her back.

"Throw her the towels," I said. "Don't go near her."

I expected curses, anger, anything, but the woman ground her teeth and wrapped two of the towels around the already swollen kneecap.

"Where's Carlos?" I said.

"I . . . don't . . . know."

"Where's Carlos?"

"He's dead," she said. "He was nothing."

Another wave of pain twisted her face and she fell on her side, holding the towels over her leg, trying not to put pressure on her knee. She shook her head, grimaced, tried to speak, shook her head again.

"Where's E210?" I said.

Her eyes flared wide open, her mouth a perfect O of surprise. "If I tell you, *I'm* dead."

"You'll have protection."

She laughed, a loud, musical laugh that had no dark edges.

"Finish me yourself, or call an ambulance. I'm done talking."

"Mary," I said. "Cock the pistol." She drew back the hammer with a double click. "Stay where you are, keep the pistol right on these perfect silicone breasts. If she makes any move toward you, just shoot."

"You can't do that," the woman said. "God-lovers don't kill."

"God doesn't roll dice," Mary said. "But I will."

"Let's make a deal. I give you E210, you forget about me."

"Deal," I said.

"You've got no proof I've done anything."

"I don't need proof, I don't care what happens to you."

"Yeah, well. What proof do I have you'll keep your word?"

"Do you believe in God?" Mary said.

"Hardly."

"Then as God is your personal witness, we'll let you go."

"That was too easy," the woman said. "There's no proof in what you said, that you'll actually let me go."

"There's no real proof of God's existence," Mary said. "But I know He's there."

"No deal," the woman said finally. "Go to hell."

"Mary. Keep your gun on her," I said. "While I look for something."

I didn't have to look far. A Tucson Yellow Pages lay open on the kitchen counter, between the sink and a portable phone and open to a page.

Storage—Household and Commercial

In red ink, a business name and address circled, with numbers in the margin of the page: 9-26-56. I ripped the page out of the book, rummaged through drawers and cabinets, and finally found what I wanted in the garage. I went back inside.

"Mary," I said. "We've got to do this carefully, so we

don't give this bitch an edge. Take this electrical tape and unroll four or five feet. I'll stand away from you, while you wrap this around her ankles. Then more tape around her arms, tape her arms so she can hold the towel over her knee."

Now the woman cursed, but we paid no attention. I wrapped the last towel around her mouth and taped it securely to her head. Furious, her eyes followed every move, but there was no edge for her, none at all.

Back inside our car, driving out of Ventana Canyon.

"Where are we going?" Mary said.

"E210," I said. Handed her the page of advertisements, bloody fingerprints and all. Mary looked at it, shook her head.

"E210," she said. "What is it?"

"A self-storage locker."

"What's in it?"

"If we're lucky, something that will lead to who's doing all this to us."

37

UStore.

The digital name itself a clue of sorts, the storage company owned by somebody with an eye to advertising on the Internet. Approximately fifty or so individual units, each fronted by padlocked, pull-down steel doors. uStore was southwest of Tucson, off Rincon and past the state prison, the pavement ending in a roundabout and a few other anonymous buildings. A graded dirt road ran to the south. I parked behind one of the other buildings, out of line-of-sight from uStore.

"Something in there," I said, "something will give us answers."

"There's no front office," Mary said. "It looks empty."

"Probably is. These self-storage places often don't have an office on the premises, there's a lot of money in this business, probably handled by a central office in Tucson. Lots of military people, from the Air Force base, they use these temporary storage units when they're not assigned adequate housing."

"E210," she said.

"And if I'm right, I've got the combination to a padlock. You ready?"

She touched her Mother Teresa medal. "Forgive me, Lord, for what I am about to do."

And the next ten minutes answered all my questions.

*   *   *

We walked quickly to uStore, no windows in sight, no cars, no vehicles of any kind until we rounded the C and D sections of the units and saw a Chevy Cavalier parked midway down the last aisle.

"This is E," Mary whispered. Her shoes clattered on the asphalt.

"Take off your shoes," I said. Removing mine, racking the Beretta's slide. "I know that car, why do I know that car?"

I stopped, thinking, couldn't recall where I'd seen the car.

Moving again slowly down the E side of uStore, number two-forty, two-thirty, two-twenty, and stopped in front of two-ten. A huge padlock hooked through matching slots between quarter-inch-thick metal bars.

"The combination," I said. "Read it to me."

"Nine." I set the padlock at zero, rotated the dial right to nine. "Twenty-eight." Right again. "Fifty-six." Right again, Beretta shifted to my right hand, tugging on the padlock. It wouldn't open.

"Doesn't it go right, left, right?" Mary said. "Like a gym locker."

Zero. Right to nine. Left to twenty-eight. Right to fifty-six.

It still wouldn't open.

"Gym locker," Mary said. "Umm, ummm, go left a full turn, then stop."

Zero. Right to nine. Left, full turn past twenty-eight, then twenty-eight again. Right to fifty-six. Our eyes locked, I pulled gently on the padlock, and it slid open without a sound. I stood two feet back from the door, motioned Mary to grasp the handle, and nodded. She jerked the door up, it rolled open on oiled tracks but still made a clatter, and we were inside the unit.

Open doorways on both the left and right walls.

"Deb?" a voice said in the distance.

"These units are connected," I whispered. "This

whole area of the storage units, they're all connected on
the inside."

"Deb? Is that you?"

"Yeah," I said. My huskiest voice.

"What are you doing here?"

I waggled the Beretta to the left, moved to the edge of
the open doorway, looked at Mary with the .357 out in
front of her, the gun steady in both hands. I stepped into
the doorway, saw a figure five units away.

"Freeze," I said. But the figure lurched sideways,
more of a fall than a jump. I ran through three more
units to find a man, crawling on the floor, trying to
reach an AK-47.

"Oh," I said. "Oh, Jesus Christ. Not, no. Not you."

Christopher Kyle scowled at me from the floor, the
AK-47 still six feet away. He dragged himself a foot
closer, but I didn't even hurry, I went to the AK-47 and
tossed it aside.

"Ah," I said. "Oh, God. Not you."

He licked his lips, propped himself against a desk.
Four computer monitors set up on a shelf along one
wall, on the other wall a rack of computers, the web
servers, the entire ChupaLuck online gambling casino.

"Who is he?" Mary said.

"A Tucson homicide detective."

"A detective?"

"Over the hill," I said. "And dirty."

"Why?" Mary said. "Why?" she said again, looking
at Kyle.

Kyle reached behind his back.

"Don't do that," I said quickly. "Christopher, do *not*
do that. Trust me this one last time, Christopher. You
move, you die."

He slowly withdrew his hand, his muscular hands
around a Glock nine.

"I'll shoot you," I said. "I've already shot that woman
today. That Carlin woman, whatever her name is, I shot
her in the knee. I'll do the same to you."

Kyle kept the muzzle away from me, moved it across his chest.

"Don't, don't don't *don't do that*," I shouted.

But he swiftly tucked the muzzle under his chin and pulled the trigger. Except the gun misfired. I kicked the gun, before he could try again, kicked the gun so hard it crushed his lips and broke several teeth.

"You always told me," I said. "You told me that killing was random and easy. Not gonna be your way out, though."

Mary knelt in front of him. She pulled off her shirt, wiped Kyle's bloody mouth, staring at him as he cursed.

"My girl," Mary said. "You threatened my girl's life. You used up a lot of young lives. I could not imagine anybody using a young woman's body like you've done, stuffing her intestines with poison."

Kyle snarled, moaned, an utterly wordless cry.

"I forgive you," Mary said. "I'm glad that you're going to live. I will pray for you every day of my life. Whatever horrible, terrible place they'll send you to, where you'll live, hopefully, you'll live a long, long time.

"For the rest of your life," Mary said. "I will pray for you. And may God forgive you."

"You would forgive him?" I said. Disbelief, shock.

"Yes."

"After everything he's done?"

"Yes."

"Will God ever forgive *me*?" I said.

"Of course."

"Then God help me," I said. "Because I understand so little of this."

Seeing a large roll of duct tape, I wound the entire roll around his body and the chair and desk and everything close enough to secure him even tighter. I looked at all the computer equipment, all of it familiar, its purpose familiar, everything about it not much different than my own office, Kyle himself not so different from me in his technical abilities.

"I don't understand this," I said.

I looked at the blood on his face, I looked for curses and defiance but all I saw was an old man's spirit and purpose sagging in defeat. Nobody moved, no sounds came from outside, the silence so profound I heard my heart beat. I held my Beretta in both my hands, I racked the slide, ejecting all the cartridges and they tinkled to the floor, one by one until the magazine was empty and I hit the magazine button and the magazine dropped to the floor.

"I don't understand this," I said. "There's no meaning in what you've done."

"You're marked women." Kyle finally spoke. "*La Bruja*'s curse is on your heads, on your daughters' heads."

"I don't think so," I said. "It's all you. When you go away, nobody will care about any of us. And you will go away for a long time."

"Kill me now," he said.

"We're going to leave," I said. "I'm going to call Bob Gates, I'm going to tell him where to find you."

"Kill me," he said. "Finish me now."

I set my Beretta on the floor.

I walked away from it.

38

"Hey, honey bunny," Ken said. "Who's paying for all this?"

I'd shifted him to a private room at St. Mary's hospital. His broken bones still needed a few more checks on the pins and screws.

"It's all on the house," I said.

"Get out of that chair," he said. "Sit on the bed."

I sat on the very edge, gingerly. He lifted the sheet.

"Get under here," he said.

"The nurse will be along any time," I said.

"Then get moving. I may be out of practice, but I'm not that quick."

I got under the sheet and he pulled down my jeans and touched me.

"Got time in your life for a beat-up retired cop?" he said.

"Years," I said.

"Whoa, wait a minute here." Feeling my lower back, naked under the sheet. "Something's missing. Where's your Beretta?"

"Forget about mine," I said, reaching underneath the front of his hospital gown. "Where's yours?"

tohono chul park

Hola, Ana Luisa.

When you read this, your English will be better than my Spanish.

I'm writing in this diary a lot, now. I have a special memory, I can replay scenes from my past, but for you, I want to write things down so I have them clearly and accurately and you will know our history.

You have been baptized Ana Luisa Emich.

Father Frank Woolever did a special baptism service in the park, at the grotto beside the puppyfish that you've come to love as much as me. He blessed the water, he ran the water on your forehead, and he said it was a symbolic burial, that you were now baptized in the name of Jesus Christ and that your new life, in Christ and God, began at that moment.

My friend Laura Winslow brought her daughter and her granddaughter, and Father Frank baptized them both.

We have many pictures.

Laura made and edited a special video.

Our lives have changed.

We are no longer threatened.

Laura says there's no end to the chaos in southern Arizona, no end to drug cartels and gangs like the *maras*. But *we* are no longer threatened, our lives are no longer in danger. Laura says that the people who threatened us worked independently of other *maras,* that all the computer records we found in the awful storage place were destroyed. Laura wiped the computer drives totally clean.

There are no records.

Just in case, and it may never come to this, Laura provided me with two completely new identities for the two of us. If we're ever threatened again, we'll use them, we'll move somewhere else and start over.

But I don't want to leave you, I don't want to leave our life together, and I don't want to leave this beautiful park and all the wonderful people who work in this sanctuary. Laura is gone. Once Ken was released from the hospital, Laura took him away and they're somewhere, out there. Someday, we may meet these special friends again.

And so I pray, Ana Luisa. I hope and I pray through Mother Teresa, may she intercede for us with God, may these dark times be over and may we live from now on in peace and serenity.

In God's name, I pray this is the true end to this story.

acknowledgments

In writing this book, many, *many* people contributed in many, *many* ways.

Thanks to all the wonderful people at Tohono Chul Park, a privately-funded, not-for-profit nature preserve in Tucson, Arizona. Fifty acres of natural beauty and quiet serenity, Tohono Chul Park is the Southwest's center where nature, art, and culture connect. Special thanks to my close friends Mary Emich and Ken Charvoz on the Park staff. Mary is Director of Visitor Services, Ken coordinates the efforts of over three hundred volunteers. Both Mary and Ken started out to be just minor characters, and wound up with major and central roles.

Thanks to *everybody* who agreed to let me use their real names for characters in the book. This is no small thing. Other than Laura Winslow and her family, just about every name here (at last count, over thirty characters) is that of a friend or of somebody who graciously contributed money at an auction so that I'd use that name for either a good or bad character. That said, don't expect me to use personal details of any of these people—*Falling Down* is, after all, fiction. In particular, the real Chris Kyle is entirely the opposite of that character in the book. Chris is kind, sweet, generous, and a good friend. The Park itself (I'm both a Park member and a volunteer) has a major role as a real and symbolic

sanctuary of peace when set against the increasing drug
and smuggling chaos of Southern Arizona.

Thanks to Mary Emich and Dympna Callaghan for
helping me better understand some Catholic mysteries.
Dympna, a Shakespearean scholar with tremendous re-
search and writing skills, always inspires me to work
harder.

I can't thank everybody who's helped me write this
book, but here are four special friends who stand in for
the larger communities they represent. As a fellow
writer, Rhys Bowen gives freely of advice and support.
The mystery community owes great debts to those who
publish genre journals and guides: Janet Rudolph (*Mystery Readers Journal*) and Kate Derie (*Deadly Directory*,
cluelass.com). Mary Jane Maffini, of Capital Crime
Writers of Ottawa, is just one member of those special
groups that promote and guide mystery writers; groups
like Sisters in Crime, Private Eye Writers of America,
and Mystery Writers of America. Thanks to my number
one fan, Sylvia Ulan of Tucson. For me, Sylvia repre-
sents the mystery book community as a whole—the hundreds and hundreds of writers, fans, and readers.

And as always, this book simply wouldn't be possible
without the support of my wife, Deborah Pellow.

Enter the World of Laura Winslow

Butterfly Lost

This first Laura Winslow mystery introduces us to the smart and resourceful computer whiz whose business is hacking onto the electronic trail of people who want to stay lost. But this time, when an old Hopi commissions Laura to find his granddaughter, she doesn't want any part of his vision of Powakas or Navajo skinwalkers—or anything else that will remind her of her old life back on the "rez" in Arizona. The Hopi's granddaughter, however, is one of too many girls recently gone missing, and only Laura can bring them home. . . .

"Are you the one who finds them?" he said.

His face was creased, lined, leathered, neutral, and expressionless. He could have been fifty or eighty years old, his breath asthmatic but steady, his body stocky and muscled. A traditional Hopi headband of faded red cloth wound around jet black hair cut at mid-ear length except in front, where short bangs hung over his forehead. He wore an old but clean long-sleeve blue cotton shirt, faded denims, and old black Nike sneakers, and he carried a plastic Bashas' Supermarket bag.

He took his hand off the girl's shoulder, and she immediately began stretching her neck and arms and legs in vague dancer's movements. Without asking, she picked up my binoculars, held them vertical with one

lens to her right eye, and scanned round and round the
driveway, lighting finally on a small pile of pebbles. She
set the binoculars on the table and sat down to begin
sorting the pebbles by size and color.

"You *are* Miss Laura Winslow?" the Hopi said po-
litely.

"Yes," I said.

"You're the one who finds the girls?"

His wide-open eyes were as black as navy peacoat
buttons.

"I only do that for the high school," I said. "And
they're closed for the summer."

"Yesterday, I went over there. I talked with a Missus
Tso."

"Billie Tso? The guidance counselor?"

"She said *you* would help."

I had a contract with Tuba City High School to run
computer searches in an attempt to locate teenage runaway girls who fled the rez for brighter lights and bigger cities. Girls who hated reservation life, girls who
were bored or curious or in trouble or just plain bad.
These girls were my soft spot, my social weakness, my
one public flaw in an otherwise mostly private life. My
own daughter disappeared when she was only two,
taken by my ex-husband to some place where despite
repeated searches I couldn't find digital tracks of their
existence. She'd now be in her early twenties, but I'm
still unable to grant her adulthood, having progressed
only to admitting that she could be twelve or fourteen
years old. By looking for other missing girls, I kept
alive my hopes of finding Spider.

"Who are you trying to find?"

He frowned, not yet ready for such a direct question.
Hopis' conversations are incredibly circular with people outside their families or clans, responses withheld
while they explore the entrails of the stranger's words

for signs and possibilities.

"What's your name?" I asked, trying to get him talking.

He pulled off his headband and wiped his neck and forehead with the left cuff of his workshirt, trying to decide how much he could reveal. After putting the headband back on, he settled the knot over his right ear and nodded.

"I am Abbott Pavatea. From Lower Moencopi. My granddaughter, she was supposed to graduate from the high school. But she left a couple of nights before graduation and hasn't been home since."

"Graduation was two weeks ago."

"I thought she'd come back," he said shortly. "She didn't."

"Okay," I said. "What's her name?"

He opened his mouth to speak, his lips moving with no sound as the unspoken name hung in the air, crackling and invisible like static electricity. I realized Abbott couldn't say the name because he believed she was dead. I stretched my arms tighter across my breasts as tears streamed down his face. For a long beat I couldn't hear the barking dogs or even the whistle of his breath, his fathomless black button eyes locked on me like those of a coyote with a lamb in sight and nothing in between them but hunger.

The Killing Maze

Laura Winslow left her Hopi self behind and came to Tucson hoping to start over. Armed with a new name and praying that her past would never find her, Laura now works as a cyber-sleuth for Miguel Zepeda—an aging private detective who lives on the Tohono O'odham reservation. Laura is hiding within the Internet, safe and untouchable . . . for now. But when Miguel suddenly disappears, and an uninvited stranger shows up at Laura's door, she is soon swept into a twisted maze of gangs, Internet scams, and cold-blooded murder. . . .

"Hello in there."

A man's voice.

"It's Rey Villaneuva."

I went to the front door and stood silently behind it, looking through the peephole. But it was too dark to see anything except that a man was standing there. He rang the doorbell again.

I reached for the twelve gauge pump shotgun beside the door.

"I work for Miguel Zepeda."

Hesitating for a moment, I flipped on the outside porch light and opened the door. He blinked at the naked lightbulb, shook his head wearily, and moved back a few steps, allowing me to look him over. His tanned and unmistakably Mexican face was topped by a shock of unruly black hair that glistened with water as though he'd stuck his head under a faucet and run his fingers through it instead of a comb. He wore brown khaki pants, creased sharply, a sky-blue shirt with some kind of dog pattern, and a light, loose-fitting blue blazer.

"Who's Miguel?" I said.

"Let me get out my ID," he said wearily, reading my distrust.

He pulled aside his blazer, revealing a dull black Glock 17 stuck in a nylon shoulder rig. He took out a wallet and flipped it opened to show me a Private Investigation Business License issued by the Arizona Department of Public Safety.

"You are Laura, right?"

"What do you want?"

"Right now, I want to come inside. I feel a little stupid, standing out here in the middle of the night."

"Okay," I said finally.

He stopped just inside the living room and carefully closed the door. Hearing the solid chunk of the door settling into the steel frame, his eyes ran up and around the door and the three dead bolts. I leaned the shotgun against the wall. It fell over and I jumped at the noise.

"Mossberg 590," he said, picking it up. "Nine slugs in the tube, four stored in the handle. Parkerized dull finish, ghostring front sight. This is a serious piece. Are *you* a serious piece?"

His intensely focused eyes were offset by a slight smile. He was either amazed or bemused by the shotgun. He ran a finger down the dull black, matte-finished barrel and laid it against the wall.

Stalking Moon

Hiding out in the Arizona desert, Laura Winslow hopes to escape the past through false names and untraceable Internet phone technology. But when Bobby, her current and elusive partner, rings Laura's cell to brief her on their latest assignment, she soon realizes that the case may risk exposure and arrest unless she can uncover a nightmarish smuggling operation trafficking in the most precious of commodities: human lives. . . .

"Here's the wiggle. Funky. I've got two people wanting to pay for the same job."

"Bobby, I don't understand."

"Two different clients. Each approached me separately. I know they've got no idea somebody else is asking for the same information."

"That *is* funky. So?"

"The first client, a package is coming your way."

"At my mail drop?"

"The second client," he continued, ignoring my question, "you're going to have to meet her."

"No. I don't personally meet clients."

"Not even for two hundred thousand?" He sucked in his breath, the sound rasping in my earpiece. "That's a minimum."

Well. Incredible. My biggest score ever. I could take months off work, I could retire for a year, I could bliss out in northern Thailand with that kind of money. The phone connection buzzed the way it does when somebody on a portable or wireless phone shifts body position and the uplink can't quite maintain the connection.

"Okay. I'll meet. Where do I go? What state?"

"No airplanes necessary. Your own neighborhood. Client's nearby. Meet her tomorrow night 4:22. She prefers Nogales. I told her you'd pick Tucson."

"Yes. Arizona Desert Museum."

He hesitated so long I thought there was a problem.

"Just checking her cell phone, had to leave a message on her voice mail about the meet. Okay. Gotta go."

"Wait! What's the job?"

"Something connected to that videotape on CNN. Today, when you get the package, you'll understand a lot more. Um, I've *got* to go."

"Um," I said. "There you go again."

"Don't have time to talk."

"Whoa, Bobby. Whoa. What's the hurry here? I know you by now. I know when you've got something unpleasant to tell me about a score."

"What's the tell?" he asked after a while.

"I'm not telling you anything. I'm *ask*ing."

"No. You know, um, like gamblers. Poker players. Get a good card, they lick their lips, sniff, hunch their shoulders, whatever. It gives away information to the other players so they can fold."

"That's called a tell?"

"Yes. Look, I'm really curious. I need to know if I've got a tell, a giveaway on the phone. Nobody's ever said that to me before."

"When you're holding back something, you say 'um.'"

"Um," Bobby Guinness said faintly.

"See?"

A long, long silence. But I waited, knowing he was

trying to figure out just how much more data to give me.

"Okay," he said finally. "Things here are getting complicated."

"*Bad* complicated? Or just . . . more difficult?"

"Both. First off. There's a Mexican factor."

"Is there data about that in the package I'm getting?"

"Second off. The package is being hand-delivered."

I was stunned.

"How do you know where I live?"

"That's my business. To know all about people. But . . . um . . ."

Uncharacteristically, he was at a loss for words. I heard a swoosh of static as he shifted his head, a momentary buzzing, like a large moth at the screen door.

"I'm going to freak you out here, I think. Tell you the truth, *I'm* freaked."

"What?"

"You're going to find out anyway," he said, "once the package arrives."

"Find out what?"

"I'm not Bobby Guinness."

Where is this going? I thought, unable to think clearly at all.

"Well. I am Bobby to you. But I'm just a voice, just a person who calls himself Bobby Guinness. Actually, I'm a cutout. I work for . . . for the real Bobby. Who's coming to see you in the next day or so. Bringing the package."

"A cutout? I don't think I like this contract at all."

"You will, once you hear the money that's involved. It's going to be a percentage, not a straight fee. Twenty percent of at least thirty million dollars."

"Jesus!"

"So. You cool? You freaked? What?"

Scorpion Rain

Laura Winslow will do almost anything to conceal her true past—a past too painful and too dangerous to acknowledge. But now a friend has been kidnapped following a bloody shootout, and Laura must risk exposing everything she's tried so hard to keep secret. In Scorpion Rain, *Laura must cross the line where civilization ends—entering a majestic wasteland where corruption, lies, and violence are bred and nurtured.*

"Laura?"

Kamesh tugged the hem of my flannel nightshirt.

"Laura, wake up. There's somebody outside."

I thumbed at my eyes to clear the sleep film, sat halfway up. My bedroom faced the driveway, and I could see bubblegum police lights flickering. Two men stood in the high-beam headlight shafts, one of them with what looked like a shotgun. Fumbling open my nightstand drawer, I took out my Glock. Kamesh winced as I racked a shell into the chamber.

My front doorbell chimed, again and again. Passing through the kitchen, I flattened against the refrigerator as a shadow flickered across the window. I moved through the darkened house to the front door just as somebody rapped loudly on the door, three times, then three times again.

"Miss Winslow?"

Behind me, I saw Kamesh in the hallway, already getting dressed. He hated guns, hated whenever I left one lying around the house.

"Miss Winslow! I'm Captain Cruz. INS."

Yeah, well, I'm Donald Duck, I thought.

Anybody can pretend to be anybody.

"Miss Winslow? Please come to the door. I have a phone call for you from Michelle Gilbert."

I punched in my alarm system code and opened the door.

"Cruz," he said. "Border Patrol. Take this."

He held out a cell phone to me, his right arm fully extended, his body slightly leaning away from me when he saw the Glock with the hammer back.

"Ma'am, please don't point that weapon at me."

I took the cell phone, shut the door with Cruz still outside.

"Hello?"

"This is Gilbert. About those other names you gave me. All four of the people are missing. I don't have much time to talk with you, but Captain Cruz will leave one of his men with you. In the morning, when I'm back in Tucson, I'll be at your house to look at whatever you've got on your computer."

"I won't be here."

"You don't have a choice."

"I have a contract job tomorrow," I said. "I can't cancel out."

"That's why Cruz and Gonzalez are there. Protection.

"I've *got* protection. I've also got a job in the morning."

"Something you can do from your house?"

"I have to be in Phoenix at four A.M. At the Perryville prison."

"When will you return home?"

"Early afternoon. Four, at the latest."

"All right." She sighed. "I'm so busy, I probably could use the time down here. Will you be at Perryville all day, in case I need to reach you?"

"No. Going from Perryville to Nogales, then back here. All four are gone?"

"No trace. But none of the families are talking. I think they've paid ransoms and are just waiting to get the person back. But these money people have rules of their own."

"It was Margaret Admiral? The body?"

"Yes. It was her. But it wasn't a body."

"The TV story about mutilation . . . was it bad?"

"I really don't know. All we found was a hand."

She paused, uncertain how much to tell me.

"What?" I said. "What else did you find with the hand?"

"A note," she said finally. "The hand was left so we could take fingerprints. But we'd never find anything else, any other . . . body parts, never find Margaret Admiral. She was dead, the note said. We have no way of knowing if that's true or not, no way of knowing if it's just a ploy for a bigger ransome. Gotta go."

Gilbert told Cruz that I'd be leaving the house at three, which was only an hour away. Kamesh tried to drive off in his '63 Corvette, but Cruz held him until Gilbert said it was okay to let him go.

A hand. All they found of Margaret Admiral was a hand.

I made up my mind right then. Do this last job with Meg, close up my house, move somewhere else. A long, long way from Tucson, far enough away so I'd never again have Hannibal Lecter leaving me messages.

Dragonfly Bones

Of all the dark secrets in her past, Laura Winslow is haunted most by Spider, the daughter she lost years ago. Now Spider is an angry young woman serving prison time, but she's agreed to help the authorities uncover an identity theft ring in exchange for leniency. In Dragonfly Bones, mother and daughter are reunited and soon face danger together at a secret burial ground near Casa Grande Monument. The discarded bones may be all that remain of dozens of inexplicably missing women, and Laura fears that unless she can uncover a terrible conspiracy, her daughter may be the next body added to the shallow grave.

"Spider," I said, lips dry, tongue in knots, my whole *head* in knots.

"Dominguez."

She cut me off, her lips barely a pencil line, they were clenched so tight, the word emerging like a hiss, lingering on the last *ahhh* syllable, teeth apart, for a moment I thought her tongue would dart out. Like a stinger. Like a snake.

"Help me here, Spider," I said.

She fingered the ID badge clipped to her orange tee. Waited for me to read it.

DOMINGUEZ, ABBE CONSUELO
ADC 49-353424-F

Finally, not knowing what else to do, I took out the photo that Jonathan gave me two years before. I traced my finger over the smiling woman, trying to discover some link, some blood, some connection between my memories of her at two years old, when Jonathan took her from me and disappeared.

Trying to make a connection between the smiling photo and the enraged face in front of me. I just kept staring at her, a tiny smile flickering on my lips, fading, more a twitch than a smile. I had so much invested in discovering this moment, meeting her for the first time in twenty years, I'd built this mythic meeting scene, I don't know what I'd built, but the daughter I'd imagined was nothing like the woman across the table.

Her concentration broke. Blinking, suddenly looking down, nothing else changing in her body, still sitting like she had a pole up her ass, years of anger at me, at somebody, and here I was as a release for the anger. And then she took a deep breath, hunched her shoulders, let the breath out with a slow sigh, and rolled her head side to side, muscle tension probably cramping her neck.

It was something to build on.

"Dominguez. Where did you get that name?"

"Run one of your hacker searchers. You'd find out." Rude.

A whole different attitude. For the first time, I wondered if she really knew what to do with me, with her mother, facing her mother, two adults, two strangers.

"I've searched for your real name for years."

"I have no *real* name," she snorted. "Like you, I have lots of identities."

"Spider Begay." She shrugged. "I filed the birth certificate. In Flagstaff."

She shrugged again.

"So Spider Begay disappeared two years after that birth certificate?"

"*You* disappeared. That's what he said. What Daddy said. When I met him in Mexico. Do you know where he is now?"

"No."

She nodded toward the steel door at the far end of the room.

"Where is he?" she asked.

"Who?"

"Mister Law."

"Nathan Brittles?"

"Oh, c'mon, Mom. You don't believe that's his real name, do you?"

"He has a lot of ID. But I really don't care about him right now."

She saw I was curious.

"Check out John Wayne," she said cryptically.

"I saw the movie. What do we do here? *Why* are we here?"

"He coming in? Or what?

"Tell me, Spider."

"Dominguez!"

"Abbie, then."

"It's not *aaaaa-beeee*." Flat A sound, long E sound, said derisively. "*Ah. Bay*. Ahbay. Don't you, like, know any Mexican?"

I swore. A border phrase, a slang phrase, the rudest I could think of. That shocked her. No telling if it was because of the insult, or because it was said by her mother. Another attitude. Negotiation with anger.

"Let's get to it," she said flatly. "Call him in."

"This is between us," I said, standing up. "You want him in here, you deal with him and I'll just go home."

After a minute of standoff defiance, I headed toward the door. I'd only gone a few steps when she surged out of her chair, slamming it against chairs behind her, grabbed a plastic ashtray from another table, and hurled it like a Frisbee, like a discus, like a deer slug out of a twelve-gauge, sailing it three inches from my head. I ducked, but she wasn't aiming it at me. Flew all the way down the room in a flat trajectory, cracking against the door and dissolving in shards. The bolt shot back with a loud click, a CO appeared with her hand on a baton.

"Get John Wayne," Spider yelled.

The CO cocked her head at me.

"Brittles," I said.

"Wait one."

She closed the door, the bolt shot home. Neither Spider nor I moved. Two minutes later the CO came in again.

"On the phone."

"Get him *off* the fucking phone, get him in here!" Spider screamed.

"Your call," the CO said to me, arms out wide, palms up, a shrug.

"We'll wait."

Spider immediately went to the other door and pounded on it with her hands. The CO quickly shut and locked her door, the second door opened, a second CO appeared. Spider held out her wrists to be hooked up. Once the handcuffs were on, she left without a word.

PERENNIAL DARK ALLEY

Be Cool: Elmore Leonard takes Chili Palmer into the world of rock stars, pop divas, and hip-hop gangsters—all the stuff that makes big box office.
0-06-077706-0

Eye of the Needle: For the first time in trade paperback, comes one of legendary suspense author Ken Follett's most compelling classics.
0-06-074815-X

More Than They Could Chew: Rob Roberge tells the story of Nick Ray, a man whose addictions (alcohol, kinky sex, questionable friends) might only be cured by weaning him from oxygen.
0-06-074280-1

Men from Boys: A short story collection featuring some of the true masters of crime fiction, including Dennis Lehane, Lawrence Block, and Michael Connelly. These stories examine what it means to be a man amid cardsharks, revolvers, and shallow graves.
0-06-076285-3

Fender Benders: From **Bill Fitzhugh** comes the story of three people planning on making a "killing" on Nashville's music row.
0-06-081523-X

Cross Dressing: It'll take nothing short of a miracle to get Dan Steele, counterfeit cleric, out of a sinfully funny jam in this wickedly good tale from **Bill Fitzhugh.**
0-06-081524-8

The Fix: Debut crime novelist **Anthony Lee** tells the story of a young gangster who finds himself caught between honor and necessity.
0-06-059534-5